THE MEANING
OF LIBERTY

By the Author

All This Time

The Meaning of Liberty

Writing as Jordan Meadows:

Proximity

Not Just Friends

THE MEANING OF LIBERTY

by

Sage Donnell

2024

THE MEANING OF LIBERTY

ISBN 13: 978-1-63679-624-6

THIS TRADE PAPERBACK ORIGINAL IS PUBLISHED BY
BOLD STROKES BOOKS, INC.
P.O. BOX 249
VALLEY FALLS, NY 12185

FIRST EDITION: JULY 2024

CREDITS
EDITOR: BARBARA ANN WRIGHT
PRODUCTION DESIGN: SUSAN RAMUNDO
COVER DESIGN BY JEANINE HENNING

Acknowledgments

Thanks to the entire Bold Strokes team for making my dream of becoming a published author keep happening.

Thanks to the many people in my life who listened to me obsess about this book through its many iterations, particularly those who listened to me agonize nearly every day while I wrote this one. I'm particularly thinking of you, Alison, but I'd be remiss not to include Haley, PJ, Anthony, Katie, and Lia. Lia, you always are ready to take up arms for me or talk me off a ledge. Thanks for nearly always knowing when to do which.

And, as always, thanks to you, reader, for giving this one a chance.

Dedication

To my daughter Haley because, as always,
there would be no books without you to inspire me.

CHAPTER ONE

TJ

W hat have you done, Tatum?"

At the sound of my father's voice, I quickly hit the key that minimizes all my open windows and brings my journal front and center. The journal is a fake, an anodyne rendering of the most boring parts of my days. My father's presence alone would have been enough for me to make that keystroke—it's a well-honed habit by now—but his tone is anguished, and it pulls me to attention even more than his presence. I quickly run through all my recent actions. Nothing. I've been being extremely careful lately. Very much toeing the line. In every way except one that he can't possibly know about, can he?

"Dad? I don't know—"

"Don't play dumb, Tatum. It doesn't suit you." His tone is still anguished, but now it's also taking on tinges of anger. He comes more fully into my dorm room, one of only a select few males allowed in the all-women's College of Glory dorms. His face is pale and tight. Maybe he does know.

I stay quiet. It wouldn't do to guess. I may tell him something he doesn't already know. I love my father, but I've learned a lot of lessons about keeping myself as safe as possible with him over the years. It's better he doesn't know my inner life. I think we both agree on that, really.

"Christina Nystrom has been taken for cleansing."

Oh. Oh no. My stomach sinks like a stone. Christina Nystrom is my ex. We didn't date long, but any length of homosexual relationship is far too long in this part of the nation, far too long for any member of the Crusade of the Redeemer Church, and far, far too long for the daughter of the head of security of the Crusade of the Redeemer Church. If Christina Nystrom spills our secrets, both my father and I could be in big trouble. If he's is in here, angry and worried, either she's been talking, or he knows about our relationship independently.

I hang my head in contrition. It's false. Aside from regret about having a relationship with a woman who somehow got caught, I'm fine with who I am and who I love. If I act contrite, though, my father will bluster for a while, then give me the silent treatment, then remind me that I'm promised to Allen Baker. What he won't do is throw me to the wolves, and he's in the right position to make sure that no one else does, either. He may not like my actions—understatement—but he won't let me go in for cleansing.

It's this that makes my feelings about him so complicated. It's obvious he loves me from the way he protects me. Not that it would do his reputation any good for me to be taken in for cleansing, but if he volunteered me, he'd make it through fine. His continued covering for my actions shows his love. I wish he showed it in other ways. He could actually seem interested in me, for example, but I know it's there.

After my mom died, it's like he didn't know how to be a father who was there for his kids anymore, aside from covering up for any actions the church wouldn't like. Except that now my brother works with him, it's different. They talk all the time. But I'm excluded from all that man stuff.

The distance and exclusion are the parts of our relationship that make me hate him more than a little. That and the fact that he doesn't accept me for who I am. He keeps thinking I'll grow up and out of liking women.

He speaks, jolting me out of my thoughts. "I see that means what I thought. She'll be naming names to clear her soul."

Oh yes. My name will definitely be one. I don't know what they expect, packing a bunch of sexually frustrated women into a school, even if we are all supposed to be holding Jesus close in our hearts. Even some of the women who would happily be with a man chose to experiment because of the availability. That wasn't my situation. I have no interest in men romantically or sexually. I haven't even had male friends, aside from my brother when we were small. If I had, it might have given people the wrong impression, that I was a sexual being period. That sort of thing isn't supposed to happen until you get married, particularly when you're my father's daughter. Although that would have been preferable to being gay.

I nearly snorted at the thought before I realized I was in trouble. "Who knows what people will say under duress?"

My father shakes his head. "Tatum Jane Rice, you will not get out of this so easily." He seems like he means it, but I know he'll save me. He always has. What he won't save me from is marrying Allen, but I have a plan. I'm going to be all right.

"I'm sorry that you're in this position, Dad."

"I love you, Tatum, but you need to repent your sinful ways and prepare to settle down and marry Allen. Once you do, all this will blow over. Until then, we need to get you out of the eye of the church until things calm down."

"The missionary trip should be just the thing, right?" Next week is spring break, and a group of us are going to Seattle to bring the good word to the poor unenlightened souls of the deviant city. It's not the only deviant city in the nation, but it's the one this year's missionary trip is hitting. I'm sure the blue and Godless Seattleites will be thrilled to hear us tell them about their sinful ways.

And I'll finally be able to get away.

"No." My blood goes cold at the word. He continues, "You will still be within the grasp of the church there. When Christina says your name, you'll be pulled in for cleansing, and there will be nothing I can do to stop it. Not only that, but I may lose my job. I'm sending to you to Florida as soon as I can arrange it. Meanwhile, you will come home with me. Now. Gather only the essentials. You have five minutes."

I sit still in shock. I had plans for escape in Seattle, plans that will not work in Florida. I'm sunk.

My father snaps his fingers. "Now, Tatum. Five minutes. We're leaving with or without your things."

I spring into action. Really, all I care about is my portie and my terminal, but there are a few other things that would be nice to have. My favorite jeans that I can only wear outside of class where long dresses or skirts are required, my favorite hoodie, my swimsuits, and all my clean underthings. I have some at home, but I'm not even sure if they really fit anymore. I take one last look around. There's nothing else. I don't care about any of the books I'm allowed to have, any of the clothes that are modest enough for school, nor any of the decorations I've put up so the room isn't just a cinderblock rectangle.

My father takes my arm and leads me out into the hall where two men, his Patriot Army guard, are waiting. They follow us past the dorm for Black women and out to the car. My dad is tense, but not even he knows exactly how my world is crashing around me. And there is no way I can tell him. He would do everything in his power to prevent my plan, my escape. And now? Christina Nystrom has handed him his wish on a platter, and he doesn't even know it.

CHAPTER TWO

BAILEY

A banner across the top of my phone appears, obscuring part of the video I'm watching and telling me I have an incoming call from Dad. I hit accept. "Hey, Dad. What's up?"

"Hey there, Bailey. I'm here with Mr. Rice. You remember Mr. Rice, right? And you're on speaker."

I remember Mr. Rice mostly because he's TJ's dad. He's also the head of security for the Crusade of the Redeemer Church, which is how he knows Dad. Not just one branch or region but their entire organization. While he's a veteran like Dad, he's not Patriot Army. He runs both cyber and physical security for the church. Mostly, that means he oversees the people who do the work, and he is the primary liaison between the church and Patriot Army. The worst thing he does is identify internal threats to the church and take the appropriate action. Send gay people to conversion camp. Put unwed pregnant people into homes until they give birth so the babies can be given to good Christian families. Round up people who express any concerns about the teachings of the church and either mandate special services for mild doubters or retreats for more serious cases.

I've luckily never encountered him in his work position. It wouldn't have gone well for me. But I'm out of his reach now and have nothing to worry about. For me, the question isn't if I remember him, it's why the fuck Dad is calling me with him there. Luckily, the training to respect the chain of command from my summers spent with Dad kick in. "Yes, of course. How are you, Mr. Rice?"

A new voice says, "I've been better, Bailey, to be honest. That's why I asked your dad to put us in touch."

"I'm sorry to hear that, sir." What in the world does he want me to do about it? I've only ever seen the man a handful of times, and I've never actually spoken to him.

"I understand you're substitute teaching up in Oregon these days. Is that right?" He says Oregon like it's a disease I have.

"Yes, sir." I had actually just flopped on the couch to scroll through the socials after getting home from a day of teaching PE to elementary school kids.

"I'm hoping I can talk you into taking a job for me."

"Teaching?" I have no interest in moving to Oklahoma, even if I could get a full-time PE position there. It is a red state, and I do not belong in a red state for a wide variety of reasons. Even if I was willing to move there temporarily while hiding the fact that I'm a lesbian, what if the threatened civil war actually happens, and I can't get out? No way.

"No, although I'm sure we'd be lucky to have you. I'm more interested in your other skills."

He would not think I was such a catch if he knew I was queer. In fact, if he knew, I'm sure he would not be talking to me at all. As for the other skills, he's talking about the skills I acquired from kids' camp when I was visiting Dad in the summers, until we decided I wasn't going to Oklahoma anymore. "I'm not super up on all of those skills, Mr. Rice," I say, trying for diplomatic.

Dad clears his throat. "I've been telling Mr. Rice about your recent accomplishments in Pukulan."

I recently went through a grueling thirty-six-hour test to become a black belt in Pukulan, an Indonesian martial art. It's my third black belt.

When I don't say anything, Dad says, "And you were telling me about getting second place in that shooting competition."

It was only a regional thing. But, yes, I like target shooting, and I have kept up the skill.

With Mr. Rice knowing these things, it will be that much harder for me to say no to whatever he is about to ask. What the hell is Dad thinking? He knows I don't want anything to do with Patriot Army and particularly nothing to do with the church. The church that has a separate wing for Black congregants, hates LGBTQ+ folks, basically rules the red states with an iron fist, and has produced every right-wing government leader in the last dozen or so years.

I clear my throat in an echo of my dad. We may be on opposite ends of the political spectrum, but we still share certain characteristics. My love of martial arts doesn't come from my mom. "Yes, sir. That's true."

"I believe you are the right person for this job." He stops speaking as if it is the end of the discussion.

"I'm flattered, certainly, but what is the job?"

"Your dad tells me I can trust your discretion. Is that true, Bailey? Even though you're living in one of those sinful cities?"

I live in Portland. People here are outdoorsy. They go hiking. The bike lanes and paths are full anytime it isn't raining and not exactly empty when it is. The rivers and lakes fill with swimmers, paddlers, and tubers all summer. We have a lot of vegans. There are community gardens and composting. Does every other house also fly Pride flags or Cascadia flags? Sure. Has the eastern three-quarters of the state—but less than ten percent of the population—left to join Idaho because of our craven ways? Yes. Did we vote in basic health care for all? You bet. Do we have a strong NoFa presence? Yes, because of the strong Patriot Army presence around us. They come at Portland all the time, and NoFa defends the city. And sometimes, lately more than ever, do they go into the red to take down leaders of Patriot Army units? The best offense is a good defense, as they say.

Does that make us a sinful city? Oh yes. In the eyes of the Crusade of the Redeemer Church, we're top five for sinful. That's at least part of the local Patriot Army's reasons for incursions, to teach us sinners a lesson. But also, they just like beating people up. And hastening the charge toward civil war.

But the question was about if he could trust my discretion. And the answer is, it depends. Will I tell the Patriot Army anything? Hell no. Will I use any information I get to discredit the church or Patriot Army? Yeah, I will if such a thing is possible. But nothing sticks. Blue already thinks they're evil incarnate. Red thinks they've hung the moon and believe everything they say, or at least, they pretend to. Any attack on them is written off as fake news. I'm told that the forty-fifth president is to thank for that playbook.

My dad interjects after the pause goes on a little too long. "Bailey, it's about Tatum. She's in trouble."

My intestines turn to water. I need to play it cool, though. I don't know if Mr. Rice knows that TJ and I were friends back in the day. He must not know there was the hint of more, or he certainly wouldn't be making this call. "I'm sorry to hear that."

"Yes." Mr. Rice's voice is tight. "I can't go into details, but she needs to get away for a while, and I need someone to protect her. Someone who isn't Patriot Army but has the training. Someone like you."

"Go away where?" Maybe he's sending her to a blue state because he's finally accepting that she likes girls. She would need an escort for that, and it certainly couldn't be Patriot Army. They'd take her to a conversion camp instead.

"Florida. I need you fly here right away, then the two of you will fly to Florida under assumed names. It is likely to be months. I'm willing to pay double whatever you're making as a substitute teacher."

I pucker my lips in a whistle but don't actually make the sound. It wouldn't be professional to accept when I have feelings about TJ. This is a seriously mixed situation. Protecting her is a draw but also fraught. Florida is beyond bad. Most states still have permeable boarders, even if they have checkpoints on their major roads. Florida has a fucking wall, even though it borders with red states. It houses the Patriot Army headquarters like Oklahoma is home to the center of the Crusade of the Redeemer. With rare exceptions, you don't get in or out of Florida without the correct travel documents. For children and women, that means parental or spousal permission. And by spouse, I mean husband. Gay marriage, of course, isn't legal in Florida. It's the worst of the worst. They're doing the most to lead the way toward breaking up the country.

Personally, I think we'll split soon. The only question is exactly how. Will we go with Cascadia here and the States of the East, with the center and south of the country all combining into one, or will the fault lines fall in a different way? Honestly, I don't really care as long as I'm on the blue side when it happens.

No, I do care. I mean, I care about the civil war part. I have no interest in fighting, nor in the repercussions war would mean for everyone. But if we could just simply go our separate ways? I think if we allowed people to shuffle where they want to be, such a separation would probably be for the best. It's that freedom of movement that's the problem, particularly from red to blue states.

The third factor is money. I need it. I've got bills and student loans. I like substitute teaching because of the flexibility, but guaranteed double pay for months? That's a real push toward saying yes.

Plus, what will happen to TJ if I say no?

"So, Bailey, can I trust you?" Mr. Rice repeats.

CHAPTER THREE

TJ

I watch the early morning world go by from behind tinted windows. My eyes burn, and my head pounds from lack of sleep. The way my future has changed from this time yesterday is staggering.

I spent about sixteen hours in my childhood bedroom while my father made arrangements. Without any input from me, of course. He sent a housekeeper to my room early this morning to tell me to get ready to travel to Florida. I had about fifteen minutes to dress and throw some things in a bag.

I don't get how this is going to work. If he sends me with a Patriot Army guard, how is that keeping me safe from Patriot Army? If he sends me alone, what's to make sure I really go? Well, actually, that's easy enough. I can't fly out of a red state without his permission. I can't just get in a car and go without him sending people after me. Meaning if he takes me to the airport and checks me in for a flight, my options become extremely limited.

But sending me away alone is not safe. There have been attacks on Redeemer and Patriot Army leadership lately, even in the heart of the bible belt. My father's position makes me a target. NoFa is getting more aggressive. Not that I blame them, but I'd rather not be un-alived. If they want to take me prisoner...well, that maybe I could work with.

"Think of this as a vacation. I'm not fool enough to think you were actually looking forward to missionary work. You'll be staying right on the water. There's even a boat." Unspoken is that it's better than I deserve, although his tone makes it clear. "You can rest, get your head right, enjoy the water, and I'll bring you home in a few months after all this blows over, just in time for your engagement party."

My stomach churns. I really thought I'd be able to evade that fate. Now I don't know how I'm going to get out of it. I want to appear to be cooperative, though. "I'm just tired, Daddy. I didn't get a lot of sleep." That isn't a lie. I had a hard time sleeping, and it was predawn when the housekeeper woke me up. I haven't seen predawn from this side in I don't know how long. I didn't even have time for makeup before I was basically tossed into the car.

He awkwardly pats my knee. The privacy screen is up between us and our driver and the passenger, both Patriot Army guards. I'm surprised they're letting this happen. I suppose if Christina hasn't started talking yet, they'd have no reason to. But how does my father know? Unless he has spies at school, so he knew to act the moment Christina was taken in for cleansing. I should have suspected. It's the most reasonable explanation. He was letting me sow my wild oats, perhaps hoping I'd get it out of my system like my brother did.

When Preston was away at college, he got up to all sorts of things. I knew about many of them because I have a long habit of digitally spying on him. But I also overheard my dad saying something about this or that thing he'd done, things Preston wouldn't have told him about. After college, Preston did the right thing and married a good church girl. He's busily following in our dad's footsteps now.

My father is clearly hoping it will be the same for me. "I'm sure you've been scared. I'm not happy with you, Tatum, but we're going to get through this."

Yes, but can I live with the life I'll have on the other side?

At the airport, we park in a parking garage, but only the guards get out. I watch as they exchange nods with a shadowy figure, likely the person selected to accompany me. The figure approaches the car and becomes clearer. It's a woman. Her movements are assured. She practically prowls as she walks. When she opens the door and slides into the seat across from my dad and me, I finally see her face clearly.

My heart stutters. What the world is Bailey doing here?

And why, oh why, do I have to see her for the first time in seven years looking like I just rolled out of bed? She's wearing black slacks and a light jacket over a T-shirt. There are white sneakers on her feet. She makes the simple outfit look good. Meanwhile, I'm in a flipping tracksuit because I couldn't be bothered. Great.

But it's also the least of my problems at the moment.

"You two have met before, correct?" my father asks.

Bailey inclines her head. "We did summer swim team together when we were kids."

We did more than that, but my dad must not have known. Or is this somehow part of an effort to find every girl I've ever so much as kissed and deal with them? Bailey looks calm, so she must have been brought here under friendly pretenses. What is she even doing in Oklahoma, much less in this car?

Then it hits me. Bailey is my dad's solution to my safety.

"That's right," I agree.

"Bailey is going to accompany you to Florida, Tatum. She will keep you safe."

And is she to be my jailor as well? I can't believe it of Bailey. However, I don't really need a jailor. It's nearly impossible to travel without permission from an adult male family member, particularly out of Florida. All red state airports require permission to fly for any woman or girl. Bailey probably has a pass from her dad. He has always been much more permissive. I'm not convinced he's even a true Christian, although he does make an appearance at church often enough.

"Your flight is in an hour. Best get in there."

I reach for the door handle, but Bailey beats me to it. She gets out first and looks around before she lets me out, even though my father's two guards are still standing out there. Maybe she's trying to put on a good show. What is her angle here?

I start for the door. My dad stops me with a low, "Tatum. Don't do anything stupid."

With that warning ringing in my ears, I take my suitcase from one of the guards and follow Bailey into the airport.

"I doubt anyone is listening to us, but until we're safely at the house, I'm Nancy, and you're Beth." Bailey cuts her eyes at me and apparently takes in my look. "I know. I didn't choose the names. I'm under strict orders not to give you your ID. I guess your dad thinks you may make a run for it."

I would if I thought it would do any good. I don't say anything as we approach the self-service kiosk. Bailey pulls two IDs out of a pocket and chooses one to scan. She taps the button for one bag and pays with a credit card.

She tucks the boarding pass, card, and IDs into a pocket. She doesn't even have a backpack. I sullenly follow her to the bag check and then security. She hands over both IDs, the boarding passes, a laminated card that I assume is her pass to travel, and a notarized form that is likely mine. I can see the raised seal. The agent gives us each a bored once-over and hands everything back to Bailey. There are no surprises in security. Great. Guess I'm really going to Florida.

Once we both have our shoes back on, Bailey says, "We've got to move to catch our flight."

It's not until we get to our gate that I know we're flying into Tampa. That's not what I expected. The church owns several large houses in Florida, but they're mostly on the east side. The one I've visited the most is a waterfront property in Miami. Maybe this house isn't even actually a church property, no doubt in an attempt to keep me further from the Redeemer gaze. But if we were going to a church property, at least I'd have some idea of what to expect.

I hate everything. Maybe being un-alived wouldn't be that bad, after all.

CHAPTER FOUR

BAILEY

We're sitting in first class, of course. TJ is in the window seat, and I'm in the aisle to be between her and anyone else. Planes are relatively safe, though. It's hard to smuggle a weapon onboard. Also, I'm between her and escape. It was made clear that I'm supposed to make sure she doesn't. That isn't an aspect of the job I plan to follow. I'd be happy to let her escape or even help her. It's something I'll bring up later. Florida will bring challenges, no doubt, but it's possible. That is, if she wants to escape. Knowing TJ, she'll probably just fall back in line. She likes to seem edgy until push comes to shove.

This is a much more comfortable seat than I had on my red-eye from Portland. I dozed a bit on that flight but didn't get much sleep. I don't intend to sleep on this flight, but I find myself waking up as we're landing. The last thing I remember is taking off.

"Nice nap?" Her tone is snarky. I don't blame her, but she must surely know I'm not her enemy.

"Yep." I raise my hands over my head and stretch. "I feel much better."

I notice her eyes stray to my stomach where my shirt rides up. So she is still into girls. That's interesting. It still doesn't mean she'll want to get away from all this. If not, I'm getting paid for what amounts to a vacation. Unless someone comes after her, which is highly unlikely in Florida. Particularly since the only person aside from me who knows exactly where we're going is Mr. Rice. And probably his assistant.

As we move through the airport, my head is on a swivel, just like I was trained. Even though the threat seems very low, that is my job. In addition to TJ's bag, I have two checked ones. One was a bag I also checked from Portland to Oklahoma. The other was one I requested my dad put together for me. He met me in the airport to give me the IDs, the bag, a credit card, and the paperwork we needed to travel.

"Mr. Rice says to spare no expense to ensure TJ's safety and comfort."

"Okay."

"And your own. Seriously, Bailey. Money means nothing to him. If you need a swimsuit or whatever, just buy it."

"Okay, Dad." I packed swimsuits. I'd be fine.

"You have two hours before you need to meet TJ and Mr. Rice in the parking garage. As Mr. Rice explained, all the details of getting to the house are up to you. The less anyone else knows, the better. So I'm supposed to leave you to sort out any details that need sorting. You got this, kid?"

I did. I checked the contents of the bag, checked my luggage, made the proper declarations, and used a new burner phone, one of several that Dad had packed for me, to book a rental car. Then, I went to collect TJ.

We step out of baggage claim and into the sweltering heat. I look around for the rental car shuttle stop. "This way." TJ looks at me askance but follows. "What?"

"I've never not been picked up by a driver."

The thought throws me for a loop, but I rally. "Well, the fewer people who know where we're going, the better." I could have at least sprung for the executive service where we'd get picked up at the curb and taken to the rental agency. It just hadn't occurred to me.

She shrugs her acquiescence. Or maybe her indifference.

We go through all the steps necessary to claim the rental car. TJ clearly has no idea how this all works, but she doesn't fuss. Finally, the agent gives us a wave, tells us to enjoy our stay in Florida, and we're off.

"Before we go to the house, you should shop for whatever you need," I say. "We won't leave the house more than we absolutely have to. Do you need anything?"

"A terminal."

"I'm afraid I can't do that."

"Because Daddy said no?"

"No, because we're going off the grid at the house. No connectivity at all. No phones or terminals." It's true. I will even keep the burner phones powered off unless there's some sort of emergency. "But if it's just for entertainment, we could pick up some books, games, magazines?" I want to offer a game console, but systems are tied to networks. To get something that wouldn't try to connect, I'd have to find something a good thirty years old. Buying something like that would make us memorable.

She huffs. "Fine. Let's go get some magazines or something."

I put bookstore in the navigation system. The closest one is Barnes & Noble. It's maybe the only one, really. Portland is so different with a used bookstore every other block. I nearly laugh at myself. This is far from the only way Portland is different from Tampa.

TJ surprises me with how many books she picks up. I don't know why, but I thought people in red states didn't read. She seems to know what she's doing, though, and I want to offer to carry her books while she browses, but I need to keep my hands free to do my job. When she's done, I pay with one of the credit cards.

The next stop is a grocery store. I get a lot of convenience food. I'm not a big cook. TJ appears completely disinterested except when she adds a couple of boxes of Cocoa Pebbles to the cart.

The navigation system is unidirectional, so I feel comfortable using it to navigate to the house. Mostly. A small paranoid part of me thinks that it can be hacked and reversed, so I commit the directions to memory and shut the system off.

"Who do you think is coming after me?"

I pull out and start driving. It could be NoFa, but it's seriously questionable that they'd go after TJ. She's not in charge of anything.

Ostensibly, they're a threat to right-wing leaders, but I've yet to hear of them going after their families. Much less in the stronghold of Florida. I really think I'm here because Mr. Rice doesn't want TJ getting any ideas. Still, I'm taking the possibility of attack seriously. I'd hate to slack on security and have something happen to her. "I have no idea, TJ. Who is coming after you?"

She scowls and crosses her arms. "I don't know if you're here to protect me from them or deliver me to them, Bailey."

"If you want to walk away from all this, I won't stop you. TJ, I'd help you."

She stares at me. "Are you serious?"

"I will pull over right now and let you out if you want. Or better yet, I'll pull over and give you the car. I'm not a jailor. If you've got someplace in Florida to go, the car is yours. But I think we both know that getting out of here isn't really an option with the car."

She folds her arms and stares out the window. "It's a false choice. I'm stuck here. Maybe with people coming after me."

"I don't know what happened or why your dad thinks you need security that isn't Patriot Army, but if I had to hazard a guess?"

"Go on, then."

"You kissed the wrong girl."

Her arms drop, and she turns to me, mouth open.

"It's not exactly hard to guess, TJ."

She smirks. "I've corrupted a few."

"And one of them told. Now you're in trouble with the church, and the Patriot Army will only deliver you to them. So your dad thought of me. Patriot Army trained but not one of them. So am I here to protect you from them? Or, as is my guess, Daddy thinks you might run off or might possibly be a target for NoFa? I'm supposed to be doing double duty."

"Only, apparently, you don't care for being a jailor."

"No, I don't."

She doesn't say anything for the rest of the drive.

CHAPTER FIVE

TJ

Bailey punches in a code at a gated house, and the gate swings open. If the church owns this property, it's subtle. Some of our properties are for retreats and things, so they have Crusade of the Redeemer splashed across them or tastefully written on a plaque or whatever, depending on the target audience, but this place is low-key. Maybe my father really did just find a generic rental.

The driveway is short and stops at a house that doesn't look like much. There's a garage, and Bailey hops out to punch in another code to open it. "Wait here while I check the house," she says.

"I thought we weren't worried about people coming after me."

Bailey shrugs. "It's my job." She goes to the trunk and rummages around.

I can't see what she's doing back there, but when she closes the trunk and passes by me, she has a gun in her hand. I don't know why that surprises me. She's a good shot or at least was as a teenager. I know she's here as a bodyguard. And Patriot Army goes around armed. But I've never seen her—or any woman—with a gun.

She pushes the button to close the garage door, takes one last look around, then goes inside. Without anything to distract me, the minutes are long. I reach for my portie, then remember that I don't have it. My father does. Both it and my terminal. He took them last night as soon as we got home, along with my credit cards and ID. I'm a little concerned about what he may find on them, but I think I've protected everything well. There are secure passwords and extra secure things behind yet more passwords.

In middle school, when everyone started passing around information about how to get around parental controls and firewalls, a whole new world opened to me. I'd been starting to think there was something really wrong with me. No matter how much I prayed or how much I tried to get myself to stop thinking about girls, the same thoughts would constantly return. I was beginning to think I was queer, and at the time, all I knew was that was wrong.

I overheard one kid telling another about how to get around firewalls. No one would have dreamed of telling me directly, not Mr. Rice's daughter. I went home and tried it. That was when I started to find my way around the internet. I was exposed to many new ideas. Not everyone thought that girls liking girls was bad, it turned out. Since that was how I felt, I really wanted someone to tell me it was okay. And there were people out there who did. I learned more and more about computers to hide my tracks while I figured out who I was.

Bailey was also a big part of figuring out who I was. I stare at the door to the house, thinking about how wild it is that she's here. Why did she agree to this?

If she really would let me go—no. It was a false statement. We're in Florida. She brought me here. If she wanted to help me escape, she'd never have brought me to Florida where there is no way out without a male chaperone. She may believe what she said, but it's likely just to make herself feel better about what she's doing. I can't trust that she's on my side.

Anyway, my father probably won't find anything beyond that fake journal and my schoolwork. A little bit of web surfing on approved sites. That's it. I hope.

Anyway, there's nothing I can do about it while I'm sitting in this crappy rental car in this garage in Florida. My life is a mess.

And Bailey still isn't back. How big is this house? It didn't look that big from the front.

And darn, does she look good. Not that she didn't look good when I last saw her, but she was the focus of my obsession then. My little fourteen-year-old self couldn't have dreamed how hot she'd be seven years later.

She was the darling of our summer swim program. Anyone would think that because she was only there in the summers, she wouldn't be popular, but they'd be wrong. The first day she walked in, people swarmed around her saying, "Bailey! You're back." Not just the girls, either. The boys were there to slap her on her back and throw playful punches. Everyone loved her. It was like a celebrity had come to town.

I remember the first time I actually talked to her. I was eleven. We'd been in the same summer swim program since I was five. She'd done it a year longer because she was a year older. But I'd been a little intimidated and a little angry at her popularity and had kept my distance. I had my clique, she had, well, everyone else.

The summer I was eleven, I got my period for the first time. Sex ed was nonexistent at our school, and my mom had died two years prior. I vaguely knew that girls got periods. We did talk amongst ourselves, but when I felt something damp in my swimsuit when we were doing dry land stretches, I thought maybe I'd peed a little from laughing with my friends. I went to the locker room to try to dry things off and saw red.

I sat there, stunned. Was God punishing me for something?

When another girl came in and went into the stall next to mine, I didn't know who it was, but I knew I needed help. "I'm bleeding," I whispered.

"What? Are you talking to me?"

It was Bailey. That was the worst. I'd have picked *any* of the other girls. Some I got along with better than others, but I'd known them all since we'd spent Sundays in the church crèche together as babies. Bailey was in interloper.

When I didn't answer, she asked more softly, "Did you start your period?"

"I…maybe?" My period. Maybe I wasn't dying.

"Is it your first?"

"I guess?"

"Has your mom talked to you about this?"

"My mom is dead."

"Oh. I'm sorry."

I didn't know what to say to that. I never knew what to say to that. Besides, most people already knew.

After an awkward moment passed, she said, "Okay, well, you need a tampon."

I'm shaken from the memory by Bailey coming back through the door. "It's all clear. We can go in."

The house *is* much larger than it looks from the front. It sprawls out the back and to the sides. There are huge windows overlooking a backyard that leads to water. I pause there, taking it in. It must be an inlet because there are no waves to speak of. There are two docks, and one leads to a boathouse. In spite of my circumstances, I feel a small stab of excitement. There's a speedboat in there, according to what my father told me. We can wakeboard. That is, if Bailey allows it and knows how to drive a boat. It isn't hard. I can teach her if she doesn't. Or maybe she's already a wakeboarder herself. I know she is comfortable in water, so maybe.

I turn to ask, but she isn't there. In a moment, she emerges from the garage, hands full. "Oh, sorry. I can get my own bags."

"It's no problem." She sets them down. "Here are the rules for safety: when we're both in the house, you can move about at will. There's a security system that will alert us to any breach." She waves at the window. "If you want to go outside, we'll go together. I don't have to be right on your heels, but I should be nearby."

"And am I allowed to swim?" I ask, a little bitterness seeping in.

"Sure. As long as I'm there, too."

"Great." I pick up the bags and walk in the direction I assumed the bedrooms were in.

I don't know why I'm being such a little brat. I mean, I do. I'm tired, for one. And, oh yeah, my plan for getting out of a life I hate is absolutely shattered. But I shouldn't be taking it out on Bailey. She's doing the best she can in this situation. I guess.

I stick my head into a couple of rooms, then pick one more or less at random. I drop my bags, plant myself facedown on the tidy bed, and briefly wonder if there are housekeepers who know this house is occupied now before I pass out.

CHAPTER SIX

BAILEY

I'm sitting in an armchair looking out at the sunset with a glass of water next to me—no drinking on the job—when TJ appears. She stands, arms crossed, shoulders hunched, and looks out the window next to me for a few moments. I wait to see if she'll have anything to say. It seems that everything I say to her, she takes offense at, so I'm not inclined to start a conversation.

"Sorry."

That's a surprise, not an unwelcome one, but a surprise. "What for?" I truly don't know and am curious. Is she sorry for disappearing without a word? Because that's no big deal. Is she sorry for biting my head off every time I open my mouth? Because that is something I wouldn't be sad to hear an apology for. Is she sorry for what happened when we were teenagers? I've forgiven her a long time ago for that. I know the sorts of pressures she was under. I simply never put myself in the same situation again. I learned my lesson, but I got it.

"I've been something of a brat on this trip. But you're not who I should be taking it out on."

"Well, thanks." Who should she be taking it out on? She came with me even after I offered to let her go, so who is twisting her arm here? Was she supposed to get to go with someone else? What trouble is she in? "TJ…"

"Yeah?"

"What exactly is happening to you? What did this trip disrupt?" It's my best guess for why she's so out of sorts.

She sinks into an armchair next to mine, still holding herself stiffly. She looks around the room.

"If you're wondering if we're bugged or there are cameras, I'm pretty sure not. I did a sweep."

"How sure is pretty sure?"

There could be new technologies of which I'm unaware, but not only did I sweep for bugs and cameras, I have a signal disrupter running. It means no internet, but it also means that we should be in the dark for outside surveillance. The house system and my own system that I set up while TJ was in her room both work on closed systems, so they're functional. "Sure enough that I'm comfortable saying that I'm a lesbian."

She sags back in the chair. "An ex of mine got taken in for cleansing."

I'm not surprised. That was my guess. "And your dad is getting you out of harm's way by stashing you down here. With me. Someone who can protect you just in case but won't turn you in."

"Exactly."

I shrug. "Seems like it could be worse. Unless you had something going that this trip disrupted." I'm not sure if it's a girlfriend or what, but she's clearly unhappy to be here.

"Exactly that." She sounds bitter.

"Did this trip pull you away from something? Are you in college?"

"I am, but that's...that doesn't matter at all. I only agreed to go because it put off getting married. I'm just going to College of Glory."

"Ah." It's an all-women's school run by Crusade of the Redeemer. The major options include homemaker, education, and assistant. I'm not sure there's anything else.

"Yeah, ah. It's crap. My father says that Allen won't want me to work, so I had to agree to major in homemaking in order to be allowed to go. I'm learning all sorts of useful things about balancing a family budget, cooking, cleaning, and child development." The bitterness is tangible with every word.

"What do you want to be learning?"

"Programming. I've been teaching myself from free courses I've found online, but those won't get me a job."

"If you're marrying, how would you be able to work anyway? And who is Allen?" I don't know for sure if TJ is bi, but I strongly suspect not. It'd be easiest to just cut herself off from half the people she's attracted to if she lived in Oklahoma and was bi. TJ, apparently, has been going around dating girls. To do that while being one of the royalty of the church is risky at best.

"You wouldn't know him. He's ten years older, so he wouldn't have been in your camps or whatever."

"Wait. Allen Baker?" He wasn't in my camps, but he was a camp counselor at kids' camp, which is what we called the Patriot Army Kids' Camp for short. All summer, I'd go to swimming in the morning, then take the shuttle with the other kids that went to camp. It was nearly all boys, aside from me. There was one other girl several years older when I started going, and Dad told me there was another who started just when I stopped, but we were few and far between. When a parent was willing to send a daughter, we were tolerated. It was useful to have some female members of Patriot Army for covert ops or things like this—protecting a woman one-on-one—even though this is clearly not a Patriot Army sanctioned mission.

We learned all sorts of things. How to prepare for government collapse, martial arts, target shooting, how to spy on each other. Honestly, a lot of it was really fun. We'd break into groups with specific missions and use all the skills we'd learned to complete them. The older we got, the more complicated the missions. The summer I was fifteen, I was hacking into keyed locks, planting bugs to spy on other teams, and lying in wait while covered in camouflage to hit opposing teams with paintballs. Anyway, older kids acted as counselors and taught the little kids. Allen was my prep teacher when I was six. I remember specifically because the boys worshiped him. I never saw the appeal, but apparently, it was enough for them that he was the son of the head pastor of Crusade of the Redeemer.

"Yeah, him, exactly."

"And you…are going along with this? Want this?"

She turns and gives me a withering look. "What do you think, Bailey?"

I hold my hands, palms up, to my sides. "I don't know you that well, TJ, at least not anymore. Things might have changed."

"What about my female ex being taken in for cleansing makes you think things have changed?"

"Again, I don't know. That's why I'm asking."

She glares for a moment longer before letting her head fall onto the back of the chair. Her words are dull when she speaks. "No. I don't want this. I had a plan to defect or whatever."

"Had? Oh. Shit. This is messing that up?"

"Yup." She pops the P.

"What was the plan?"

She sighs. "I was supposed to go on a missionary trip to Seattle over spring break. I was in touch with people who were going to help me. I have some money hidden away." She stops abruptly, making me wonder what she's leaving out. "Anyway. I was just going to walk away in Seattle."

"If I got you out of Florida, could you get to your money?"

She sits up. "Yes. I need to get to a blue state, and I need a terminal. Can you do that?"

"I have an idea, yes." Meanwhile, I'm pretty sure she hasn't eaten all day. Well, she could have eaten on the plane while I was asleep, but that was a long time ago now. "Are you hungry? We can talk while you eat."

"I'm suddenly starving."

That's likely due to having some hope. "I ate a little while ago. It's a help yourself situation."

"From all the delightful selection of frozen meals you purchased?"

To be fair, I also got stuff for sandwiches, snack foods, and cereal for breakfast. "Exactly."

"Great." She pops right up and heads to the kitchen.

The sarcasm in her voice compels me to call after her, "You know, you were in the grocery store, too, if you didn't want convenience food."

She turns around and grins. "Yes, but I was busy pouting then."

I laugh and go back to watching the water while I wait for her to return. She really does seem ready to leave. Maybe she has changed.

CHAPTER SEVEN

TJ

I'm bored. And filled with nerves and excitement but bored. After our talk last night, I am filled with hope again. That is the excited part. I may not have to marry a man—and a man I can't stand—after all. Bailey thinks it's best to wait until after her first check-in with my father to lull him into a sense of complacency. The first check is after we've been here one week. She's going to suggest two weeks after that so that if we leave right away, we can be long gone before anyone is looking for us. It's a good plan.

But it means a week of hanging out here. I've only been up a few hours, and I'm bored. I've done all the reading I care to do for now. I want to swim, but going to Bailey to ask permission makes me feel like I'm about six. So I wander aimlessly through the house. I find the bedroom Bailey claimed right next to mine. I have an impulse to look through her room, but I resist. Not only do I respect others' privacy because of not always having had it myself, but she's likely to pop up at any moment.

I move on. I open drawers, doors, and cupboards. There's not a lot of interest, but I do find a stash of games. I pull out a deck of cards, thinking I'll play Solitaire.

One whole side of the house is a great room, with windows for walls that overlook the inlet. At one end, where the door to the garage is, the kitchen is delineated from the dining area by a breakfast bar. The dining table seats about a dozen. On the other side of the table is the sitting area where Bailey and I talked last night. Furthest away from the garage is a family room with the TV and a few couches arranged around a coffee table in a U. It was in one of the built-in cupboards that I found the games.

I wander the length of the great room, the tiled floor cool under my bare feet until I reach the breakfast bar where Bailey sits. She does have a terminal, even though she said we'd be off the grid. It annoys me. If she's not my jailor and is connected, why can't I be?

"Is the outside world still there?" I ask.

"I assume so." She lays the terminal facedown on the counter.

I gesture at it. "You weren't checking news or whatever?"

She glances at it, then back at me. "No. I told you, we're internet-free here. I meant me, too. I was just checking on the security system, making sure everything is as it should be."

"Oh." My annoyance drains away. She keeps telling me she's not my jailor, but it's still a surprise every time I see evidence of it, even after our talk last night. The terminal is plugged into the wall with a USB cable. That must be how she's connecting to the isolated security system.

She eyes the cards in my hand. "What kind of games do you like to play?"

I put the deck on the counter, having lost interest in Solitaire. "I dunno."

She lets out a soft sigh. "We have a week to wait. We might as well figure out some way to entertain ourselves."

Images of ways we could entertain each other flash through my head. Where did that come from? I mean, Bailey is sexy, yes. She's all legs. She has an athlete's build. The way she moves is akin to a leopard on the prowl. Her eyes are a piercing blue. So, yes, amazingly sexy. But. I tried kissing her once when we were teenagers. She was so appalled that we never spoke again. There's no way she's talking about that sort of entertainment. She's talking about cards.

"I haven't played a lot of cards. I was thinking of Solitaire, but I'm not even sure I know how to play. It's been years," I admit.

"I know some games. I could teach you."

I consider the offer. It'd be a way to kill some time. I'm not against it, but I set my pride aside and ask for what I really want. "What I'd really like to do is go wakeboarding."

"We need to check out the boat anyway. Sounds like as good a way to test drive it as any. Let's go." She picks something the size of a charging case for earbuds off the counter and leads the way.

We walk down to the boathouse, and Bailey produces keys to unlock the door. Inside is a beautiful speedboat. It's nicer than I'd anticipated. Our escape will be done in relative comfort. Along the walls are a selection of equipment, including boards, life jackets, and right next to the door, keys for the boat.

"Okay, then. Let's go put suits on." Bailey glances at me. "Or, I guess, me. I don't know if you've got one on under there."

I'm wearing a sundress, and I do not have my swimsuit on underneath. We go back up to the house. I don't wear one of the skimpy bathing suits I packed. I don't know why I even packed them. They're expected of girls my age, but I prefer bike shorts and a sports bra for wakeboarding, so that's what I put on. In less than fifteen minutes, we're out on the dock. Bailey is in a two-piece that looks built for being active in as opposed to showing off her body. Not that it doesn't end up doing that, too. There's a long stretch of toned abs between the sports bra top and the bikini briefs that hug her curvy butt. I try not to stare. I feel like a twig next to her.

She climbs into the boat first and sets something into the recess of the dashboard where the gauges reside before starting the boat. It purrs like a dream.

It's an excellent time. I push myself to do harder and harder tricks because when I'm doing a backflip above the water, I'm not thinking about anything else. When I was a kid and my brother and I were still friends, this was what we did all summer and as often as we could get to Florida in the winter, which was often enough. My mom brought us down all the time, mostly because she liked to be in Florida, I think. Afterward, we had a nanny. Our father would send us and the nanny down to get us out of his hair. Family tradition was to fly down the day after Christmas. Was. That's all in the past.

That's fine. While I always loved being out on the water, after my mom died, it got a lot less fun. Not only was she gone, but Preston got mean.

Anyway, driving the boat while keeping an eye on Bailey as well as being out here myself takes my mind off all that. Bailey isn't as good, but she can do a few simple tricks. When I come back aboard after my third turn, she looks at the dashboard with a worried frown.

"Do we need gas?"

"Not yet, but if we want to come back out, we should head in."

"You're telling me we can't get gas?"

"We can…" She sounds reluctant. "But it's just one more time to be noticed, so I'd like to avoid it."

I fall into the seat next to the driver's seat and cross my arms. "This is the worst vacation ever. Stuck in a house with no connectivity and nothing to do except maybe once or twice go out on the boat before we run out of gas."

Bailey sits as well. She'd been standing in front of the captain's seat. "And only me for company."

"You're not bad company, but you are being a little bit of a stick-in-the-mud."

"I think that's the first time anyone has ever said that about me."

"So let's get some gas and keep having fun."

She's tooling slowly back in the direction of the house and continues to do so in silence for a few minutes. I figure she's not going to budge and resign myself to playing Go Fish for the week.

"I think I saw a gas card next to the key. Let's call it a day today, but tomorrow, we'll figure out which pump around here it goes to. If we can get gas without drawing attention, we will."

"Fair enough, I suppose. But if we don't think anyone is coming after me, why all the precautions?"

"After what you told me last night, I wouldn't put it past the church to send some Patriot Army people after you to bring you in for cleansing."

I consider that for a few minutes. Wouldn't my father prevent that? That was why he sent me here. Maybe he doesn't think he can protect me this time. Maybe he'll decide it's best to turn me in.

There are different kinds of cleansing depending on the supposed sin. Cleansing for queer people means conversion camp, where they go through all sorts of different therapies and treatments to cure them, like it's some sort of disease to be gay. There are plenty of opportunities to purge oneself through giving up others.

I wonder if Christina has named me yet, and if so, what lengths the church would go through to pick me up. Or if they threaten my father's position enough, will he give me up? If he does, I'm really sunk. Not only does he know where I am, he knows who I'm with.

If the church decides to put its mind to picking me up, then Patriot Army would be looking in all the likely places. They'll also put my picture out to all the local branches of the church and Patriot Army. So if they're looking, my face could be everywhere. And turning people in that the church is looking for leads to rewards. Maybe Bailey is right.

Now my optimism for escape is tempered by fear that I'll be picked up before we get the chance. I hate everything about this. I hate that I was raised in a society where just being me is a sin and worthy of punishment. I hate that I keep getting my hopes up for escape, then having them dashed. Well, in this case, not entirely dashed. Bailey is on my side now. Given all we've divulged to each other and our shared history, I really believe it. And I know she's capable. I need to heed advice from my trusted expert, as much as it rankles.

"Lying low it is, then."

CHAPTER EIGHT

BAILEY

Our days fall into a rhythm. I'm always up first, checking the security systems. We eat cereal for breakfast, then do yoga on the dock before we go out on the boat. We come home for lunch and chill time. We play cards or read. In the afternoons, we go back out. We have to get gas regularly. We've been really blowing through it with all the wakeboarding and admittedly, some joy riding. Sometimes, other people are at the pump. We never wait because that would be drawing attention to ourselves, so we pass on by and try again the next time we go out. After our afternoon outing, we come back for dinner and more card games or reading. We sit and watch the water a lot.

We don't talk much aside from basic pleasantries and about the games. I'm not sure why, but I respected TJ's seeming desire to keep to herself. I honestly don't know if I want her to talk to me or not. The crush I had on her makes me care, but if I can avoid getting further attached, that will make my life easier. Still, I can't help but be curious about who she is these days. Also, despite the fact that we're keeping each other at arm's length, she draws my eye all the time. She's a striking woman.

All the more reason to keep my distance.

One night after dinner, we're in our usual armchairs watching the sunset. TJ surprises me by asking, "What's it like living in Oregon these days?"

It shouldn't be that much of a surprise; she used to ask about living in Oregon when we were kids. It's just I hadn't expected a conversational gambit at all. "It's good. I mean, for me, it's good."

"What's good about it? Are you ever scared for your life?"

She's probably asking because we don't have a police force anymore. A lot of people in red states think that means we're lawless and at the mercy of criminals. We're not. We still have traffic enforcers, but they're unarmed. We also have crisis responders. They're the ones who show up for domestic violence type calls. As for solving crimes, well, the police didn't have a very good record of that. It is true of all police forces in the US, current and historic. They're bad at solving crime. Worse, they tend to commit sanctioned crime themselves. Portland defunded them years ago and established a completely new, small, community-based system for investigating crime. There have been some kinks, sure, but it's no worse than before, and these days, things run fairly smoothly. Maybe some crime goes unpunished, but it's a fair trade for all the wrongful imprisonment and outright fear many people had of the police before.

One of the major pushes to defund was because when Patriot Army came calling, the police blatantly favored them. Many of them *were* Patriot Army. Most lived outside of Portland and thought we were all criminals. "Only when Patriot Army yahoos come into the city looking for trouble." I belatedly realize that maybe I shouldn't have called them yahoos to her. "Sorry."

"What are you sorry about? You're probably more Patriot Army than I am."

She has a point. Patriot Army and the Crusade of the Redeemer Church aren't the same. The Venn diagram of Patriot Army and Redeemers would show Patriot Army nearly entirely inside the much larger Redeemer circle. But Patriot Army has its own hierarchy and doesn't answer to the Church. However, they do offer themselves as a militarized arm of the Redeemers when necessary.

She continues, "And aren't you insulting your dad when you denigrate them?"

"Sort of. I mean, as far as I know, my dad isn't part of any arm that goes and harasses blue cities. Honestly, he just likes to play army."

"What does he do when he's not playing army?"

"He's a nurse. That was his army training, same as my mom. She did more school when she got out of the military and is now a nurse practitioner. Dad is an ED nurse. Emergency department."

"Huh."

We're quiet again for a few minutes. "Why did you stop coming to summer swim?" she asks.

My head swings in her direction, and I try not to let my mouth hang open.

"What?" She seems surprised at my surprise.

"Because you kissed me."

The summer I was fourteen was the summer I became TJ's tampon supplier. After I happened upon her in the bathroom the day she started her period, we went through a whole awkward explanation of tampon application. After she had it in, she burst into tears.

"Are you okay? Does it hurt or something?" I was back in the stall next to her after having gone and gotten a tampon for her.

"No. I just don't know where I'm going to get tampons."

"I mean, they sell them at the store. But what you really want is a cup."

"I can't just go in and buy either of those things."

I was still mulling that over when someone came banging into the bathroom. "TJ? Are you in here? I got sent to check on you."

No one had come to check on me. Figured. People liked me. I had friends. But I was an afterthought. I wasn't anyone's person. They all had best friends or groups that were cemented in the fires of going to school together. I only showed up in the summers. People talked to me, were happy to see me, and were happy to have me sit next to them. But no one thought of me when I wasn't around.

TJ, suddenly sounding put together, said, "I'm fine. Be right out."

Her friend left, and I heard TJ leave the stall. I followed. We washed our hands side by side. She said, "Thanks," and disappeared.

I figured that was it. She'd never talked to me before, and she wasn't likely to talk to me again. At the end of swimming, though, I shoved a couple more tampons into her hand before I went to the bus. My dad bought them for me but had no idea how many I actually needed. If he didn't buy me any more before college, I'd probably be fine. I only used them on occasion because I had a cup, but everyone I knew back home carried a tampon or two just in case. They were smaller than cups and could be passed out to friends in need.

I'd always thought it was stupid when girls sat out swimming several days a month here, but maybe it was because they weren't allowed to wear tampons. Maybe they had to deal with stupid pads. Maybe only adults were allowed tampons.

I brought in extra for her the next day.

I wasn't sure when I'd give them to her. I didn't want to do it in front of her friends. She hadn't even told the girl yesterday what was going on. Maybe she was embarrassed. Even if she wasn't embarrassed about the tampons, maybe she'd be embarrassed about me talking to her.

That sounded paranoid, but there were cliques at swimming. It was a little different in kids' camp because we were a smaller group of kids whose dads were in the Patriot Army or we were labeled high-energy individuals, those whose dads weren't Patriot Army, but someone had looked at them bouncing off the walls and decided they needed a lot of activity that kids' camp absolutely provided. As well as discipline. The rest of the kids went to Redeemer camp after swimming. Or went home. There were a lot of stay-at-home moms in Tulsa, which wasn't the case in Portland.

Out of my loose group of a dozen or so friends in Portland, only one had a mom who was a homemaker. A couple had moms who worked part-time from home. One had a dad who worked part-time from home, and a few more parents worked from home full-time or outside of the house. Also, three of the parents were same-sex couples, and one of my friends had a group of parents who were polyamorous. Of course, I never shared that information with anyone in Tulsa.

For whatever reason, swimming was a popular thing to do in Tulsa. I think it was one of the few activities that both boys and girls could both do. And it was considered wholesome. There were Redeemer kids—really, everyone was, but some more than others—Patriot Army brats, sporty kids, and a lot of regular kids. They were different from regular kids in Portland, though. They mostly went to Crusade of the Redeemer on Sundays; they just weren't as involved as kids like TJ. I went to services with my dad when he wasn't working, and we weren't camping. Or more accurately, we went when he felt like he needed to put in an appearance so as not to look unfaithful. Which meant I didn't hang out with the core religious kids that much.

I tried to catch TJ's eye in the locker room, but she seemed to be ignoring me on purpose. Finally, just before it was time to leave when the buses and moms showed up to pick us all up, I caught TJ alone when she ducked into the bathroom.

"Here." I pulled a small bag out of my backpack.

"What is this?"

"More tampons."

"Oh. Thanks."

She ducked into a stall, and that was it for that day. The next day, though, she said hi when she saw me. The day after that, I stretched next to her before swimming. Within a few weeks, we were inseparable. Her friends looked at me askance at first, but after a while, they just accepted that I was part of the group now.

That started a couple of golden summers of being friends with TJ. I had a person in Tulsa who noticed if I was gone, who looked for me rather than just accepting me when I showed up. I was crushing on her so hard, but I also knew that wasn't allowed in Tulsa. I went to church more. If Dad was at work, I'd go anyway so I could hang out with TJ. I knew what was happening even while the pastor was preaching that being gay was a sin, even while the youth pastors were telling us we should be honest and come forward because there was help for us. And I knew what was happening even while being pretty sure TJ didn't have any idea what I felt. I'd never tell her, not in Tulsa.

We weren't together all the time. I still went to kids' camp. She still went to church camp. She never came to Dad's house. I only went to her house a couple of times. Her brother, who was only a couple of years older than me, paid me attention that felt uncomfortable. I never met her dad aside from a time or two in passing. However, when we could find time to hang out, we did. We emailed to stay in touch year-round. Yes, it was quite old-fashioned even then, but TJ was limited in the sorts of apps she could have. When she later got around that problem, email was both habit and easier for her to explain if her dad looked over her shoulder.

She had lots of questions for me about life outside of the red states. I think that part of why she eventually started seeking out more and more forbidden information was because of me. By the time I was fifteen and she was fourteen, she was skilled in the ways of the internet and sometimes surprised me with the media she consumed. She was no longer the model religious kid she'd been when I'd handed her that tampon. I wasn't even sure if she believed anymore. But she put on a good public front.

It was that summer that I was talking to my mom one afternoon about TJ. I hadn't noticed Dad come home. When I got off the phone, he came into my room. "Bailey, we need to talk."

My stomach nearly dropped out of my butt. Had he heard? Was he going to try to talk me out of being gay? Was he going to put me in conversion camp? It was close to the end of summer, and I was supposed to go back to Portland in less than two weeks. He couldn't keep me legally, but that didn't make much difference in reality. The federal government was too weak to enforce anything, and I was too deep in red territory to hope for NoFa to come to my aid, particularly then. They were still being very defensive rather than launching offensive missions.

I had training in defense against interrogation, though. I stayed calm and didn't offer any potentially damning information he might not already have. "Okay."

"I heard you talking to your mom." I didn't say anything. Dad smiled a proud smile. "Smart girl. You need to continue to be careful, though. Not just with me but everywhere here. You're home and feel safe, but what if I'd brought a friend home?"

I cocked my head as if I didn't know what he was talking about. I gave a long, drawn-out "Okay?"

He chuckled. "Very good. I'm laying my cards on the table. I heard you talking to your mom about TJ and how you feel about her. Never, ever do that again. Never act on that. It's not safe. If anyone were to find out, I might not be able to protect you. Do you understand?"

"Yes." I did. I'd been going to Crusade of the Redeemer. I was aware of the policies. A boy from swimming who was one of the Church camp kids had suddenly stopped showing up earlier this summer. He acted like a very stereotypical gay boy. The gossip mill worked overtime to inform us all that he'd been taken to conversion camp. Apparently, his dad was the one who made it happen. So, I knew.

He patted my knee. "Good talk. Feel like burgers for dinner?"

A week later, TJ kissed me. It changed everything.

CHAPTER NINE

TJ

Wait. You stopped swimming because I kissed you?" It amazes me that anything I did as a fourteen-year-old would have had any impact on Bailey at fifteen. She'd been cooler, wiser, and much more confident.

"Not only stopped swimming but stopped going to Oklahoma at all."

She didn't say it with any sort of judgment, but she still stopped spending summers with her dad because I kissed her. "You hated kissing me so much you gave up a whole state?"

She stares at me for a long moment. That must be the case. What the hell is she doing here protecting me if she hates me that much. Is she really just that altruistic? Finally, she says, "No. It wasn't the kiss, TJ, it was the aftereffect."

"What?"

"You also stopped talking to me."

"Oh." It was true. I stopped talking to her after the kiss. It had been my first. It overwhelmed me, to say the least. I knew by then that I liked girls and Bailey in particular. I was also sure she didn't like me. I was a year younger, scrawny, and had all sorts of hang-ups from how I was raised.

One day, when it was nearly time for her to leave to go back to Portland for the school year, we snuck away from a rambunctious youth group to find a quiet corner to talk. We were talking about her friends in Portland and if she was excited to see them. She mentioned one girl in particular. Something came over me, and I suddenly stopped her talking with a kiss. Then, I ran away. And, yeah, I avoided her at swimming the next day. I was too embarrassed, too unsure what she'd say. The next day, she didn't come to swimming, and I never saw her again until that morning at the airport.

"Yeah. I told Dad, and he decided that I should leave and not come back. I went back to Portland early."

My mouth drops. "Why did you tell him? Did you know he would be that mad that you kissed a girl?"

"No, it wasn't that he was mad. It was that he was worried you'd tell your dad, and I'd get hauled off to conversion camp."

"Oh." As the import of that statement hits me, I raise a hand to my once-again open mouth. "Oh!"

She nods. "Yeah. I had no idea what you were thinking. Dad had just had a talk with me about how careful I had to be. I thought you might tell your dad that I'd kissed you and then…yeah. Dad wanted me safe."

"Shoot, Bailey. I'm so sorry. I never intended to tell anyone. I was so embarrassed that I kissed you. I figured you wouldn't want to talk to me, little kid that I was. Or that you'd be all…noble about it or something. I had no idea about those repercussions."

Bailey doesn't so much shake her head as do a side to side nod. "You know, it was the impetus to me leaving early, but it was probably time. Both my dad and I knew I wasn't safe there being who I am."

"A living monument to the fact that people living in blue states aren't monsters?"

She scoffs. "No. Gay."

"Did you know you were even then?"

"Yes, of course. I think I always knew."

I'm quiet for a minute. I didn't know until Bailey. Not just her but the world she opened up to me. So, yes, in that way, she was a threat to our way of life. It's not that I'd have been straight and happy if she hadn't come along, but it might have taken me a lot longer to figure out why I was so unhappy. I might not have figured out how to break free of the firewall to explore the internet.

I can't tell her she was my gay awakening, can I? I mean, why not? She's being very honest with me. "I didn't know until the tampon summer." I'm looking at her as I say it, but she's looking out the window until I get to the word *tampon*, then she cuts her eyes at me. When she sees I'm looking, she turns fully.

"Are you saying…"

"That having a crush on you was what made me realize I was a lesbian? Yes. That's why I kissed you. But I got scared. I didn't know how you were going to react, so I withdrew. I'm sorry about that. I really didn't mean to cause you so much worry. And I super didn't mean for you never to come to Tulsa again. You never emailed, either, so I didn't know what was happening."

"You didn't email, either."

"I know. Again, I was young and scared of my feelings and embarrassed. I'm sorry about that."

She groans and touches her fingers to her forehead. "Same here. I mean, I wasn't that scared of my feelings or embarrassed, but I was scared. I was scared of conversion camp and of never getting to back to my mom. Dad knew it was better for me in a blue state and loves me enough to let me go. I'm just sorry that I never reached out. I really thought you regretted it, and I didn't know what you were going to do."

"Well, we both kind of blew that, didn't we? But mostly me. I'm really sorry. You had every reason to be scared with who my father is."

She grins wryly. "Well, we were kids. What can you do?"

Her crooked grin is so darn sexy. I really, really want to lean over and kiss it off her, but after the fiasco of last time, I know I shouldn't. Besides, we barely know each other now, despite the days we've spent together. At least that's something we can change if we want to. I can start really talking to her like we're doing tonight. We can build a new relationship, possibly a friendship.

The friend part would be a lot easier if she weren't so wildly hot.

CHAPTER TEN

BAILEY

I'm in the kitchen stirring half-and-half into my coffee when TJ comes in. She greets me with a smile, but I'm so distracted by her tousled morning look that I barely register it. Every other morning, she's appeared in the kitchen dressed and with her auburn hair neatly in a ponytail. Apparently, our conversation last night is making her feel more at ease around me. This morning, she's wearing what are apparently her pajamas: a loose shorts and tank top combination. Her hair has clearly been slept on. It's flopped over, with many strands loose around her face and neck. Some are darker, some nearly blond. I wonder if she has highlights done, if it's a result of time in the sun, or if it's how it naturally grows.

Overall, the impression is messy and comfortable. That's all I should feel about it. But the sensations in my lower body are a strong indication that I feel more. A lot more. I push it aside.

The smile has fallen off her face, but it's not until she says, "Is everything okay?" that I shake myself out of the inappropriate haze. I muster up a smile, trying to make it as natural as possible. "Nope. I mean, yes. Everything is fine. All secure." I touch the indicator I've been carrying as proof.

She squints at me for a second before thankfully turning her attention to getting coffee.

What is going on? Of course I think TJ is attractive. Who wouldn't? She has cheekbones that could cut glass. Her brown eyes have a darker brown ring around the outside that makes me want to stare into them. Her exposed shoulder sports a distinct tan line where the sports bra she's been wearing on the boat sits. I want to trail my finger along the line.

No. We're working on a friendship here, and I don't want to mess with it. This is all temporary. When it's over, after I get her to safety, we'll go our separate ways. I don't want to get involved in anything that I'll need to recover from again. Plus, I'm her bodyguard. Bodyguards aren't supposed to get involved.

She turns to me, mouth open to ask a question, and my gaze zeros in on her lips. They're full and naturally a light shade of pink. I want—

"Are we—" She abruptly stops speaking.

I'm again jolted out of thoughts of the things I want to do with her. I try to cover by taking a drink. When I lower my mug, she's looking at me speculatively. "So," I say loudly, "should we get outside and do our yoga?"

But now thoughts of her in her various yoga poses are running through my head. I want to weep. Shoving my desire aside is not working. How did my thoughts about TJ change from protective and a little annoyed to this overnight?

If I'm honest with myself, it wasn't just overnight. This has been building. I've just been supplanting any thoughts of her attractiveness with annoyance about her attitude and how it's my duty to keep her safe. But now, I can't seem to do that. Something shifted after our talk last night.

"Sure." She lifts one shoulder, drawing my attention to the muscles playing under her skin. "Let me go get changed."

I flee to my room to put on sunblock before my face can betray how the thought of her changing affects me. "Pull it together. Just because you're both lesbians and you've admitted you were interested as teenagers does not mean that you should be interested now," I mutter to myself as I put lotion everywhere. I have fair skin to go with my blond hair, and even though we've been out in the sun every day for a week, I'm not tanned. My back has odd bits of sunburn from places I can't reach. The spray stuff doesn't work as well.

No matter what I just said aloud in an effort to convince myself, I'm interested. Very interested. I struggle to reach my back but give up and spray it as best I can. When I step out of my room, TJ is standing in the hall, wrinkling her pert nose. "What?" I ask.

"Did you use that spray stuff?"

"Yes."

"I can smell it." She grabs my shoulder and pulls me around. "Plus, it's not working very well. You have a blotchy burn back here."

"Yeah. I've felt it. I can't reach, though."

"Get the sunblock. I'll put it on for you."

My mouth goes dry. I stumble over nothing as I go back into my room to get the bottle. Wordlessly—I don't think I could speak if I wanted to—I hand it to her. Her fingers linger on mine as she takes it. Was that on purpose? She lightly touches my shoulder to encourage me to turn. I hear the squirt of the lotion, and I feel like a million tiny little needles are lightly touching my skin. The anticipation of her touching me has amped up my sensitivity. I'm glad she can't tell how fast my heart is beating.

The first sensation is cold, the lotion against my burn. Then, she begins to rub it in. Her hands smooth across my back over and over. She lifts my suit straps with one hand and my suit bottom gets prematurely wet. I clearly did not talk myself out of being attracted to her. She rubs under the straps with her other hand. I want to lean into her touch. I do.

She slips her other hand under the back strap, smoothing along both sides of my spine, around the curve of where my back meets my sides. Is she going to—

Her hands pull out from under the suit, and it snaps back into place. "Sorry."

I clear my throat. "Um, are you?" I'm still facing away from her.

"Should I be?"

"No." I say it so softly that I'm not sure she hears me.

"No?" Her voice is equally soft but suggestive.

My heart beats even faster when she lays a hand on my shoulder. I turn, causing her hand to drop, and I miss the contact, but then her hand is in mine. I'm not sure if I took hers or she took mine, but we're connected again, and it feels right that we are.

I find myself focused on her lips that are slightly parted. They are pulling me like a magnet, but I wrench my eyes away. I shouldn't kiss TJ. I'm supposed to be protecting her. Getting involved would be messy. Besides that, what future would there be? I'm not against flings in general. I've had a couple, but I don't like them. I want to be in a relationship with the person I'm physical with. It matters to me that there are feelings.

Could I have feelings with TJ? No doubt about it. I already care about her. There's a history that only deepens the relatively new adult association. Oh yes. I could develop feelings. To be honest with myself, they probably already exist. If not, I wouldn't want to kiss her so much.

She squeezes my hand, and I bring my gaze back to her face. She's looking at me intently. Her eyes flicker to my lips and back.

If she initiates a kiss, I don't know that I have the strength to resist.

Chapter Eleven

TJ

I want to kiss Bailey so badly. I've wanted to kiss her since I watched her sleeping on the plane, if I'm honest with myself. Not only is she exceedingly hot, which I noticed the moment she sauntered to the car in the airport garage, but she revealed a whole plan to get me out of red. She's been nothing but gallant and accommodating, even when I was a brat. It should be annoying, but after our talk last night, I haven't been able to get over the thought of kissing her.

And after rubbing lotion on her back? Kissing her is all I can think about. We're standing face-to-face in the hall, fingers entwined. We're nearly of a height. She's just a little shorter, which is cute with her being the more masc one. Not that she's particularly masc with her long blond hair. It's up in a ponytail like mine. I long to rip the tie out and run my fingers through it. Her hair is so fine that it slips out of her holder all the time. When we're out on the boat, strands whip around her face. It's caught and held my attention more than a few times.

For a moment, she looks like she is going to kiss me, but she looks away. I want to groan with frustration. I know I shouldn't be kissing her. Kissing a girl is what got me into this trouble in the first place. But she's Bailey. She's sexy. She's here. No one else is. Who will even know?

I squeeze her hand to bring her attention back to me. When her gaze meets mine, I nearly combust with want. I lean in, taking my time in case she really doesn't want this, giving her time to pull away or say no. Instead, she meets me halfway.

And then we're kissing.

It's nothing like our other kiss, my first kiss that consisted of me hastily pressing my lips to hers before running away. It's not like any other first kiss I've had with any of the three girls I've since kissed, all of whom were other students at Glory. I was the first girl each of them had kissed and the first kiss at all for two of them. I'd been the driver in each instance.

Bailey, though? She is a confident kisser. She hugs my lower lip with her two, then runs the tip of her tongue across it. I feel that caress in my core. It only deepens when she sucks the lip in. Our mouths continue to move together. I'm doing my best to give as good as I get. I feel like I'm taking a master class. I thought I knew what I was doing, but this is next level. It's a good thing that her arms are around me, holding me up. Otherwise, I may collapse into a puddle of goo.

She eases out of the kiss by withdrawing her tongue from my mouth, giving one last caress of my lip. She ends with a kiss that would be chaste if it hadn't followed on the heels of the expert make-out session she just led me through.

She leans her forehead against mine. "Okay?"

I'm pretty far from okay. I'm fairly certain that I've gone from thinking that kissing Bailey would be a fun diversion to being ruined for kissing anyone else. I let out a groan.

"TJ? What is it? I'm sorry. I shouldn't have—"

I have to stop her. I was the one who kissed her, and I don't want her thinking I regret it. "No. It's not that. I...really enjoyed that."

"Good." She hesitates. "But, you don't have to...I don't want you to think that..."

I'm not sure what she's trying to say. She's usually very straightforward, so this stumbling, while I've seen it a couple of times, makes me think that she feels awkward about whatever it is.

That's when it clicks. "Oh! Bailey, I'm not kissing you so you'll help me. I'm kissing you because I want to kiss you."

A smile blooms on her face, and she kisses me again briefly. "I want to kiss you, too. Obviously. But what I mean more than that is that I don't want you to think you owe me anything for helping you. When we get to a blue state, you can do whatever you want. You said you had people who were going to help? I can take you to them."

My heart sinks. She's not interested in me other than having a little—I don't know—dalliance. That's okay. That's fine. That's all any of my relationships have been, all they could be. There was no future for any of them, and clearly, there is no future here. It was stupid to think there was. It was one kiss. I don't even know why my heart sunk a moment ago. What was I expecting? It's fine.

I let my arms drop and stand back. "Thank you."

Some expression flits across her face that I can't identify, but what she says is, "It's the least I can do. This is a bad life for women like us."

I start walking down the hall, my back to her. "Yeah. Let's go do yoga."

CHAPTER TWELVE

BAILEY

I wish I knew what just shifted between us. I was very much enjoying the kissing, and this slight chill between us is not nearly as fun.

I keep sneaking glances at her while we do our individual yoga routines side by side. We brought the yoga mats we found in the house down to the uncovered dock, our routine during our stay. Every time I look, she looks like she's deep in her own thoughts. We were just kissing each other's faces off, and now it's like we're back to before we really talked.

I'm doing a downward dog and looking back at the house between my legs when I see movement. I freeze. There are people there, and my button isn't flashing. Shit. It's probably flashing on the table in the hall where I left it after getting distracted by kissing TJ. Fuck.

"TJ." I try to infuse my voice with both urgency and calm focus. She pauses in her flow. Low, she says, "What?"

"We're going to slip into the water. Right now." I'm not sure they've seen us yet. If they have, wouldn't they be out here? Who are they? NoFa? Patriot Army come to take TJ to conversion camp? How would either know we're here? Unless Mr. Rice decided he had no choice but to give her up.

She straightens and looks at the house.

"No. Fast movements might draw attention." She's right next to the ladder. "Go slowly and smoothly to the ladder. Go now."

She moves a little too fast. I'm worried they'll notice. I glance back at the house. I don't see anyone now. When I look back, she's already treading water. I descend the ladder and join her. "We're going to swim to the boat. We can go under the dock. Swim underwater as far as you can. When do you come up for a breath, try to go slow and easy. No big splashes. Got it?"

Her eyes are wide and nearly black. She's scared, but she's listening. That's all I can ask. I glance back at the house and see someone come out the back door casually. It's clear we haven't been seen yet.

"Go now. Smooth movements."

She takes a deep breath and goes under. I follow. I thank our combined years of swim training for how long we're both able to stay underwater. When we're under the dock, I take her arm and pull her up for a breath. The boathouse has some infrastructure to make it a challenge to get in without a code or the remote installed in the boat. However, it's not completely secure. We'll have to dive deep, then shimmy under the wall that comes near to touching the inlet floor. I went over this possibility with TJ after I checked it out, shortly after we got here.

We are facing each other and treading water in the dim light under the dock. The tide is high, so there's not much space between our heads and the planks. Her pupils are still blown, but she's holding it together. I think we've got this.

"Do you remember what we talked about?" I ask.

"Catch your breath, then go under. Do you think they saw us? Who are they?"

I don't know the answer to either of those questions. If they're smart and saw us, they could well be keeping quiet and planning on ambushing us. As far as who, I have my suspicions but no facts. "I don't know. Right now, we just need to get away. Ready?"

She takes in a deep breath and nods.

"Okay, follow me." I take a few deep breaths and prepare to dive. Keeping my eyes open in the saltwater is unpleasant, but I need to see where we're going. I pull down and down and down. When I reach the bottom, I'm really wanting a breath, but I still have to get under the wall and up inside. I hold on to the bottom of the wall with one hand and look to see if TJ needs a hand when she grabs me. There are little bubbles leaking from the corner of her mouth, reminding me of our mutual need for air.

I put both hands on the bottom and pull. It's a tight fit against the muck on the bed of the inlet, and I have to squirm to get through. TJ should have an easier time because she's skinnier. As much as I want to pull to the surface, I pause to make sure she's through, but she is even faster. I find her already pulling for air. I hope she's got her eyes open and is paying attention because if she bangs her head on the bottom of the boat, it could spell disaster.

I follow her and watch as she slows and puts a hand on the bottom of the boat. She's on her back, using her hands to pull up along the curve of the hull. It's as good a plan as any, and importantly, she didn't smack her head.

Our heads bob up at nearly the same moment between the boat and the dock. We both gasp for desperate breaths. We're near the bow. There are only a couple buoys between the boat and the dock, and it would have been hard to squeeze through there.

I motion for TJ to stay where she is, treading water while I kick to get my head farther out of the water and look around. The boathouse appears empty. With one more signal to TJ to stay where she is and keep quiet, I scramble onto the dock. There's no one there. I gesture to TJ to follow. I stand and watch in case she needs a hand, but she scrambles ably up. I grab the key fob from the hook.

I put my mouth next to TJ's ear and say, "Get onboard. Be ready to start the engine. I'm going to release the ties. Then we'll start the engine and open the door at the same time. Both will be loud and blow our location. Stay low just in case. You're driving." I push the key fob into her hand.

I don't bother to tell her that if they've planned this well and mean to kill her, they will likely succeed. They may have boats waiting in the water. I didn't see any, but that doesn't mean they aren't nearby. The one man I saw come through the door to the backyard wasn't even holding a weapon, though. My strong suspicion is that Patriot Army has been sent to collect TJ. They won't expect a struggle. That means that surprise is on our side. Probably. If not, we'll find out soon enough.

I make quick work of the ropes and step onto the now loose boat. I retrieve the gun I left in one of the many storage compartments. I tap the button to raise the door, and as soon as it starts, TJ pushes the start button. I brace myself against the side of the boat and hold the gun at the ready. I don't know if an attacker will come bursting through the door on the dock or if boats will be waiting when we clear the door. I feel woefully underprepared for what may happen.

The door from the shore side of the boathouse flies open just as TJ decides we have enough clearance to exit. The man who comes through is almost certainly Patriot Army. He's wearing a flak jacket with a camo pattern and a red hat. Typical. He has a gun strapped to each thigh, but he hasn't pulled them. He's waving and yelling, but we don't wait around to hear what. We're clear, and TJ guns the engine.

CHAPTER THIRTEEN

TJ

G o out to open water," Bailey directs.
We've stuck mostly to the inlet while we've been here. It's smoother water for the activities we've been doing. But we did take a little cruise out to the Gulf of Mexico once for fun. I follow that route.

"What's the plan?" I ask.

"I think the plan is that we're bailing early with no preparation and people chasing us." She speaks loudly to be heard over the engine.

My stomach clenches. Are we going to get away? What happens if we don't? I still don't know who's after me. Us. Do they want to kill or capture me? If capture, for what purpose?

The radio crackles to life. "Swanson? Come in, Swanson."

"Well," Bailey says, "I guess we know for sure who the people are."

I glance at her, trying to read her expression. She's not going to turn me in, is she? Technically, she is working for my dad, and if he sent Patriot Army to collect me, she should turn me over. I know she was just planning my escape, but now that they're here, it's much safer and easier for her to just turn me over. Sure, we were passionately making out less than an hour ago, but she also said she doesn't want to be my girlfriend, so that doesn't really signify anything, does it?

She picks up the radio, and my heart sinks. "Who is this? Over."

"Thanks for picking up, Swanson. It's Mark Holder. You were in my camp some ten years ago. I understand why you took Miss Rice. It was a good piece of evasion." Even over the crackling radio, there are notes of pride in his voice. "But it's us. Come on back. We're here to take Miss Rice back into the fold. Over."

Bailey pushes the button. "Copy. Over." Her arm drops to her side, and she taps the fingers of her other hand on her bare leg. She's staring at the watery landscape in front of us, the picture of pondering. What exactly is she pondering, though?

"Bailey?"

She looks at me and must see the worry in my eyes. She puts a hand on my shoulder. "I'm not taking you back, TJ. I'm just thinking about the best way to proceed. We've got less than half a tank of gas. Once they know we're not coming back, they'll be looking for us. It'll make refueling much more challenging than I was hoping for. Also, we've got…" She trails off and moves to the built-in cooler. "Three bottles of water." She opens the small fridge. "And a granola bar and two oranges. Our best bet is New Orleans, at least a full twenty-four hours away, and we'll be in the sun the whole time. It's not a lot to work with." She looks around. "They don't know we're not coming back yet. This is as good a time to fuel up as we're going to get. Go to the pump."

We just passed the community pump that the card provided with the boat is associated with. I bank left to circle back to it, hoping like crazy this isn't some elaborate scheme to hand me over. But what she said makes sense. We need gas. It's only going to get trickier from here.

"Go in slow and easy, casual," she instructs.

While I do my best to follow her directions, despite the fact that all I want to do is roar off in a blaze of speed, I notice that she is hawkeyed. She's leaning against a seat, mostly likely in an effort to look casual, but her eyes are scanning.

"You stay on the boat. If anything happens, take off," she says as she scans the pier.

I don't say anything. Why would I leave her when it's me they're after?

"TJ." Her voice leaves no room for misinterpreting. It's the voice of a parent who means business.

"I hear you." I pull alongside the thankfully empty pump.

Bailey steps onto the pier and uses the card to initiate fueling. I want her to get back on the boat while we wait, but I realize it's impractical. It will be faster for her to disconnect the nozzle if she's already there. I look at passing boats, then back to the pier, then behind.

"TJ, remember to look casual."

It's only at her reminder that I realize how jerky and hunted my movements must look. I settle on the captain's seat and look at her.

She smiles a comforting smile. "Deep breaths."

It's no doubt because she's looking at me and trying to comfort me that she doesn't see the figures step onto the pier behind her. "Bailey!"

She's already disengaging the nozzle as she turns. The men start running. She leaves the nozzle hanging and leaps onto the boat. "Go, go!"

A crack rends the air. They're shooting. Shit. I push hard on the throttle in a panic and almost hit a fishing boat trolling by. Bailey nudges me aside and takes the wheel. I look behind. The men are already fading into the distance. I slump onto the bench. We're okay. For the moment.

There's a drop of red on the white seat next to me. My head snaps up. Bailey is bleeding. My voice wobbles when I ask, "Bailey?"

She looks at me, then follows my gaze to her arm. She lifts the elbow to look at her bicep and winces. "Yeah. They nearly got me."

"Nearly? You're bleeding."

"Just a graze. It'll be fine."

I take a shaky breath. She got shot because of me. For me. This isn't a game. I knew it wasn't. I've lived under this threat my entire life. And yet, I've never actually seen a consequence for me or someone I care about. My father has always set things—if not right—then some semblance of it for me. I couldn't live the life

I truly wanted, but I've never gotten anyone hurt. Even Christina. There's no way her cleansing has anything to do with me, not after all this time. She must have slipped up elsewhere, with someone else.

I wanted out, and I knew it required careful planning and would be a challenge. But I didn't want anyone to get hurt. And now there are people shooting at Bailey. I take a deep breath to steady myself as she suggested back at the pump. The least I can do is hold it together and take care of her arm. I get up and search for a first aid kit. I've just found it when the radio crackles to life once more.

"Swanson, I take it this means you're not bringing Miss Rice back to us. Over."

Bailey glances at the radio but doesn't pick up. There is no further message. I guess everyone knows where we all stand now.

"Here. Let me dress that arm for you."

"One second. Take the wheel. Go, I don't know, in as random a direction as possible."

I'm worried about the fact that she's still dripping blood, but I do as she asks and watch as she bends and looks at the panel under the steering wheel. "What are you doing?"

"I need to check for a GPS tracker." She moves to a storage compartment and takes out a small toolkit. "A lot of fancy boats have them so the owners can find them if they're stolen or lost at sea. They could have just randomly checked that fueling station, but I suspect that's how they located us."

She lies on the deck, her head practically between my feet. I sit back on the bench to give her room to work and try to decide what direction to take us in. She said random, but going to open ocean still seems like a good idea. There're more options for getting away. I head in that direction.

After a few minutes, she pops up and throws something overboard. "Got it."

"Did they teach you these skills at kids' camp?"

"They did, in fact." She looks around. We're almost to the mouth of the inlet. "Ah."

There's something in her tone that makes me feel like I've done something wrong. "Should I not have come this way?"

She puts a reassuring hand on my bare shoulder. "We had to go through here sooner or later. And sooner gives them less time to prepare. It's just that with the tracker only just ripped out, they'll know we're headed to the gulf."

I gulp. "What should we do?"

She looks around and seemingly comes to a decision. "We go for it. You drive. Once we go under the bridge, hit it."

I would ask what she's going to do, but from the way she's bracing herself and lifting the gun, I don't have to ask.

My chest gets tighter the closer we get. There's all sorts of room getting in and out of Tampa Bay, room for cruise ships, but as we approach, it feels like I'm taking us into a trap. Bailey obviously feels the same way with how she's prepared to shoot.

We go under the bridge, and nothing happens. I start to relax a little. I'm wondering if I should turn north or swing south first so as not to telegraph our eventual destination.

We're just passing the point and heading to open water when I realize my relief came too early.

CHAPTER FOURTEEN

BAILEY

I might not have chosen to leave the bay while we had the tracker—I'm kicking myself for not thinking of it sooner—but I didn't lie when I told TJ it was okay. More time would have given the Patriot Army longer to gather reinforcements. It's clear that when they came for TJ, they expected my cooperation and didn't send a full extraction team. If they had time to plan for a hostile kidnapping, there would have been boats in the water. At least, there would have been if I was planning it.

Now, they'll be scrambling. Still, I expect there to be trouble as we exit. There's plenty of Patriot Army around here. Even if the team that came to the house are from Oklahoma, they've now alerted the locals, who will most definitely have boats. I can't discount the possibility that there will be at least a boat or two waiting for us between the points.

And there is.

In fact, there are two. One is a fishing boat that we can definitely outrun. The other, though, is a police boat. This shouldn't be a surprise. The Venn diagram between police and Patriot Army is practically a single circle. It's one of the reasons Portland disbanded their police. They weren't there to serve the people but to keep the poor and minorities down.

At the moment, that's neither here nor there. We still have to get away.

"Hit it," I yell at TJ as the police boat turns on its lights.

She does, either as a response to my command or according to the plan.

An amplified voice comes from the direction of the police boat. It hails us, then says we're in violation of some code. I have no idea what the code is. It doesn't matter if it's made-up or if we're actually violating a real code that could be something to the effect of being gay while in Florida or being a woman running away from her father. Either way, they are coming. The voice goes on to say, "Cut your engine and prepare to be seized."

TJ shoots me a panicked look.

"Keep going," I tell her grimly.

The fishing boat is closer. It's doing its best to intercept, but it's easy to evade. We cut a curving path around it, but shots ring out as we pass, making my heart rate increase, even though it would be a miracle to hit us at the distance and relative speed. I don't bother to return fire. It would be a waste of precious bullets.

On the other side of the fishing boat, the patrol boat is angling to come alongside. The voice, back on the loudspeaker, says, "Cut your engine, or we will be forced to use lethal force."

Because our relative speed is much more closely matched, that threat is real. But our boat is faster. Mr. Rice went all out with our accommodations. Did he foresee us needing to flee? I can't imagine that he'd have sanctioned that, unless maybe he was thinking we'd be fleeing from NoFa. Whatever his reasoning, we have a fast boat, and we'll need every bit of its speed to get away.

"Go north. There are islands. Maybe we can lose them there."

TJ makes the adjustment. The police boat does, too. They have a gun mounted on the back of their boat, and it swings around to point at us. Unlike the guns on the fishing boat that are getting farther and farther behind, that gun I'm worried about. It has range.

I pick up the radio. I hope they are monitoring the same channel the Patriot Army guys were using. "This is the *Mary II*. Repeat, this is the *Mary II*. Over."

"This is the police boat, *Mary II*. Cut your engine. Over."

"Back off or I will shoot Miss Rice. Over."

TJ shoots me a look. I shrug. I'm just trying to buy us time.

A few precious moments pass before the loudspeaker booms again. "Nice try, *Mary II*. Cut the engine, or we start shooting. Over."

Maybe if I'd been willing to hold the gun to TJ's head, we'd have had a little longer. As it is, the distance between the boats is slowly lengthening with the brief window I bought us. However, we're nowhere near out of range. I need more time. Will the police really shoot at us, or are they bluffing? They may be bluffing. Who wants to kill the daughter of Thomas Rice? It's possible that he's been fired, in which case, all bets are off. If that's the situation, things are worse than they seem, bad as it is already. No, I have to believe that they'd be in a world of trouble if they harmed TJ, even if some of the army yahoos have already fired near her. The police are better trained and less likely to go off script than the folks who are only Patriot Army volunteers. So if they're not really going to shoot, what's their plan? They must be trying to get more boats in the water to corral us. Or they're banking on us running out of gas. That's a good bet, actually. I scan our environs, trying to come up with a plan.

Being out in the ocean isn't like a car chase. We can't turn a corner and hide down a side street while the pursuing car goes by. But maybe we can approximate that. We're flying past the archipelago of islands that span the northern peninsula that juts into the opening of the bay.

"I have an idea. Let me take the wheel." It won't do any good to shoot at the police boat anyway. We're way outgunned. I shove my gun into a compartment on the dash. She doesn't question me, just slides down the bench to make room.

I take a quick turn between islands into the Mullet Key Bay. I made a point of studying the area, and part of why the name of this bay stuck in my head was that the mullet part made me laugh. I zoomed in and checked it out. It's a paddling area. No motorboats allowed. I go in anyway. I see immediately why it's a motorboat-free zone. I can easily see the sandy bottom. Thinking quickly, I come up with a new plan.

I slow, looking for ways through. There are kayakers dotting the area. I also see a canoe and a couple of stand-up paddleboarders. Excellent. It'll hard to justify shooting at us if they might hit bystanders.

A man in a kayak shakes his fist at me as we pass, wake rolling away from us. I get why he's upset, but needs must. I see a sandbar with what looks like a decent-sized channel beside it. I make for it. There are two boards pulled up on the bar. The paddlers look at us in open amazement. One cups his hands around his mouth and starts yelling. I have no time for it. I can't hear it anyway.

I look behind. The police boat has slowed but is keeping pace.

In the channel, I gun the engine again, building up speed. I push a button on the console and swing left, cutting just around the tip of the sandbar. When the water looks deep enough, I push the same button. I'm watching carefully to make sure there's enough depth for the motor, so I ask TJ, "Did it work?"

With glee in her voice, she says, "Yes, they're stuck."

I was banking on them following and not having the snazzy feature of pushing a button to stop the motor and pull it up that the *Mary II* has. I was right. We're in the clear. As long as they haven't gotten more boats in the water, we should be able to make a clean getaway.

"Bailey!" TJ's voice is piercing, and it's the only warning I get before they start shooting. Fuck. They are willing to risk TJ. Even if Mr. Rice hasn't authorized it, these particular goons don't care. This changes the game.

Thankfully, they've waited too long. I've just cleared the shallows and gunned the engine. Shots hit the water to the side of us but start falling behind.

We're clear.

I stay focused and watchful as I drive north, but it seems we're good for now. I head to open water. When we've lost sight of the shore, and there are no boats around, I relax a little. A few minutes later, my arm starts throbbing.

CHAPTER FIFTEEN

TJ

I'm still watching anxiously for pursuit when Bailey slows a little. I whip my head around to see if something has gone wrong, only to find her frowning at her bloody right arm.

"Do we have time for me to dress that now?" She was right that it only grazed her arm, but it looks painful. I wince in sympathy.

"I can do it myself." She sounds a little uncertain.

"Then who will drive? I'll do it. You drive."

I find the first aid kit. During the wild turns of the escape, it slid off the seat and onto the deck before lodging under one of the side seats. I take it back to Bailey, who is now sitting before the wheel.

"Why did you slow down?" I ask as I pull open the kit on the seat. "Shouldn't we be running as fast as possible?"

"Our fastest will be a little slower than max. The sweet spot for a boat like this in terms of gas usage is about twenty-six knots per hour. By going a little slower, we'll minimize refueling needs."

I have no idea how we're going to refuel. We have whatever was on the boat this morning and the swimsuits we're wearing. That's it. No credit cards, although I assume using them would be a bad idea anyway in terms of being traceable. No extra food or water. Nothing. All of that is a problem for later. Right now, I need to get Bailey cleaned up.

Actually, water is an issue. I need to clean her arm to see what's happening. The cooler contains two bottles, like Bailey noted. That's not a lot. Still, her arm needs to be cleaned. I take one out of the cooler and carry it back to the bench.

Bailey glances at the bottle. "I'm sure you're thirsty, but we should ration the water."

I huff annoyance. "This is for your arm."

"No, don't use that. Use seawater to clean it off, then antiseptic. We're going to need all the fresh water we have to make sure we don't dehydrate. At least until I can get us more."

How in the world is she going to get us more out in the middle of the Gulf of Mexico? "Won't it get infected?"

"Nah. Just use the antiseptic after."

I'm still holding the bottle. I think she's lying about the infection part. "But…there are things in the water. Little organisms?"

"TJ, it's fine. I'll be fine."

I'm still skeptical, but I have to admit that she likely knows more about first aid than I do. With a sigh, I return the bottle to the cooler and collect a bucket I came across in one of the compartments. I use it to scoop up some water, nearly dropping it in the ocean as I do so.

Back at the bench, I use my hands to lift water to Bailey's arm. We don't have any towels or rags or clothing to use instead. She sucks in sharply, and her left hand tightens on the wheel when the water hits the gash.

"Sorry."

"It's okay. It needs to be done." Her wheel hand loosens.

When I've washed off the caked blood, it's clear that the wound is still seeping. "I'm no expert, but this looks like it needs stitches."

Bailey lifts her arm and turns her head to examine it. "Yeah, stitches would be best. But I can't do it with my left hand. Are there butterfly bandages in there? That should do."

I look, and there are. But there's also a suturing kit. I've never stitched a person before, but part of my education in housewifeliness included learning basic sewing, much to my dismay at the time. What a useless skill, it seemed, when everyone bought new clothes as necessary. Now, though, it can come in handy. If I can get myself to do it.

"Are there not any?"

"No, there are. But I think I can put stitches in. If you want me to try."

Her hand tightens on the wheel briefly, then relaxes. "Yes. That would probably be best."

I lay my hand on her arm just above the gash. "I'll be as gentle as possible."

She smiles at me. "I'm sure you will."

I rummage around in the kit a little more and find numbing spray. It may help some. First, I rinse it again. Blood has accumulated in the time we've discussed the plan and while I've gotten my supplies lined up. Then, I spray it with the antiseptic. This causes more hand clenching on Bailey's part. I don't say sorry. I'd be saying it with every move from here on out if I say it every time I cause her pain. I do squeeze her forearm in sympathy. Her muscles are firm under my hand.

Next, I spray it with the numbing spray. It says to wait fifteen minutes, but if I wait, I'll have to clean the blood again. I decide to use one of the wound pads in the kit to apply pressure while I wait.

Bailey, still driving, looks at where I'm holding the pad to her arm. "Are you nervous?"

"Yes, but that's not why I'm hesitating."

"Then why?"

"That last spray is supposed to numb the skin. It should take the sting out of doing the stitches. A little."

"That's thoughtful."

We wait the fifteen minutes. She's driving. I'm holding her arm. I'm very aware of the feel of her skin under my hand. I wish I was holding her arm for any reason other than that she's injured, and I'm about to hurt her more. I'm telling time by the clock on the console, and the third time I glance at it, a thought occurs to me.

"The clock is syncing somewhere."

Bailey glances at it and back. "Yeah."

"Is that a problem?"

"Oh. For tracking? No. It's download only. That clock won't send any signals. Just don't use the radio. They can triangulate that."

"Oh. Cool. Okay. Well, it's been fifteen minutes."

"Okay."

"So stop the boat."

"What? No. Just do it while we're going."

"Bailey." I do my best taskmaster voice, which I don't think is all that great, but it seems to get her attention. "We're bouncing up and down. I can't stitch you while we're bouncing. Plus, I need you to hold this here while I get everything ready."

"Ah. Fair point."

She eases off the throttle, and soon, we're drifting. We're still moving around a little thanks to the swells, but it's better than bouncing over the top of them. Her hand covers mine briefly while she's replacing the pressure on the bandage. I selfishly take comfort from that before I pull my hand out and open the pre-threaded suture needle.

"Shoot."

"What?"

"I should have put the gloves on first."

"Oh well."

"No, there's more than one of these in here." I pull gloves on, then open a new one. "We already have too many vectors for infection already." I have to hope we won't need the other.

I glance up at Bailey's face. She looks amused. "What?"

"Just watching you work."

"Well, excuse me for not wanting you to die from a staph infection or whatever."

"No, no. I appreciate it. Proceed."

"Thank you," I say with mock dignity. Then softly, "Ready?"

She nods somberly.

I take a deep breath, let it out, and start sewing.

Bailey is a trooper as I pull the needle through her flesh. I'm grateful. I don't know that I could keep doing this if she was freaking out. Still, when I finish, her face is pale. Mine probably matches. The stitches are sloppy, but they're holding the sides of the gash together, and that's what's important.

"Well, I'm not exactly ready for a career as a plastic surgeon, but I think it'll do."

"I think you did a great job for your first stitches."

I pull out what I need to bandage her arm. "Have you ever stitched anyone up?"

"No. I've only practiced. My dad had a kit I liked to mess with, and at kids' camp, we stitched dead pigs."

I shudder. "Gross."

"Not as hard as a person, I think." She wipes her arm with the pad we used to apply pressure.

"Maybe so. Here. Let me see." I take her arm and try to decide if I should apply more antiseptic. Better safe than sorry. I spray the whole area again before putting a fresh gauze pad against the area and wrapping the whole thing with self-adhesive wrap. "Is it too tight?"

She flexes her arm, and I get a little distracted by the play of muscles. "Seems good. Thanks."

I trail my fingers down her arm before I start trying to clean up. Trying because there's not much I can do about the blood, aside from throw seawater on it. But I pick up all the trash and shove it into the trash area that until now, has only held granola bar wrappers. While I'm working on that, Bailey gets us moving again.

Once everything is as tidy as I can make it, the reality of our situation hits. I sink down on the seat next to Bailey. "So…do we have a plan?"

CHAPTER SIXTEEN

BAILEY

This would have been much easier if we'd been able to go on a supply run and slip away unnoticed as planned. As it is, things could be worse. There's water all around and the boats in the distance haven't launched into pursuit, so they likely aren't looking for us.

But if they catch a good sight of us—two women traveling unaccompanied by a man—they may report us. There's a big push in red states that if someone sees something, they should say something. It covers situations from someone acting suspiciously to us here and now. So we stay well clear of any boats we see. At a distance, they won't be able to tell who is on our boat.

Our supplies consist of a gun, a ransacked first aid kit, a couple of bottles of water, a single granola bar, a few tools, a bucket, wakeboarding equipment, a bottle of sunscreen, a fueling card that only works on the pump back in Tampa Bay, and a rapidly dwindling half a tank of gas. It's not ideal.

Not to mention that we're in our swimsuits and have no other clothes.

Per my original plan, we need to be underway for approximately thirty hours with a solid five fill-ups. I planned on picking up some five-gallon gas cans to minimize our need to hit up gas stations, both for flying under the radar and because there are stretches of the west coast of Florida where it may be hard to find a gas station. We can survive thirty hours with a granola bar and two bottles of water, but it will be ugly out under the sun and in the saltwater spray. We can in no way, shape, or form make the gas we have last for that entire journey.

My original plan was also to make our way to New Orleans, a blue dot in a sea of red. Now I have to consider if that's still the best plan. "I'm still thinking about our plan, as it happens," I say.

"Perhaps we talk it out?"

So we do. TJ asks good questions. I'm impressed with her intelligence and problem-solving skills. We discuss and discard the idea of moving to land. The main problem is leaving Florida with its wall. It's well-guarded and nearly impossible to scale. Our only chance to leave on land would be to procure fake IDs and fake travel permission. I don't have contacts in Florida to get either of those things, nor access to the tools I'd need to attempt them myself, even if I was any good at forgery. We decide to stick with the boat and discuss various options for getting gas.

The best has us returning to the coast, dangerous as that is.

The last thing I want to do is put us in view of people who may be looking for us. No, scratch that. The last thing I want to do is run out of gas in the middle of the Gulf of Mexico. What we have going for us is that the coast of Florida is lousy with boats. With any luck, we'll blend. What isn't great is that we're two women in swimsuits on a wanted boat.

When we come within sight of land, TJ squeezes my forearm and hides as we planned. I feel the ghost of the squeeze for several long minutes after she's tucked into the foot space between the benches in the bow.

We've been traveling north, but the Tampa area is large, so we're still well in civilization, if I can call anyplace in Florida civilized. It's not Tampa anymore, really. I rack my brain to remember the names of the small towns. I think we're probably in the vicinity of Clearwater. It doesn't really matter. What matters is finding a marina. Someplace with a lot of boats. I eye every boat we pass with suspicion. No one makes to follow us.

It's not long before I find what I'm looking for. It is Florida, after all. Everyone has a boat. Well, everyone who lives on the coast and has money. And they need marinas to dock at. I spy a bustling one and casually make for it. There's an empty berth, and I slip the boat into it rather than using a short-term guest spot where there may be eyes watching. I quickly tie the boat off at the bow so it won't take long to undo.

There is a yacht on one side. While this boat is a very fancy speedboat with amenities I've never enjoyed before, it is not a yacht. A yacht would be a much superior vessel in which to take this journey. That sleek boat has a much larger fuel capacity and at least one bed and also plenty of ways to get out of the sun. It is also not currently being hunted. If I could do it without drawing attention, I would absolutely steal it. Unfortunately, yachts have robust antitheft systems. Given a lot of time and privacy, perhaps I could do it, but even then, it would be questionable.

I turn my attention to the sailboat on the other side. I'm not going to steal it, either. I have very little in the way of sailing skills. I get the general concept but actually sailing? Nope. I've never done it. However, it's an older boat, so there probably isn't much security. I cross the dock and step on it as if I know exactly what I'm doing. Confidence is what sells it. I'm just stopping by to pick up a few things from my sailboat, don't mind me.

I note the pair of flip-flops on the deck. I feel better and lighter in bare feet for now, but we will eventually need shoes. There are several towels hanging on the railing. I grab them all. Actual clothes would be better, but at least the towels will give us something to cover up with and will also be useful for things like cleaning wounds and getting blood off the seats.

At the cockpit, I find an insulated bottle with some sort of liquid in it. There's a bucket with some rags hanging around the edges. We have a bucket and the towels, but something to carry my collections is useful. I put the bottle in it. I skip the sunblock. We have some. But I toss in the ChapStick next to it. There's a ball cap attached to the helm. I add it to the bucket. I eye the umbrella jerry-rigged to shade the helm. Shade would be great, but it would just blow away at our speeds. I leave it.

I walk to the cabin, casually looking around to see if anyone is paying attention. I don't see anyone. I can't see TJ from here, so she seems to be staying hidden. I try the door. It opens. I drop down into the galley. There are shelves with rubber bands holding things in place, but it's spices, oils, and sauces. Also on display are plates strapped in vertically and cups in a clever holder. The jackpot is a netful of oranges. I take six. If we don't have food, we'll get hungry, sure, but we won't starve in the day and a half I expect our trip to take. Hydration is by far the bigger issue. The fruit will help.

Speaking of hydration, I pull the water bottle out and open it. A casual sniff reveals that it seems to be water. To be safe, I dump it down the sink and fill it with water from the tap.

I need to get moving. What would help immensely is clothing to make our gender more ambiguous. I see an unmade bed through the door on the other side of the tiny table. The walls in there are made up of drawers and small doors. I open a door at random and find a stack of T-shirts. I stuff one in the bucket and pull another over my head. It's oversized, which is great. It'll help disguise my figure. The next door reveals shorts. Considering the shirt, they won't fit, but I grab two of them.

My nerves are jangling, telling me I've stayed too long. They're not necessarily right, but they could also be signaling something my subconscious noticed. Maybe I heard something that altered me. There are sounds all around the harbor. I haven't noticed one stand out, but my conscious mind might have missed it. It also might just be accumulated stress, but I heed the signals anyway. I don't like leaving TJ, and I've probably gotten most of what will be useful here. On the way back though the galley, I lift a roll top door and see two bags of bread. One is full while the other is half-used. I grab the half-used one.

Time to get out of here. I stuff the cap on my head, tucking my hair up under it. I want a casual observer to think me androgynous as I leave the boat. Before stepping onto the deck, I listen, then peek my head out to look around. There's someone on the dock. I pull my head back in, heart beating fast. There's a narrow dock between this sailboat and the speedboat. It leads nowhere except to these two. The person on the dock must be the owner of the sailboat or someone checking out the speedboat. Neither is a good situation. Either way, I can't stay here.

I look again and see the man looking over his shoulder at the wider dock running between the bows of the rows of boats. I quickly exit the cabin and slip around the other side where the only thing between me and the next boat is water. I glance at the wider dock. There's no one there to see me sneaking around. I creep to the front of the cabin and peer around. I don't see anything.

"Where'd my towels go?" It sounds like the man's on the boat now.

Shit.

When I ease a little farther around the bow, I see him, older and potbellied, leaning over the railing, looking at the water, mostly likely for the missing towels. It's quite a drop from the deck, but it's my best bet for getting off the boat unseen. And I need to do it now. I loop one arm through the handle of the bucket and prepare to go over the railing.

Someone is walking down the dock. Instead of going over, I turn and walk back to the side of the cabin I was just hiding behind. *I'm invisible. No one sees me.* Despite my mantra, I'm ready for shouts at any moment. When none come, I breathe a quiet sigh of relief. But I'm still on this boat that I just pillaged along with a person I presume to be the owner.

I climb up on the railing and jump across the couple of feet of water to the boat on the other side. Not our boat. Worse, it's a yacht, so there are probably cameras recording my movements. Hopefully, no one reviews the security tape until we're long gone. Maybe they never will because I don't plan to steal anything off this boat. I'm just passing through.

I disembark on the other side on the narrow dock between it and the boat next to it. That boat, three away from ours, is a fishing boat. The stern bristles with long fishing poles. What snags my attention, though, is a red fuel canister tucked into the corner, secured with a bungie cord. I can't quiet reach it from the dock, so I climb aboard. It's the work of a few seconds to free it. When I go to scramble back, I notice one more thing I'd hoped to find. I shove it in the bucket and get off the boat.

The gas can is sloshing in a way that indicates it's close to full. Perfect. I pass in front of the sailboat with the bucket on the far side in case the owner is looking. He's probably realized that more than just the towels are missing by now and may be searching for the thief. I'm just past it when I realize that the speedboat and, more importantly, TJ are missing.

Chapter Seventeen

TJ

When I first hide in the bow, I tuck up in child's position. I feel like a fool right away. It's like pretending that if I can't see, no one can see me. I shift around, discovering that I can lie flat on my back. My feet do stick into the passage between the console and the panel opposite, but they're not in Bailey's way. And I can see a little of what's happening. Obviously, I'm not going to be completely hidden, but I'm about the same amount of noticeable I would have been in child's position.

The boat slows, then slows even more. There's a slight bump. I see Bailey pass from one side to the other, a blur as she moves across the dock. Then just the tops of a couple sailing masts and the sky. I stay still.

I flash back to playing hide and seek with my brother when we were kids. Waiting to be found was both boring and sometimes terrifying because he liked to scare me. Those emotions made time stretch and shrink like taffy, depending on if it was hot or cold. This is like that on steroids because the scary moment could mean capture or even death.

It feels like an hour passes, but it can't be more than minutes when I see a face. It's not Bailey's face. It's a man's face. He's older and has a weathered look.

I smile and wave, then pretend to close one of the doors that leads to under-the-seat storage and stand.

"What're you doing here? That slot belongs to Murray."

"Right. Sorry. I just needed to grab something real quick. I'll be on my way."

He gives me a skeptical look, so I start untying the line to prove it. He looks around as if searching for someone to complain to about me being where I'm not supposed to be. I drop the rope in the boat and go to the cockpit. He's looking again, so I start it.

He gives me one last glare, then boards his boat. "Hey! Where are my towels?" He leans over and looks at the water, the deck, me.

I shrug, mustering as much nonchalance as I can, then back out. My nerves are buzzing. I don't know where Bailey is. Is she on his boat? A different boat? I go slowly down to the end of the dock. It's one of several branches of docks at the marina. Bailey said that if people come for me, I'm supposed to go. I never intended to do that, though. Even if I was willing to abandon her, how can I make it on my own?

I scan for her on the dock between the boats. It's a busy marina. There are other boats coming in or out. There's a garage on the dock producing lots of clanging and motors and power tool noises. There are some people, like a family preparing to board their boat.

If I keep puttering along, I probably won't draw attention, but maybe I'm wrong. Maybe someone will notice the same boat with the same woman passing by over and over. Shoot. That would be a "see something, say something" situation for a lot of people. I can't go back by the sailboat I was just parked next to. That man is certainly on the lookout.

I pull up to the end of the next dock over, out of sight of the sailboat. I tie off loosely, wanting to be able to make a quick getaway if necessary. It's the best I can do. I can't stay long, and if Patriot Army has eyes here, they will certainly think to look at the short-term docking spots. Still, I think it's my best bet.

I'm scanning this dock and the neighboring arms when I notice an orange can with a nozzle sticking out of it sitting on the dock. Gas. It's our highest priority. Is it worth me disembarking and grabbing it?

The boat moored in front of it has a man bent over, doing something I can't see. When he straightens, he's wearing a mask and snorkel. He steps off the stern and into the water.

I hop onto the dock, walk the thirty or so feet to the gas can, pick it up, and saunter back to the end of the dock. My heart is pounding a mile a minute and does not stop when I'm back on the *Mary II*. I can't stay here. Not with my heart about to pound out of my chest and the incriminating evidence sitting right in the open. I untie. As I start to leave, I realize I could tuck the canister into a compartment, so I do so.

"Watch where you're going," someone yells.

I straighten to see I've drifted while away from the wheel. "Sorry," I yell at the man as I straighten my course.

"Shouldn't be out here alone anyway, pretty little thing like you. Where's your man to do the driving, honey?"

My insides shrivel at the words. Not only are they horrible and hateful, but now I've made an impression on this man. Plus, Bailey is still missing. Everything is super messed-up. I don't plan on answering, but he's stopped next to my boat now.

"Oh, um, he just ran back to the car for something. I'm just waiting."

"Well, wait tied up. He won't be happy if you scuff that pretty boat."

I force out a giggle. "No, you're right. I'll just tie off."

"Need any help, darling?"

I gag and try to hide it. I look around to see if anyone else is clocking this interaction and think about just driving off. A lifetime of being forced to respect men is a hard habit to break, though. I'm looking back when I see someone at the end of the dock we'd originally moored at. At first, my eyes slide over the person, but something about the figure catches my attention, and I look back.

She's androgynous in a baggy T-shirt and ball cap, but I recognize those legs, even if I can only see about the knee down. It's Bailey. She's looking enough like a man that I can pretend. "Oh, there he is. Oops, silly me. I should have stayed at the first dock." I titter again and reverse.

I glance back to see the man in the other boat looking between me and Bailey. He finally lifts a hand at Bailey and drives away. I breathe a sigh of relief.

It's short-lived because behind Bailey, a man—the man from the sailboat—is running down the dock, shaking his fist. Bailey beckons for me to come faster. I do, but I'm reversing, so my aim is poor. I'm too far away from the end of the dock as I pass it. I slam the boat into gear to move forward and pass again, but I'm moving too fast for Bailey to board.

"Darn, darn, darn," I mutter frantically, already planning my next pass.

Bailey doesn't wait. She leaps for the boat.

CHAPTER EIGHTEEN

BAILEY

I hesitate briefly with one foot in the air the moment I realize TJ and the boat are gone. I don't know what happened, but there are various reasons why she might have taken off. The possibility of us reuniting range from meeting at the end of the dock—like we talked about—to me never seeing her again. My heart clenches at the thought. Not only because I worry about her. I have faith she can do pretty much anything she sets her mind to—she already had an escape plan, after all—but also because the thought of never seeing her again hurts. That's something to think about later. Right now, I need to figure out my next move.

I turn, cursing the fact that I have to pass the sailboat again. I can't see the owner, but that doesn't mean he's not currently discovering more missing things. I hurry just a little, not so fast as to look like I'm running from something. Hopefully, I just look like I'm moving with purpose. Going this way has the downside of heading toward the end of this branch of the dock. I'll be trapped with nowhere to go if sailboat man comes after me. But that's where I have the best chance of finding TJ if she's not miles up the coast already.

I'm nearly to the end when I see two boats nearly collide. The *Mary II* has its stern pointed at me, The other stops, and TJ's head pops into view. I can hear voices but can't make out what they're saying. I watch, feeling powerless. Yelling doesn't feel like the most under-the-radar thing I could be doing right now.

Finally, TJ looks over her shoulder. I see the double take as she realizes who I am. She starts moving toward me. The man in the other boat stares for a long moment, then raises a hand in my direction and moves off.

"Hey, you!" The yell comes from behind me. "That's my stuff. How dare you?"

Fuck. Sailboat man is coming my way. A glance over my shoulder confirms that he's coming down the dock at me. Shit, shit, shit.

TJ is backing up erratically. I think she's coming toward me, but at the last minute, she veers away. I consider jumping in the water. She could pick me up. We'd lose everything I collected, though. I consider turning and fighting sailboat man. I'm pretty sure I could take him. But that would draw a lot of attention.

TJ is moving forward now, but she's going way too fast, and it looks like she'll pass a few feet away. I take a step back, then run a couple of steps and launch into the air.

I throw the bucket and the gas can as I soar, hoping to get them both onto the boat and clear of my landing, which is not going to be an easy one, I can tell.

I land with an *oof* as all my breath is knocked out of me by the edge of the boat. I've landed behind the cockpit, right by the sink. Thankfully, I didn't land on the spigot, or I'd have done myself some serious damage. As it is, I'm clawing to cement my purchase. My legs are dangling over the side.

TJ reaches for me.

"Go," I gasp out, still clawing.

I'm surprised she can hear my breathless plea, but she turns back and pulls the throttle. The movement of the boat doesn't help me, and I spend a suspenseful moment trying to get one leg in. When I am finally on the right side of falling—into the boat, not out of it—I glance back at the dock to see sailboat man still shaking his fist at me.

This will get reported. The Patriot Army will know we were here, and worse, they'll know we're headed north.

I sink onto the deck. I can't muster the strength to climb onto the seats yet. I haven't taken a full breath since my leap. My arm is throbbing in pain, with occasional sharp stabs to spice things up. I hope I haven't pulled my stitches.

"Are you okay? Bailey? Talk to me."

"Fine." It's constricted by needing air. "Go."

I lie there and concentrate on breathing while I watch wispy clouds come in and out of my field of view.

There's something under my hip. I shift and pull out the half a loaf of bread. It's pretty well squished. I imagine we'll still eat it. But now I'm wondering what all made it onboard with me. I roll over and push to my knees. I touch my head and feel just hair. I must have lost the hat in the struggle.

Oranges are rolling around. I gather them up and put them in the fridge with the half loaf. The bucket is here, and there are still towels inside. I got the gas can, thank the universe. I right it and inspect it to see if it's leaked. It seems intact. I wedge it into a corner to try to keep it in place. There's a pair of shorts in the sink. I don't know where the second T-shirt or shorts went. I look for a few moments, but it becomes clear they didn't make it. When I straighten and go to check on TJ, the red water bottle I filled catches my eye.

Besides the clothes, the other thing I can't find is the permanent marker I found on the fishing boat by the gas can. That's a loss. I had a plan for it.

I slump next to TJ on the cockpit bench. "Hi."

Her eyes are worried as she looks me up and down, finally settling on my face. "Are you okay?"

"A little bruised but otherwise, right as rain."

She faces forward to see where she's going. We're already well out to sea, so there isn't much to worry about hitting. I check the map display. We're going north-northwest. Good enough. Because I disabled the GPS tracker, all the map display is showing is a compass. Before the disabling, it was a full map feature. I wish there'd been a way to keep the navigation without the tracker but not on this system.

"And your stitches?"

I lift my arm to look at the bandage. There're some new bright red spots, and it hurts, but since it's not soaking the bandage, I figure I'm fine. "I think they held."

"That was an amazing leap. I thought you were going to end up in the water for sure. Sorry I left."

"I'm sure you did what you needed to do. What happened?"

We relay our dock experiences. When she tells me about the gas can she got, I grin. "Me too. I mean, I also got a gas can."

She smiles. "I think mine is only about a quarter full, though."

"Mine is full. Still, it won't get us far. We need more." A lot more. Our gauge is rapidly falling below half. I get up to check on the can TJ procured, but I step on something round and hard.

"Ouch." I realize I've lost the flip-flops when I step on something that hurts my bare foot.

"Are you okay?"

"Yeah, just stepped on something." I lean down and pick up the fat-tipped permanent marker. "Hello, you."

"You seem really happy to see a pen." TJ sounds amused. And—dare I believe—a little jealous?

"I am." I tuck it in the band of my swim bottoms. "I have a plan for this little guy." I pat it, maintaining eye contact with TJ the whole time.

"Wow. Just wow."

It would be inappropriate to kiss her right now, right? It doesn't really matter. I've got things to do. I open the compartment where she stashed the canister. It has a long nozzle, which mine doesn't and is an excellent feature, but she's right. There's not much gas in it. Between our two canisters, we've likely got another five gallons.

The question is, do we stretch it and wait to get gas until we're desperate? Or do we try to get more gas now, when maybe we won't be expected yet?

"How far do you think we can go on what we've got?"

"Maybe another couple of hours at this speed." I squint at the sun. "It's still only about noon. We've got a long way to go until the cover of night."

"When stealing gas will be easier?"

"Yup. Meanwhile, how about an orange?"

She shrugs her acquiescence.

I peel one and hand her a section. She pops it in her mouth and chews. I watch her throat move as she swallows, the rest of the orange forgotten in my hands. "Oh, my. I didn't know how hungry I was until just then. How many of these did you get?"

I swallow. "Six. No. Five. I only found five. I must have lost one in the jump."

"I think I could eat them all right now. That's probably not a good idea. Or is it?" There is a distinctly hopeful tone to her question.

"Probably not. But maybe some squished bread to go with it?" I hand her another orange slice and remember to eat one myself.

She shoots me an orange grin. It's adorable. "You make that sound so appetizing."

"I know," I say modestly. "I'm quite the chef."

"I mean, this orange is the best thing I've eaten in a long time, so I'd say you know what you're doing."

"Hunger is the best seasoning."

"You do know how to make a girl hungry."

Was the double entendre intentional? Either way, my body responds with a rush of sensation to my core. I consider putting a hand on her thigh, but it's sticky with orange juice, and there's still half the orange to go. It's not really the time for romance anyway. Plus, I remind myself, she backed away when I told her I didn't expect her to date me just because I was helping her escape. I'm probably reading the situation wrong.

With the last slice eaten, I go to the stern to rinse my hands in the spray. I continue to keep them to myself.

CHAPTER NINETEEN

TJ

I'm lying on my back in the bow again. Bailey, wearing the T-shirt and shorts belted on with a rag—and another rag tied around her head to disguise her hair—is driving again. We're headed to a marina. Again.

We've only progressed an hour up the coast. There are some long stretches of not a lot of civilization, so we need to fill up the tank and the cans and a couple more cans if we—Bailey, really, I'm supposed to stay right here, but we know how that went last time—can find them.

She isn't the only one disguised. We used the permanent marker to make the *Mary II* into the *Maty III*. It's not exactly convincing, especially if you get close, but the hope is that it'll pass a casual look and buy us some time.

I wish we had a plan that felt less risky, less like we need all the luck in the world. While things went wrong at the last marina, they went wrong in a salvageable way. No Patriot Army attack. We're two people, one nearly useless: me, as evidenced by the fact that I'm lying on the deck trying to hide. We have one gun, not that me having a gun would help at all. And the enemy is like Medusa: cut off one head and more sprout up. A well-armed Medusa at that. It's pure luck they weren't at the last marina, or at least, they weren't where we were. Maybe they were watching the fueling stations and not the docks in general. Now they'll know we're heading north and that they need to watch whole marinas, not just the fueling stations.

The whole plan is that Bailey is going to slide in there on this poorly disguised boat with her poorly disguised self and try to steal us some fuel.

I wish we'd waited until dark, at least.

But Bailey is worried that the more time we give them to organize, the harder it will be for us. She knows more about this sort of thing than I, for sure. I have to trust her.

The thing is, I do trust her. I more than trust her. What I really want is to be somewhere safe where we can figure out what we are. Where I can kiss her again, take her to bed. I shift a little. My discomfort stems more from the images in my head than from the hard bumpiness of the deck.

I cast about for anything to think about aside from Bailey, but I land on my father. Why would he let this happen? Did he give me up or lose power? But if the latter, how did the Patriot Army know where we were? Did he give me up to save himself from a worse fate? It's hard to imagine the father I remember from before Mom died sanctioning any of this. One of the memories I hold on to when I need to bring my love for my father forward flashes into my head.

I was maybe seven. We were in Florida at one of the church's properties. My father was rising in the church but not in his current position, so we weren't right on the water and had to walk a few blocks from our house to the marina where the boat we were using was docked. I was pouting because Mom was ahead talking to Preston. I wanted her attention.

Dad noticed I was falling behind. He circled back. "What's got you down, squirt?" His voice was kind. Even then, I knew to sometimes be wary of him. He was the disciplinarian. If I pushed him, it would be good for a swat on the butt or time in my room. Right then, I had the kind father.

"Nothing." I dragged my feet.

"Clearly something." There was a tiny edge in his voice. It faded as he regarded the sky. "But it's a blue sky day. We're getting on the boat." He cast a fond look at Mom and Preston, then down at me. "What's to be sad about?" He leaned down and swooped me off my feet and into the air. He paused with me on his hip and tickled me. I giggled. He lifted me to his shoulders. I was too big for it, but I couldn't help be delighted. He carried me to the boat, and I felt like a princess the whole way.

Bailey shifts her feet, drawing my attention. When she stands before the wheel, I can see the top of her head. When she sits and kicks her leg out like she likes to do, I can see the toes of her left foot. I'm waiting for her signal, so I need to keep my eye on her rather than let my attention drift.

I'm supposed to cover myself with towels before we pull in. I, too, will be more disguised this time. I still think it won't be enough, that we'll face a confrontation this time. Bailey has so much she is trying to do. She's going to attempt to steal credit cards for fueling but also find a hose for siphoning fuel from other boats. That will work better under the cover of darkness but is likely to be necessary.

While she works, I'm supposed to just lie here doing nothing to help. My stomach clenches with nerves and frustration at my impotence. I get that I'm a liability. We don't have enough clothes to disguise me. And Bailey is much better at, well, everything. But lying here for however long it takes her to do what she needs to do while hoping that nothing happens to her and that I'm not discovered? It's a tall order.

I see the top of Bailey's head over the windshield. Well, I see the rag. She isn't signaling, just standing for a while. I wonder if it's nerves that has her unable to sit. Even though she told me earlier that she gets nervous, I haven't seen any evidence of it. She always looks calm and put together, even when I was stitching her up.

I feel like I've perfected a poker face over the years when hiding who I am, but Bailey is next level. I study her head for clues about what she's thinking or where we are. The rag is giving nothing away. Her hand lifts above her head in a stretch. It's the signal. I scrunch up, trying not to seem so body-shaped, and pull the towels over me.

We're here.

CHAPTER TWENTY

BAILEY

I don't envy TJ her job, lying on the deck and trying not to look like a person. I'm glad my role is the active one. Involuntarily, I watch out of the corner of my eye, seeing just the movement of the towels as she situates herself. I yank my attention back to the marina ahead. I need to focus on the job, not TJ, even though I find her captivating.

This marina is smaller, which isn't good. We're more likely to be noticed. Although, it's also possible that the Patriot Army will focus their attention on larger marinas. Maybe they won't even be here.

That is almost certainly wishful thinking.

The last marina had a ramp coming down to the water from the parking area above a wide dock running both to the left and right, with narrower docks sticking out like so many capital Es on their sides. Each jutting prong spiked off even smaller docks running between the boats.

This one has also has a ramp that feeds into a dock going in both directions. However, to the north, there are only some temporary tie offs and at the end, a fueling station. To the south, there are some docks jutting off the main one with numbered mooring spots for perhaps a couple dozen boats. It's not much for getting lost in.

There is a police boat tied off at the north. Shit. I nearly flee, but that would be flagged for sure. And we need gas. There's nothing to do but hope the flimsy disguises we came up with and a confident air win the day. I make for the south side of the marina, trying to look like I do it every day. My heart is in my throat, and I'm ready for shouts, revving engines, or even gunshots at any moment.

A man on his boat eyes me as I practically drift by in my attempt to be casual. I raise a hand in a bro-to-bro greeting I perfected while going to kids' camp and interacting with lots of bros. He raises his in return and goes back to whatever he was doing. The relief is real, but we're nowhere near out of the woods.

I pull into an empty berth and tie off. I grab the two empty cans and step off the *Maty III* with purpose, ostensibly walking to the fueling station. It's a little unusual to walk over with canisters but not unheard of. But I'm carrying them in case I see an opportunity to siphon gas. It's a long shot in broad daylight, but I'm taking a scattershot approach to the gas problem.

Trying to look casual, I look for any of my laundry list of items. I would take a hose, a stray wallet or purse, more gas cans, or clothes for either of us. I luck out at the end of the dock. There's a boat with a water hose curled up on deck. I won't even have to step onboard to grab it. I shift both canisters to my left hand while I languidly look around to make sure no one is looking my way before snagging the hose with my right hand.

No shouts. So far, so good. Better than I'd imagined.

This is a much quieter marina. That's mostly to do with size. There are simply fewer boats for people to come and go from. Still, I hear at least two engines puttering along nearby. I'm keeping my gaze averted so my face won't be recognized, so I'm not completely sure where they are. I have some idea due to sound. I deem them far enough away to make my next move.

I step onto a boat that doesn't have a security system and look for anything useful. I come up empty and try again with another. I can only do that so many times before people notice me. I opt to work on filling the tanks.

The hose will need some modifications to suit my purpose. I kneel between two sailboats tall enough to disguise what I'm doing unless someone walks down the dock I'm on. I slice off each end, toss them in the water. Sorry, fish. I slice a short length off. It's the part I'll blow into to get the gas moving down the other hose.

I straighten and am evaluating my options for pilfering gas when I hear a voice. At first, I act like I don't hear it. The person calls again. "Hey! Ya, there."

I look out of the corner of my eye and see a woman in a boat that's something of a junker. She's just on the other side of the moored boats. For a split second, I'm not sure if I should respond, keep walking, or run away. I settle on giving her a puzzled look. I really am puzzled, She's a woman alone, unusual in red states, although it does happen, particularly with older women if they're alone in the world. I just have no idea what she wants with me. Did she see me on the boats?

"Come closer." She beckons to me.

Shit. Will she kick up a fuss if I run or just let me go?

"I ain't gonna hurt ya."

From this angle and what's between us, I think she can't see the hose. I drop it and walk to the edge of the dock. Complying will draw less attention than running, but there's no need to be obvious about what I'm up to. There's still a boat between us, but unlike the last marina, there aren't little docks between boats, so I can't get closer without getting on someone else's boat.

Her engine is rumbling but not super loudly. She speaks just loudly enough to be heard over it. "You in some kind of trouble? Is that even your boat?"

I'm not entirely sure how to play this, but I feel like she isn't out to get me. There's something in the way she's looking at me that makes me think she wants to help. Still, I don't want to just give up my secrets. "Good as."

She eyes me. "I saw that hose. You clearly don't have any good options for fueling up if you're looking to steal some. I can buy you a tank, see you on your way."

That's a surprise. I don't say anything. I'm not sure if I should accept. On the one hand, having someone buy a tank helps enormously. On the other, I don't want to take the boat so close to the police boat. They will definitely be looking for us. Additionally, her boat looks one strong wave away from not functioning. I don't know that I should take any of what must be her precious funds.

She narrows her eyes. "I can see you have need in spite of that pretty boat. Running away from something, are ya? You should ditch the boat. Too flashy."

I decide to be at least somewhat honest. She doesn't seem like the sort to turn me in. She seems like the sort to know a thing or two about how to get by in red country without being part of the mainstream. "I don't have other options right now. Can't sell it. And I need a boat. I'll make it work. Alone."

"Don' be proud. You need help, and I can help." Her gaze travels up and down me, not in a "checking me out" sort of way, but in a "I recognize you" sort of way. "We womenfolk have to look out for one another."

That clinches it. I nod. "Okay."

She nods back at me once, decisively. "Okay. Can you follow me to the pump and fill up?" She glances over my shoulder, then back. "Or is that police boat going to be a problem?"

I look her directly in her eye. "It'll be a problem."

"Give me those canisters. I'll fill them and a couple others." She jerks her thumb at the back of her boat where I see some faded red cans. "That'll get you a little ways. Money? Food?"

I nod. "And water if you have it."

"The police boat is moving. You should get out of here. You're way too obvious in that thing. There's an island just up the coast. Little cove on the leeward side. Go wait up there." She holds her hand out. I step on the boat between us and pass the canisters off, then step back, collect the hose—because we are likely to need it later—and walk casually back to the *Maty III*. Moving fast will only draw attention.

I untie and pull the rope in with me as I jump. "Change of plans," I say to the towels in the bow. "Stay hidden. I'll fill you in in a minute."

The police boat is in the first branch of moored boats. We're at the end. They'll see us move, but I'm hoping to mislead them by heading south. And being the only one on the boat. And hoping the newly adapted names helps.

I back out. The police boat doesn't seem to notice. I head south. The police boat pulls out of the lane it was in and comes my direction. I don't change speed. They follow for a few minutes but don't gain on us. Then, they peel off.

"Stay down, but you can uncover if you want. I don't think anyone is following us."

I see the towels being thrown off. TJ's voice comes just loudly enough for me to hear, "Did you get gas?"

"Not yet. There was a police boat, and I thought it best not to stay. I think gas is coming. I'm pretty sure it's coming. If not, we at least have a hose now, so we're better set up for stealing it."

"How is it coming?"

"An older woman offered to help." My stomach clenches a little. If she doesn't come through, not only will we not have gas, we won't have our cans. It was a big gamble deciding to trust her, but I'm nearly certain it was the right choice.

"Huh."

"Yeah, I know."

"If you trust her…"

"I know it's a risk, but it seemed less a risk than any of the other options."

"And I take it she knew you were a woman, as opposed to the boy you're trying to look like."

"What? This old thing?" I pluck at the oversized T-shirt, even though she can't see me.

"I knew it wouldn't work. You're too beautiful to be a boy."

I feel my cheeks heat. She thinks I'm beautiful. "Not nearly as beautiful as you."

"Matter of opinion."

Maybe TJ is interested in me as more than a way to get away from her dad and the church. If that wasn't flirting, I don't know what is.

I take a wide circle back to the north and tell TJ I think it's safe to get up. When she joins me on the bench, I place my hand on her thigh. It's hard not to touch her, particularly after the flirting, but I try to keep it friendly. "Sorry about having to lie down there. I'm afraid you'll need to go back into hiding for the gas pickup. I want to trust…shit. I don't even know her name. Anyway, I want to trust her, but we should keep what she knows to a minimum, just in case."

"That makes sense." She sounds resigned.

"For what it's worth, after that, you shouldn't need to hide. We'll be stealing gas under the cover of night, and if anything, I'll need a lookout."

"Glad I can be of service and not just baggage."

"TJ, you're not baggage. You've helped me problem solve and have held your own on a really rough day."

She covers my hand. So much for friendly. "Thanks."

We go along for a while without talking. I'm thinking about the rendezvous. How long can we stay if the old woman doesn't come quickly? Will she show at all? If this is some sort of elaborate plot to cause us harm, what are my options for getting us out of it?

I keep scanning the horizon, looking for her. I don't know how long she'll take. I don't want TJ to have to hide too long, but I also don't want her to be seen. We're approaching the island now, having come at it in a roundabout way, and she could have come directly.

"Should I be hiding again?"

"I don't want to make you, but it's like you read my mind."

"I'm just paying attention, is all."

"If it helps, I think as long as you sit in the footwell, you'd not be very noticeable. You don't have to lie down yet."

"Great. I'll settle on a towel for comfort. It'll be the height of luxury."

I'm relieved that she's joking about it. "Well, it's not lying directly on the hard, nubby deck, but I suppose it'll do."

She laughs. I'm a little surprised when she kisses my cheek before she goes to hide. I feel like a teenager with a crush on her again, even though we were just making out this morning, and I'm a few years away from being a teenager. I briefly put my hand over my cheek as if to hold her kiss there. I drop my hand when I realize that when she's sitting up, we can see each other's faces. I'm not quite quick enough, and she shoots me a knowing grin. What do I have to lose by leaning in? I blow her a kiss. Her grin turns to a full-fledged smile.

I pull into the cove that I think the woman was talking about. I'm torn between staying near the mouth for a quick getaway and tucking as far back as possible to stay hidden. I settle on tucked far enough back to not easily be seen by someone passing the mouth but close enough not to feel trapped. Although, if she set this up for us to be captured, it won't really matter. I also can't see when someone is just outside the entrance. It'd be easy to set up a blockade. With the engine cut to save gas, I imagine I'd hear them, though. Plus, why go to these elaborate lengths? If she'd just stood by while I pilfered gas and called the police, it would have been easy to trap us at the marina. No, I think she's really helping.

It's not long before I hear her boat. TJ settles in with the towels over her again.

The woman and I raise our hands at each other in greeting. She pulls her ramshackle trawler alongside our sleek craft. The boats are about the same length, but hers would be much better for the sort of voyage we're doing. It has a much wider bottom and likely gets better gas milage. However, I could definitely outrun her, which is important. There are our two stolen canisters—plus another three faded ones—sitting on the stern of her boat. My eyes go wide of their own accord. She's dropped a lot of money helping a stranger.

She must see where I'm looking because she says, "All full. Should help ya get on your way." Unspoken but hanging in the air is the understanding that it won't get me all the way. She seems to understand that there will be theft in my future.

She throws me a rope. I catch it and pull until we're touching. I tie it loosely. We do the same at the other end before she starts handing me the cans. While she passes them over, she says, "Ya don't have to tell me what you're running from, but I imagine someone is missing that pretty boat. I hope you've at least disabled that GPS system?"

"Of course."

"Of course," she echoes. "Hard to tell if you've got a good head on your shoulders when I met ya trying to pilfer gas at a small marina in broad daylight."

She's not wrong, but I have very few options. It made the most sense at the time. Switching to land travel is out of the question because of getting across the border. We could conceivably switch to land, steal a car, and then steal another boat father north. However, that's a lot of points at which our presence would be flagged and a lot more eyes on us overall. Now that we have this gas, if we find some private docks where I can siphon gas off boats and maybe cars, we may be able to stay hidden for the remainder of our flight to New Orleans. "I hear you, but I had my reasons."

She nods as she hands me the last can. "Desperation will do that to a person." Her eyes flicker to the lump that is TJ in the front of the boat, and my heart quickens. "I hope you find safety." It's clear to me she means the plural you, but I am still not going to let her lay eyes on TJ. It's better she thinks I'm running away with my girlfriend so we can be together than that I'm smuggling Thomas Rice's daughter out of the state.

She leans down and comes up with a gallon of water. "Here's the water you asked for."

I take it with thanks.

From another hidey-hole, she produces a greasy white bag. "I stopped off at my favorite waterfront fish fry. This should give you a few calories to make some distance on."

As I take the bag, scents of fried fish and potatoes waft toward me. My stomach rumbles. "Thank you. This is…incredibly helpful." I nearly said it was too much, but what I would have meant was that it was too much for her, given the state of her boat and clothes. That would have been presumptuous of me. I don't know her situation. If she can help, I will gladly take it. And I certainly don't want to offend her.

"We have to do what we can for one another." She gives me a meaningful look. "Pass it on when ya can." She darts another glance at the towels in the bow. "Not that ya aren't already. Get goin' before some Patriot Army yahoo comes by."

I stand like a ninny for a moment before untying. Does she know who we are? Then I get moving, untying the loose knot and tossing her the rope. She lets it fall into her boat rather than catching it, and our boats begin to drift apart.

"It's all over the news to watch out for two women on the run. One of them is supposed to be the Rice girl. Just so ya know." She raises a hand again.

I raise one back and thank her fervently.

We're back out in open water and moving at speed when TJ throws off her towels. "Are we clear?"

"Yes." It doesn't matter if the woman, whose name I still don't know, sees her. She knew all along. It's a harsh reminder that everyone will be looking for us.

She sits up and scratches vigorously at her ankle before coming to join me on the bench. I wonder if she'd been under there itching all the time. The job of hiding is definitely the harder job. "So," she says, echoing my thoughts, "did she know I was with you or..."

"Oh, she knew. She kept looking at you."

"Do you think...I mean, she seemed like she was on our side?" TJ looks back over her shoulder as if to gauge the expression on the face of a woman nowhere in eyesight.

"She is. I'm sure she is. She...there was an understanding." I pause to take in how much she risked for us, how much she gave up. Those gas cans in the back are clearly ones she's had a long time. I need to honor her by really appreciating what she's done, not second-guessing her abilities to do so. "Besides, look what she brought us." I point at the bag of food.

TJ smiles big, picks up the bag, and brings it to her nose. "Oh my."

I go weak at the knees. Oh my, indeed.

CHAPTER TWENTY-ONE

TJ

This smells amazing. How do you think she does it?" After I say it, I'm not sure Bailey will get what I was going for with the question. I want to know how the woman who helped us is out on her own, apparently unbound by the rules, or at least, cleverly subverting them.

"In kids' camp, one of the things they talked about was flying under the radar. It's easier for some than others. For example, a woman with children at the grocery store. Even if the kids are acting up, it's just part of the scenery, part of what's expected. They told us that we should endeavor to not be noticeable rather than going with some elaborate disguise." At first, I'm not sure she did catch my drift, but then she continues, "I think older women are overlooked because they're discounted. I think that's how she does it."

"Well, you know women of any age don't really count."

"Which is why Patriot Army is spending all these resources to try to hunt you down."

"We only count if we're a problem, obviously. Is your dad a nonbeliever?"

Bailey's been looking all around, marking our progress or looking at the gauges. Now, she looks at me. "Does it matter?"

"Only because he let you train with Patriot Army. My father always said that we needed some women to be trained, but a father who would allow it must not be right with God."

"Are you a nonbeliever?"

That means something very specific to the Church of the Redeemer. It means you don't believe in all the tenants of their doctrine. You're allowed to sin, everyone does, but you should know it's a sin and feel bad about it. You should try not to do it. And that alone should tell Bailey I'm a nonbeliever. Not only have I repeatedly sinned in my past, but I kissed her this morning. Was that really this morning? It feels like a different lifetime.

On the other hand, she may be using the specific term in a nonspecific way. That is, she may be asking if I'm religious at all. "I believe that Church of the Redeemer has a faulty interpretation of Christianity because one of the main precepts of Christianity is love and acceptance. I'm not sure if there's a God at all." I shrug. "You?"

She looks me right in the eye. "I'm a nonbeliever. So is my dad. So maybe your dad isn't wrong."

She's trusting me with this. If I get caught, I could give him up for points that would accelerate my assent into a more comfortable hell. Or maybe she is really that confident that we'll make it, rather than truly trusting me. But I want her to trust me.

I maintain eye contact while I nod to show I understand. I want to ask about why her dad chose this life if he's a nonbeliever, but I have an idea why. I can see how Patriot Army would be a draw for someone who likes to play with weapons and doesn't mind the rest, even if they don't believe.

I look at the food in my lap. I'm hungry, but I'm more thirsty. "Did I hear we got more water?"

"Yes, quite a bit. Drink your fill."

I could really go for some sweet tea right now, but the water tastes nearly as good. It's wet and almost sweet. I am clearly very thirsty. I drain one of our original water bottles before I think to ask if Bailey has gotten any yet. She tells me no, so I hand her the other one. She's a little more restrained but goes through that one in short order.

Being out of immediate danger and having quenched my thirst, my stomach rumbles. "Should we eat?"

Bailey shoots me a grin. "Oh yeah."

The fish and fries are still a little warm, and nothing has ever tasted so good. We make quick work of the bag.

I look sadly into the empty bag, hoping for one more fry. "I feel like that was a lot of food, but I still want more. I don't think I've been this hungry since I was a teenager. I remember coming home from swim practice and absolutely devouring a couple of peanut butter and jelly sandwiches and a bag of chips. And I'd have had a smoothie before practice."

"My dad always used to complain, mostly playfully, about how much his food bill went up when I visited. He said he was pretty sure I ate more than him when he was a teenager. I mean, he had me out doing physical activity all day, every day. Of course I was hungry. I'd like to tell you to break into something else, but we should probably ration."

I lean back and put my feet up on the dash. "I'll live, I suppose."

"That's good news. I'm fond of you and would be sad if you perished from this earth."

Her tone is teasing, but there is a note of sincerity that makes me brave enough to take her free hand. She wraps her fingers around mine, giving me the feels. I'm beginning to realize that she's interested in me. While the kiss this morning made that clear, the following declaration that she didn't want me to be her girlfriend when we got to safety had me doubting. Playing the conversation back, she did say something about not wanting me to feel obligated. Perhaps she really meant just that she's interested but doesn't want me to think that her helping me escape means I have to with her.

But maybe, just maybe, if we're both interested, we could date. Or something. Dating seems odd after all this, but I suppose that would be the next logical step.

"What are you thinking about?" Bailey gives my hand a tiny squeeze. "You look pensive."

"I was thinking about you."

She looks at me with a touch of worry. "Good things or…"

I laugh at her insecurity. Orchestrate an escape from a police boat when it seems impossible? Fine. Saunter onto a boat and steal supplies? No problem. But not being able to read the mind of a romantic interest? Doubt.

She smiles as if in reaction to my laughter, but the worry around her eyes also looks a little more pronounced.

I pat her hand with my free one. "Sorry. I didn't mean to laugh at you. It just occurred to me that we're, I mean, just humans. And while you seem like you've got it all together, you're over there wondering if the girl you like likes you. And I do." A touch of worry creeps in around the edges of my newfound confidence. "I mean, you do like me, right?"

Her smile goes big, and suddenly, she's kissing me. I kiss her back, tasting salt and a little bit of sunblock and her. We hit a swell at a strange angle and bump apart.

"Oops." She disentangles her hand from mine, puts both hands on the wheel, and rights the boat. "I guess I should be paying attention to the road. So to speak."

"So to speak." I can't help feeling smug. I've still got it.

She spares me a quelling look. Piloting the boat takes some attention, yes, but at least out here, it isn't like driving, where she has to worry about lots of other cars crowding her or anything.

"Where'd you learn to drive a boat anyway? Kids' camp?"

"We did learn there, yes, but a friend of mine in Portland, her family has a boat. I've been going out with them since I was little. That's where I learned to wakeboard, but I didn't get to do it as much as I'd have liked until I stopped going to Oklahoma for the summers. How about you? Seems like a skill that girls aren't supposed to have."

"Well, girls who wear little swimsuits and do fun things are encouraged. You have to catch a man's eye, after all. It's after marriage that you're supposed to don the skirt and all." I don't mean this exactly literally. Redeemer doesn't require skirts. But a lot of women seem to adopt them after marriage. There are a few families where even the little girls are put in modest clothes, but mostly, teen girls are supposed to be sexy. That's also unspoken. But it's true. "But the real story is that my mom was big on the water. She was the one who wanted us to have a boat and insisted on Florida vacations. Her family had a house on the Keys when she was little, but of course, that was gone by the time I was born. There are plenty Redeemer properties elsewhere in Florida, and we made good use of them. By the time she died, it was ingrained, I guess. And, yeah, she insisted both Preston and I learned so the three of us could go out by ourselves."

I think about my mom and about going out on the boat for a long moment. I think it was one of those things that made life worth living for her. I know she passed that on to me, at least. I don't think the drive is as strong for Preston. "My father loved her so much that he was willing to overlook the impropriety of her being in charge on the boat. I mean, it wasn't that big of a deal. She wore tankinis and swim skirts and all that. But her taking us out alone was a little unorthodox, I guess. He never fussed about it, though. I think that when she died, he broke down in some ways. He was never the sort of father who cuddled us on the couch and read to us or anything, but he was more present before we lost her. After, I think…I think he covered for me when I did things I wasn't, you know, supposed to do because of his love for her. I know I look a lot like her. I think…I don't know. I think he just chose that path. Not getting close to me but still protecting me."

Bailey takes my hand again. "You never talked about your mom much when we were kids."

"It was hard. I missed her so much. Life was so much worse when it was just my father parenting. I couldn't even…I couldn't talk about her without breaking down."

"I'm sorry."

"It was a long time ago." I stare at the horizon. "I don't know what might have been different if she lived. For all she was into boats, she was—or at least, seemed to me—pretty devout. I can't imagine she'd have been pleased with the way I turned out."

Bailey is quiet for a few moments before she says, "She might have struggled to accept that you like women, but I think she would have been proud of you. You're confident and resourceful. You know what you want and go for it. It's admirable."

I like that view of me. I don't disagree, but those traits aren't valued in women in my community. I'm not convinced that my mom would have agreed with Bailey, but that doesn't mean I'm not basking in the praise. It's been a long time since anyone thought I was admirable. Even the few times I was in a mockery of a relationship—it's hard to be real when we know we're going to have to marry men—I was a dirty little secret, not something treasured. Craved, yes, but not treasured.

"Thank you."

"TJ, you are someone special."

I hunch my shoulders and look away. I like hearing it, but it's also hard to accept. I change the subject. "So, your mom. Is she still a nurse?"

Bailey accepts the topic change and fills me in on her mom and her maternal grandparents, both of whom she's close with. "I'm sorry. I know all your grandparents have passed. It's inconsiderate of me to go on about mine."

It's thoughtful of her. I put my hand on her knee in appreciation. And a desire to be in contact with her. "It's okay. I never knew any of them. I am sad about my mom still, but that doesn't mean I don't want to hear about yours."

She covers my hand. "Tell me more about your mom. If you want to."

I find that I do. I tell her all the funny, sweet stories I can think of, then move on to times we fought but circle back to funny and sweet. It's cathartic. I've never really gotten to talk about her, and it feels good. We take a break to fill the tank, then keep chugging north with me now in the captain's seat and Bailey next to me. The words keep tumbling out, things I didn't know I remembered. Bailey is an excellent audience. She laughs, places a comforting hand on my thigh, and asks questions at the right times. How is she so amazing? She's basically G.I. Jane but also empathetic and so sexy.

The sun is getting low in the western sky, and we've been going along in silence for a little while when Bailey says, "We'd best go through the night. We should take turns trying to get some sleep. Do you want to lie down?"

"Nah. I'm feeling really awake. I'll drive for a while."

"Okay. I'll try to nap. Wake me up if the tank gets to a quarter, and I'm not up yet or if you get tired."

She kisses my cheek and pulls her arm off my shoulders. I miss its weight immediately.

CHAPTER TWENTY-TWO

BAILEY

I lie on the back seat watching the clouds gathering. I am tired, but I fall asleep best if I take a few minutes to let my mind wander before I try to sleep. That way, when I close my eyes, I'm ready to drift off. It works a lot of the time, at least.

Looks like we're in for some rain. I sit up. The water has been getting choppier, too, now that I think about it. I look around. Shit. I think we're in for a storm. I move back up to the captain's bench.

TJ smiles at me. "Couldn't stay away, huh?"

I smile back, but I know it's a little weak. "I think a storm is coming." I point at the water. "Look how choppy it's getting. And the swells are growing." I look at the darkening sky. It's not only the sun going down. The clouds are getting dark.

TJ takes it all in and clearly comes to the same conclusion. "Do you think we should risk going to shore?"

"Maybe. I—"

The radio squawks to life. I left it on thinking that if anyone from the Patriot Army tried to contact us, that would indicate that they were within sixty miles or so. Plus, anything else they say can provide more information. I don't intend to reply, of course.

"Swanson...Holder. Over." His voice is staticky. I'm not sure if that means he's at the outer range of the VHF radio or if it's because of the weather. I wish he wasn't close enough to get through, even if it's at sixty miles. It's too close.

There's a long pause like he thinks I'll answer.

Finally, he speaks again. "I don't...if you're even still... *Mary*...sure...suspect...heading north. Swanson, listen...hurricane warning. Mr. Rice...about his daughter. I've been...offer you a deal."

Even without the over, there's a pause, as if he still hopes I'll respond. I look at TJ. She's staring at the radio.

"Turn...in...any police station. Miss Rice...home and do her cleansing there. Swans...you'll be...Portland. No repercussions. Just come in."

TJ looks at me. There's a frown line on her brow, and her face looks tight with worry. "We're not doing that, right?"

Holder begins repeating the offer. We definitely got the gist the first time. There's a hurricane warning. People are evacuating. It's not safe. If we turn ourselves in, TJ goes home rather than to conversion camp. I get sent to Portland.

"Bailey?" TJ asks when he's gone through it a second time.

I put my arm around her. "No. No way. Unless you want to go home."

"No." She's emphatic.

"Then, no. We'll figure out another way."

She breathes a sigh of relief incongruous with the danger we're now in. At least if Holder, who is going through the spiel a third time, isn't lying. They could be taking advantage of a brewing storm to make us worry it'll be worse.

That thought is disabused quickly when the radio cuts into Holder talking with loud blares, followed by an announcement that a hurricane is approaching the area, and we should seek shelter.

"Guess he wasn't lying," TJ says, echoing my thoughts.

"Start for shore," I say. "We'll find some place to hole up."

I just hope we don't also find the Patriot Army waiting for us. We're a couple miles offshore, and they could be anywhere within sixty miles to get through to our radio. That's a large radius. We should be able to slip in.

"Hurricane season starts in April. That's totally normal," TJ deadpans as she heads for shore. The boat is jostling around more now. The weather is shifting quickly now. The first drops of rain hits us.

"It's just God punishing us for our sins. If we repent, he'll fix it all." I'm parroting the Redeemers' line about global warming. There are very few people who don't believe it's happening these days, but the how-to-fix-it part is still very much up for grabs. Meanwhile, we have hurricanes in April, and there's no going back.

We're offshore from an area of Florida that is not super-developed. As we approach the coast, we're greeted by mostly green. While that's lovely to see and I'm glad there are still areas of the country that remain wild, it's not super helpful right now.

"North?" TJ asks.

"Yes. Let's not lose progress, at least."

The rain is still light, but we're not dressed for it. Or maybe we are in our swimsuits. But not really because the rain and wind make it cold. In the interest of disguise and a little bit of warmth, I give TJ the T-shirt.

I'm scanning the water for danger and the coast for both danger and shelter. It's getting harder to see with the dark clouds, rain, and sun now below the horizon. Are we better off making a landing and moving inland or continuing along the coast? We're getting tossed around now. Waves are crashing on the shore that obviously doesn't get much in the way of crashing waves. The section we're passing right now is green, not beach.

"There." I point. I'm holding on to the top of the windshield with my other hand.

"Where?" TJ squints. "Oh, it's an inlet."

The conditions are so bad, we both almost missed it. "Yeah, go in. It should be more sheltered, and maybe we'll find a building."

We're nearly dashed against the rocks on one side of the mouth of the inlet, but TJ manages to get us in safely. It's not deep, and my hopes are falling. I'm about to suggest we attempt to get back out and keep looking when a house catches my attention. It's all boarded up, and hopefully, that means the inhabitants have evacuated. There is a dock, too.

TJ gets us there. The waters are surging, but it's not as bad as on the open ocean. We manage to tie off. We collect what we can carry and head for the house. The wind is staying high, and now the rain is picking up. The rain drives horizontally from our right side. We're already soaked, and the rain feels like ice chunks pelting us. We hurry inland toward the house.

My heart sinks as we approach. Up close, I can see that it's big and fancy. What that means is a big fancy security system. While it's highly likely no one will come check out a break-in right now, our location would be known once the storm ended, if not before, making it that much easier for the Patriot Army to find us.

I stop and look around for options.

"We're not going in the house?" Even though we're off the boat, TJ still has to yell to be heard.

"Only if it's that or the hurricane."

"I think it is that or the hurricane."

I stop when I see a pool shed. I'd think that a shed wouldn't be the first choice for shelter against a hurricane, but these people obviously wanted their shed to last through the increasing number of hurricanes and didn't care about how attractive it is. It's cement, painted so it doesn't stick out like a sore thumb, but there are no windows, and I can tell from here that the walls are thick. It's practically a bunker.

I jerk my head at it. "The shed."

TJ shoots a longing glance at the large, comfortable-looking house, then follows me to the shed.

It's locked, but I make quick work of that with a couple tools I pull from our kit. I open the door and feel around for a light switch, hoping the power isn't already out. An overhead LED illuminates the dark space, filling every corner with brightness. I wince against its intensity.

Once inside, we pause and drip on the cement floor for a moment. TJ's eyes are wide, and she's breathing hard. Her hair is plastered to her face and neck. I probably look the same. She sets down two gallons of water she was carrying, pulls the T-shirt off, and wrings it out, only breaking eye contact briefly as the shirt passes over her head.

I swallow and lick my lips. I can't look away from her. She's standing there in just her swimsuit. While that has been the case most of the day, my attention is newly drawn to all the exposed skin. She's lean, with toned muscles that flex as she wrings out the shirt. And she's looking at me like I'm a meal after days of hunger.

I'm drawn to her like a magnet.

I drop the buckets I'm carrying and close the distance between us. I'm a pace away when she tosses the shirt aside and reaches for me. I take that as consent for the kiss I'm driving toward. Our lips meet, and the kiss is passionate and intense. The tension has been building between us not just since our kiss this morning, not just since the parking lot at the airport, but from when we were teenagers. Our intensity is fueled from that tension but also from the situation we're in. We've been running on adrenaline all day. We need an outlet.

I pull a pool mat down from the shelf next to us and lay TJ down on it. It's a matter of minutes before we've each climaxed. We're lying there, still wet in more ways than one, still breathing hard, my injured arm throbbing, tangled in one another, with part of me hanging onto the cement floor when I fully realize what we've just done.

"Oh, TJ, I'm sorry."

"Why?" She regards me with what looks like genuine curiosity.

I rest my forehead on her shoulder. "I wanted this to be... different."

"This? Sex?"

I lift my head and look her in the eye. "Yes. I wanted our first time to be slow and wonderful, not a quickie on the floor of some shed under harsh lighting."

Her face softens. "You thought about our first time?"

My cheeks heat. I'm sure they're bright red. "Yes? Lots?" I'm asking as if I'm not sure it was okay.

"Me too." She cups my cheek. "And maybe our second time will be slow, but this was still wonderful. At least, I thought so?"

Along with the lift of the last couple words, I see doubt creep into her eyes. I rush to dispel it. "It was. I mean, it was amazing. I'm not sure I've ever mutually gotten off so quickly."

She laughs. "I think it was exactly what we needed."

The sound of the door rattling in its frame brings me back to our situation. "I think we need to take care of a few things."

TJ pulls my head down for one more kiss, then says, "What do we need to do?"

I consider going out to try to find more supplies, but that is risky on a number of fronts. Getting into the house would set off alarms, notifying people that we're here. Even if the power cuts out, I noticed the house has a backup solar power system that will turn on automatically to keep the house systems going. The growing weather situation is another factor. We have water. We have four oranges, two granola bars, and a half a loaf of squished bread. We have what remains of the first aid kit. It's enough. The important thing is to make sure that door doesn't give way. We shove and pull until we get a shelving unit in front of the door to reinforce it. We find some heavy items and add them to the shelves to increase the heft. Then, we retreat to the back of the shed with our supplies and several mats with which to make a nest.

"Let's look at your arm," TJ says. "I'm sure you need a new bandage. That one has gotten wet a couple times now."

I hold my arm up and look at the dirty wrap. She's right. I just don't know if there's enough usable things in the first aid kit to do a good job of it. TJ lays out the supplies.

"Those bandages are wet, too," I point out. "We could cut strips from the towels?"

We do that. The resulting bandage is a little bulky, but it's cleaner. Also, there is enough antiseptic to douse it again. It's nice to think it may not get infected.

While TJ is putting the supplies away, I get up and look at the pile of pool toys. I'm wondering if noodles or an inflatable swan would make a better pillow when TJ wraps her arms around me from behind. We're both still naked. There didn't seem to be a point in putting our wet suits back on. They're currently hanging to dry. All of which means I feel all of TJ pressing against my back in the most delicious way.

"How about we try for slow this time?"

I decide that the pillow question can wait.

CHAPTER TWENTY-THREE

TJ

I wake up periodically during the night. Pool mats on a cement floor don't exactly make the most comfortable bed. I'm very aware of Bailey, too. Every time I shift and come into contact, I fully wake and consider waking her up, too, but one of us should be getting some rest, I suppose. The howling winds outside don't help.

I'm woken from a dream involving trying to catch a flight when everything is going wrong to Bailey shaking my shoulder gently. What a weird dream to have in the middle of this. It was a stress dream, for sure, something to do with travel. But the stress of missing a flight seems insignificant in comparison to the stress of fleeing for our lives.

I squint at the sunshine coming through the door. Bailey must have shifted the shelving unit by herself without waking me. I guess I finally fell into a deep sleep.

"Sorry to wake you, but we need to get moving."

I stretch and rub my eyes. When I lower my hands, the stretching has dislodged the towel I was sleeping under, and Bailey's eyes are on my exposed breasts. They're small, and I've never considered them my best asset, but the way she's staring is giving me life. She swallows, then looks at my face. Her cheeks go bright red, which is adorable. She clears her throat and looks away.

I put a finger on her chin and guide her back to me. I kiss her lightly. Her cheeks are still pink, but now she looks pleased.

"So, yeah, good morning," she says. "We need to get moving before people start coming back."

"Okay." I sit up and look around for my swimsuit. Bailey already has hers on. She hands me mine, plus the T-shirt. I refuse it. "You wear it. You need more sun protection." I tan, and she burns.

She hesitates, then nods and pulls it over her head. "Here. I peeled an orange. Breakfast of champions." She hands me a half.

We eat quickly before gathering our things. Bailey picks up the two buckets, and I take the water again. We drank some, so my load has gotten lighter, but Bailey has added a rope to one of her buckets.

When we step outside, I see that the hurricane hit hard. There are palm trees down, one onto the house, meaning someone will be around to check on it soon, I imagine, given the security system Bailey was sure they have. Debris is everywhere. We're both still barefoot, so we're careful as we pick our way down to the dock. When we're in sight of it, we both stop dead in our tracks.

The boat is gone.

"Shit," Bailey says.

The water is much higher than last night. It's sloshing across the top of the dock. There is one frayed rope still dangling from the tie off. "It must have rubbed on the dock too much." She straightens and looks around.

I follow her lead. This inlet seems private. It's small, and the only structure I can see is the dock. Maybe the *Maty III* is along the shore somewhere? But it's fairly flat, and I see no sign of it.

Bailey leans far out on the end of the dock and cranes her head to the left. "I think I see something over there." She points. I follow her finger. There are some trees between here and where the inlet dips in over there, obscuring whatever may be in the tiny bay. Maybe, possibly, I see the end of another dock? I'm not sure, though.

"Is it the *Maty III*?" Bailey asks.

"I think it might be another dock."

"I think you're right. Let's go check it out." She looks back at the house. "Or we go see what's in the garage up there. But our time for doing that is likely running short. I bet the owner's security team is en route." She hesitates for just a couple of seconds, then says decidedly, "Water is better. If we don't find a boat, maybe we can wait out the security team and try the garage after they leave."

She sets off back up the dock, water sloshing over her feet. I hurry to follow. There's another path that leads in the direction we were looking, and we take it. When we get through the trees, we're greeted by the sight of a covered boat dock like the one at the house where we were staying.

"Jackpot," Bailey says and hurries.

From the outside, the boat garage looks intact. "I sure hope there's a boat in there."

"Me too." She sets the buckets down by the door and examines it. "I think I'm better off going under. Wait here." Without waiting for an answer, she executes a shallow dive into the water. She surfaces, takes a few deep breaths, then dives under.

I nervously look back and forth between the path and the water where Bailey disappeared. I get that we're in a hurry, but I'd rather be diving under the dock with Bailey than standing here exposed and wondering if anyone is going to come strolling down the path. I nearly jump out of my skin when I hear a beeping noise from inside the boathouse. It stops after a few moments, and Bailey opens the door.

"Security system. I think I disabled it before it really went off, but we need to hurry." She grabs the buckets.

Inside, it's clear there's been some damage from the rough waves, even back in this sheltered area. There is a speedboat—a smaller, less fancy one than the *Maty III*—that has been crashing into the walls, as evidenced by the broken boards on the far side. An inflatable tube has been pulled off the wall and popped. There are two stand-up paddleboards and two kayaks that look like they should be on wooden arms but are lying helter-skelter. One of the boards is half in the water and must have gotten smashed between the boat and the dock. On the inland side of the boathouse is a wide dock that holds two different craft that look largely untouched. One looks like a bike on pontoons. The other is a Sunfish.

I learned to sail a Sunfish at one of the houses we stayed at for vacation. I check it out while Baily checks out the speedboat. It looks nearly exactly like the one I learned on, except this one has a red-and-white sail instead of green. I pick up the mast experimentally, wondering if it's lying across the deck because it snapped or if it was being stored this way. It looks intact. The hole it fits in likewise looks functional.

"Shit," Bailey says.

I whip around, not sure what the latest calamity is. Bailey is standing on the dock looking at the stern of the boat with her hands on her hips. There don't seem to be any people showing up to attack us, at least not yet. "What is it?"

"There's a hole in the gas tank. We're not getting out of here on this boat."

"How about this one?" I lift the mast.

She eyes the hull skeptically. "It looks small. And I don't know how to sail."

"It is small, but what choice do we have? And I know how to sail this sort of boat. It's easy. And we wouldn't have to stop for gas."

"Can we both fit on it without sinking?"

I laugh. "It'll be tight, but it can hold us, no problem. Help me get it in the water."

She follows my direction to prepare the small boat in the space between the speedboat and the water side garage door. "If there are people here, they'll hear the door opening. We'll need to get out of here as quickly as possible. I'll push the button, then run back. You pull the boat out of the garage as soon as it'll clear. We'll need to go as fast as possible. I'll stay out of your way unless you need help."

"I won't. It's designed for one. You just hop in, sit there"—I point where I want her—"and keep your head down so I don't hit it with the boom."

She looks at me nervously. "Is this going to work? Is there enough wind?"

"Plenty. Don't worry. I've got this." The winds haven't completely died down from the storm, and it's rare that there isn't wind at the coast anyway. We really will be fine.

"Confidence is extremely sexy. Do you know that?"

Before I can answer, she puts a hand on either side of my face and pulls me in for a kiss. I do know. It's part of her appeal. It's also cute to see her nervous. I smile at both the kiss and her nerves. But when she hops onto the dock and goes to push the button, reality crashes back in. We're not out for a day of sailing fun. We could be attacked the moment we try to leave. In fact, it seems highly likely that there is a security team already checking the property.

The roof is high enough to have the mast up, but I fold it over so I can exit as soon as the door is a couple feet up. I'm holding on to the deck, ready to start pushing along when Bailey pushes the button.

She pushes. I start running, and I'm already halfway clear of the door when she steps onto the stern, making the boat rock. As soon as we're out, I lift the mast and maneuver the sail to catch the wind.

I'm ready for shouts or worse, but nothing comes. I have to tack to get out of the mouth of the inlet and worry about the extra time it's taking but still nothing. And then, we're clear. I turn to high-five Bailey and find her scanning the horizon in all directions. I lower my hand and go back to sailing. We're not yet in the clear. Who knows when it'll ever feel like we really are?

But it's only ten minutes later that Bailey rests her hands on my shoulders. "I think we've done it. You did such a good job."

I lean back into her. "Thanks. But we've a way to go yet, no?"

"True, but we don't have to stop for gas now, and we don't seem to have a tail. And I doubt our stay will have attracted much notice. I suspect it'll be chalked up to hurricane damage. So I think our major hurdle is getting to New Orleans without another hurricane. Or storm of any sort."

"I'm a little concerned about navigation. This thing doesn't have squat in terms of tools. Do we just go by the sun?"

"I mean, sure. That'll get us close. We can adjust when we hit the north side of the gulf." She pauses, perhaps thinking about dealing with that. "It's possible they'll be trying to find us there. They're probably expecting us to go to New Orleans. But it's a big, porous coast. We should be fine." Another pause. "It's a problem for then. For now, we're in a functional craft and safe enough."

I pull her from her perch to sit inside the recessed area with me. It's tight in here, particularly with our supplies at our feet, but I don't mind snuggling in. The current winds are chasing the hurricane north, making my job easy. The prevailing winds in the gulf are north-northwest, which could require tacking on my part and mean more work, more boom movement. For now, we can just let the wind carry us.

Bailey looks at the sail stretching overhead. "You'll have to teach me to sail so we can take turns being in charge."

"Right now, there's nothing to do. If the wind shifts or when we hit the coast and need to figure out where we are, things will change. Just now, you know all you need to know."

She puts her arm around me, making me feel protected. "Well, I guess we're just out for a lovely sail."

I laugh a little. "Not sure that squished bread would have been my picnic choice for that, but sure."

"Speaking of, we might as well eat that before it gets moldy, if it isn't already."

It's not, but it does make us thirsty. We spend some time eating and drinking, finishing off the first gallon. There's one left. But if these winds keep up, we should get to the coast before midnight, so we'll be fine. But thoughts of what happens after eating and drinking go through my mind. At some point, I'm going to have to hang my butt over the side of the boat in front of Bailey. Maybe I should keep that in mind before I guzzle any more water. Last night, we set up a bucket in the shed, which was bad enough, but at least it was dark. This will be right out in the open with nowhere for the other one to move away.

And now that I've thought of it, I can't think of anything except that my bladder is starting to feel full. Desperate for distraction, I say, "Tell me about life in Portland." I've asked her before, when we were kids, but I suspect her answers will be different now that she's an adult. Plus, things have changed in the last few years. We're getting closer and closer to civil war.

With no motor and no hurricane howling, this is the quietest it's been for talking since we left the house. She doesn't even have to raise her voice to say, "What do you want to know?"

"Everything. Is it scary walking around there, or is that just propaganda?"

She laughs. I feel small for a moment before she starts speaking. "I'm sorry. I don't mean to laugh at you, just at the idea that Portland isn't safe. I get that's what you've heard. We're fine up there. If you choose to live there, you'll see."

And there it is again, the question of what will happen after I get to safety. My plan had been to live in Seattle. The org that was going to help me has a safe house and offers resources for people building a new life for themselves. What will I do now? I don't know. It's hard to tangle out what I really want for my life with my feelings for Bailey. And if I choose Portland because I want to be close to her, is that so bad? Does she not want me to? I know she's interested in me, at least for now, but that doesn't mean she'll still be interested when we're out of the heat of the escape. Maybe when she gets back to Portland and her life there, she'll realize that helping someone freshly escaped from the heart of the red states isn't what she wants to do, especially someone who thinks Portland may be dangerous. Maybe this is just a fling for her.

Is it a fling for me? Honestly, I can't parse that right now, either. Luckily, I don't have to. She keeps talking.

"Portland is mostly like any other place but greener. Well, part of that is historical. We're not as green as we were when I was a little kid. It's still greener than Tulsa, though. Anyway. There are houses and stores and places of business. We do have more houseless people than you see in Tulsa. Unless that's changed. It's been a while since I've been there, aside from the airport." She pauses, maybe to see if I have anything to say about houseless people in Tulsa.

"Still not very many visible houseless, no. I'm not sure what happens to them, but they're not anywhere I spend time." I want to ask if they're dangerous, but I know from my time online that the question would be offensive. But everything I've been taught is that they're all drug addicts who will cut anyone for the money they have. I don't have direct experience. I do know some drug addicts, though, and they're more likely to lie than to cut. I keep all this to myself.

"Yeah, that's what I remember. Patriot Army patrols take anyone sleeping on the streets or in parks or whatever, and well, I've heard stories. The best of the outcomes is that they're put on buses elsewhere."

"Yikes."

"Yeah. Anyway, we don't do that in Portland. I'm not saying our system is great. If it were, we'd have homes for everyone, but at least they're mostly left alone. You'll see some people living in their cars or tents, which can get messy, I'll admit, but mostly, our houseless population chooses to live in city-maintained designated camping areas. There are resources there ranging from toilets and showers to help finding housing. Not that there is enough for everyone." She looks at the mast for a moment. "Honestly, I wish it was better. I wish we had rooms enough for everyone, but even in Portland, there are differing beliefs about how to handle the housing situation. But the solution isn't locking them up or bussing them off."

"You seem to have a real passion for the subject."

She shrugs, her arm around me. "Yeah, I had a friend in second grade whose family lived in their car. One day, she just disappeared. I hope her family moved to stable housing, but I don't know. I think about her anytime I encounter a kid in the classes I substitute for who is struggling in that way."

"Wait. You're a teacher?"

She looks as surprised as I feel. "I thought you knew, but I don't know how you would."

"I guess we have a lot to discover about each other." Or maybe that's too much for two people who may not have a future together. "I mean, if we want to."

"I'm interested in all things TJ," she says.

A bubble of pleasure nestles into my chest. "Same. Except, all things Bailey. Tell me about teaching. Do you want a classroom of your own, or are you happy subbing?"

We talk for hours. Our only other job is to occasionally make adjustments to the sail or tiller. Soon, we get back on the topic of family.

"Preston went to Liberty University and came back even more insufferable," I say after tweaking the sail. "He puts on a front of being even more conservative than my father." The wind is starting to shift, and I suspect that we'll need to start tacking if we want to keep going north. As I settle back in next to Bailey, I think about telling her more about Preston, but before I have the chance, she asks a question. "You know what's always been a little wild to me?"

"What?"

"That *liberty* is somehow a conservative thing. It seems that generally, they're dead set on taking liberties away from people. You can't be queer, you can't be an independent woman who looks out for herself, you can't be religious in any way other than what's outlined by the Crusade of the Redeemer Church, you can't be an atheist, you can't—I don't know—what else can't you do?"

"Sex before marriage. Unless you're a guy, then it's okay, but if you're a woman, you've *ruined* yourself. And as a woman, you're supposed to be appealing to men but not too appealing, or you're the problem. If you get raped, well, clearly, you've gone too far. You can't skip church on Sunday unless you have a very good reason. You can't sleep all tucked in because arms have to stay outside the covers so you can't masturbate. Well, again, unless you're a dude. In addition to not being queer in any way, you can't look queer or think that queer people are human and deserving of rights." I take a moment to breathe. "I think I might have gotten away from concrete can'ts."

"Maybe, but those are still very valid points. So if the red side is the one restricting liberty, why do they get the word? The very meaning of which is being free to do what you want."

I shift, looking for a comfortable spot. I end up on my back with my legs on the higher deck and my head resting on one hand. My other hand is on Bailey's thigh. "It's a good question. I think it's because they think that they're being truer to the creators of the constitution, so life, liberty, and the pursuit of happiness are concepts that belong to them."

Bailey snorts. "Pursuit of happiness. Reds definitely suck the joy out of a lot of people."

"Yeah." Tears gather in my eyes. It's unexpected, but maybe it shouldn't be. I've lived my whole life missing so much joy because I don't fit into the mold. I know it, yet hearing Bailey say it touches something deep inside.

"Hey, hey. I'm sorry." She shifts until she can gather me into her arms. I go willingly. "I didn't mean to hurt your feelings."

"No, no you didn't. I'm not crying because you offended the culture of my youth or anything like that. It's that I feel—I don't know—seen. I've missed out on so much joy." I move from tears rolling down my face to full-on sobs and can't seem to stop.

Bailey just holds me, strokes my hair, and lets me cry. When I slow, she's still there. She kisses my head. "I'm sorry it's been so rough for you."

"It's not your fault."

"I'm still sorry. It's really unfair and wrong."

"Yeah."

I feel her shift as she looks around. "I hate to push you to recover, but I think we're heading northeast now. Can you show me how to fix that?"

I laugh a little, which dispels the last of the tears. "I think keeping us on course is reason enough for me to pull myself together." I sit up and make the necessary adjustments, explaining what I'm doing. The wind has decidedly shifted, and we need to pay more attention to staying on course.

CHAPTER TWENTY-FOUR

BAILEY

It's been full-on night for about an hour when we see a dark mound ahead and know we're close to shore. This stretch appears to be uninhabited because there are no lights. The question is, the shore of which state? It's Florida, Alabama, or Louisiana. That's all we know for sure. Or if we're super off course, it could be Texas. Considering the time it took to get here, I'm pretty sure it's not Texas. That would have taken longer.

"Do we just…approach the shore?" TJ asks.

"I think it's the only way to figure out where we are, yeah. If we can even figure it out without a town. We're dark, so we won't be sticking out like a sore thumb." I'm not exactly being truthful. There is a lot of white on our sail. The moon is out. But it's also highly unlikely anyone is looking for us on an uninhabited stretch of shore.

When we get close, I realize we're approaching an island. And there are buildings. They must have lost power due to the hurricane or the storm surge that followed. I'm not familiar enough with the coast here to know exactly where we are, but I did spend some time looking at a vintage Gulf of Mexico map that hung on the wall in the house. I'm pretty sure we undershot and are east of New Orleans. At this point, we could just go west along the coast until we hit New Orleans. However, I'm not absolutely sure if it's to the east or west. Large ships would help us find a big port like New Orleans, but we've only seen some at a distance. We need more clues.

We circle the island, getting a good look. There's a bridge to the mainland that we pass under. There are no lights from the streets to the houses.

"Looks like some houses but not many?" TJ says. "The island looks thin, right?"

It was made thinner by the storm surge. There isn't much beach where it looks like there should be. These could be empty houses, mostly vacations homes and rentals, but any inhabitants have likely evacuated and aren't back yet. "That's exactly what I was thinking. It looks like a place to find shoes."

One of the many things we discussed before the wind shifted—causing us to pay more attention—and the sun went down—causing us to become more watchful—was how we need shoes and something other than bathing suits and one shirt. We'll need to sneak into New Orleans, which means not making a direct approach, which means walking in undeveloped areas. We agreed we'd take a chance with visiting someplace to procure what we need.

"Can you pull in among the trees? We can tie off in there and not risk a marina."

"Aye-aye, Captain."

That startles a laugh out of me. "In no way, shape, or form am I the captain of this ship. You're the sailor."

"You're the metaphorical captain of the mission, though. Clearly." She's not wrong, and the moment of levity passes as we approach the trees and potentially trouble.

"We can navigate between the trees, right? I mean, we won't hit them?" We're moving at a decent clip. It makes me a little nervous.

"We'll be fine. Take the tiller for a moment."

I do, and TJ lowers the sail, which drastically reduces our speed. I'm relieved when she takes the tiller back and threads us into the trees. Trees that are clearly not supposed to be standing in the water.

I pull us to a stop by grabbing a thin tree and tying off on it. "If you have to run, take the boat. I'll meet you in New Orleans. Jackson Square. You remember the plan?"

"We've only gone over it seventy-three times. Don't go straight in. Go in via a bayou, then make my way into the city. But you'll be there with me."

"That's the plan." I hesitate. Should I take TJ with me so I know she's safe, or leave her here while I plunder? She'll likely be safer not tagging after me, and I'll be less noticeable. But I'm thinking one of these flooded homes is our target, so there's not a lot of chance of being seen.

I'm still dithering when she says, "I'm not staying here by myself. I'm coming with you."

"Are you a mind reader now?"

"No. You're just obvious."

"That's excellent to hear. That makes me feel good about my various skills."

She pats my arm. "There, there. Now, let's go."

"Okay, but stay close, if I tell you to wait somewhere, do it, and if I say run, run. Even if you think you're leaving me behind. I may be able to get away when it's just me. So if I say go, go. Agreed?"

"Yup."

That sounded far to flippant for my taste. "TJ?"

"Agreed. You say hide, I hide. You say run, I run. And I'll stay close because that's where it feels safe anyway."

Even though my entire purpose for being with her is to keep her safe, meaning that sentiment should be a given, hearing her say she feels safe with me makes feel like I've just taken my first sip of a really good mocha with whipped cream. Warm, awake, and special. I wrap my arms around her briefly. The longer we linger, the more likely we'll be noticed if there is anyone on the island.

"Okay, let's go."

We take turns gingerly stepping out of the boat. The water only comes up to our knees, but that's enough that we can't see underneath, which makes walking in our bare feet fraught with danger. Also, there are…things in the water.

TJ lets out a muffled scream and grabs my arm. Almost immediately, she chuckles a little. "Sorry. I think it was a fish." But she doesn't let go.

I should tell her to. Having my hands free gives me the most options, but I like the feel of her hands on my arm. The danger of attack seems low on this currently uninhabited-looking island.

I step on plenty of questionable things, bruising my feet up nicely, before I feel asphalt under the water. Then, it's much easier going. There are still things floating and swimming in the water, but now there aren't roots and such tripping us up.

We're just settling into the easier going when I feel a much larger bump against my leg. That isn't a fish. Maybe it's a piece of debris, but I don't think so. I extract my arm from TJ and peer into the water. My night vision is quite good. If it's what I think it is, I should be able to see it coming in this shallow water if it comes back.

I don't hear the rest of TJ's question because I see a long shadow moving quickly toward us. Its mouth is wide open. An alligator. Attacking us.

I don't have any alligator training. The only alligators in Oregon are in the zoo. I'm unarmed. But in the few moments between the bump and this charge, I've come up with a plan.

"Wha—"

"Run." I launch myself at the alligator.

I shove the bucket I'm carrying into its mouth, then go for its eye. It has to be the most vulnerable part. I miss because it's thrashing its head, trying to dislodge the bucket. I run after TJ while it's occupied.

I don't think alligator attacks are common. Maybe we stumbled close to its nest. I hear the crunch of plastic behind me. This isn't over. I grab a floating branch and turn to face the scaly beast.

It goes flying past me toward TJ. I bang on its back with my stick, but it pays this no mind. I take a flying leap and land on its back. It's like landing on a log with spikes. The breath is knocked out of me, but I ignore that and go for its eye.

It turns its head back to snap at me.

"Bailey!"

I hold on tight while it thrashes, slowly working my way up its back. It snaps at my leg so close, I feel the water move. I yank my leg back, which nearly knocks me off. Prone in the water with a homicidal alligator on the attack? That would be a disaster.

I desperately wind my arm around it, hoping for any purchase, clinging to its neck. I'd planned on using the branch on its eye, but I've lost it in the struggle. I cling on with one arm and jab it in the eye with my fingertips. It growls, sounding like a motorcycle, and rolls.

Shit.

I'm underwater. Everything is confused. I don't want to let go and find myself on the business end of its mouth, but if I don't, I may drown.

It growls again, and I feel it more than hear it. It thrashes again, and I lose my grip. I'm scrambling for purchase when it steps on me, then off. I surge to my feet, adrenaline coursing through my system, and see TJ standing there, brandishing a thick branch. "I think it ran off."

I don't see any shadows underwater. I take a deep breath and let it go. "Are you okay?"

"I'm fine." She sounds eerily calm. "I hit it in the stomach when it rolled, and it ran off." Her calm breaks, and she lets out a sob. "It ran off."

"Okay," I say, trying to infuse my voice with calm. "I think it's okay now." I put my hand on her shoulder and feel her shaking. When she doesn't hit me or flinch, I put my arm around her shoulders. "I think it's over."

She lowers the branch but doesn't let it go, and I blame her not a bit for that. I'd like to have a branch of my own. She leans on me. "I thought it got you."

"I'm okay." I am, but I'm also starting to feel the scrapes and bruises. I smell like a swamp, and I'm worried about infection. Plus, we've lost the bucket and everything in it. We need to find supplies now more than ever. "Let's get moving."

TJ starts walking, head turning as she goes. "Yes. Let's get out of this water." She practically starts running, and I keep pace. I have no more interest in finding another alligator. Or the same one back for more.

The first house we come to is a no go. It's a single story, and the water is halfway up its walls. There's not likely to be anything salvageable in there. The next few are the same, but I can see a house that's higher coming up.

The first floor is half-flooded like the others, but there's a second story. That's where clothes are likely to be, so this one is worth going in. The water will have dismantled any security system already. So far, the entire island seems deserted. That means I can be loud about breaking in if need be.

We circle the house, looking for the best entry point. We get lucky. One window's protective boards must not have been properly secured. One came loose and broke the window while flapping in the wind. I reach in and unlock it so we don't have to climb through broken glass. There's barely any climbing necessary because the water overflows the sill by a foot or so.

There's a lot of floating debris but also heavy furniture that is still submerged. We proceed with caution. I'm hoping this is someone's vacation house and not a rental. The best we could hope for then would be to add to our towel collection. Or sheets for togas. Which would stick out like a sore thumb. Probably. Who knows? In New Orleans, maybe we'd fit right in.

It's dark, so my first move is to look for a flashlight. I find one in a kitchen drawer. Turning it on is a risk because people may see the light through the gaps in the boards, if there are any people around to look, but we're going to have a hard time finding things in the dark.

The kitchen looks stocked for a family rather than generic. I think we're in luck. We look in the pantry first. The pantry is stocked. This is definitely not a rental. The bottoms shelves are wet, and things are floating, but the upper shelves hold a few things that will be useful, and there's a hook on the wall holding reusable shopping bags. We load one up with some granola bars, fruit snacks, and boxes of juice.

"Here." I take a box and stick a straw in it before handing it to TJ. "Drink this."

"Is this really the time for a snack break?"

"We need it." I hold my shaking hand in the beam of the flashlight. "It'll help with the adrenaline crash."

I punch a straw in a juice box of my own and suck it down. When I'm done, I drop the empty. There's nothing better to do. This house has more problems than me littering. TJ hesitates a moment but follows suit.

The second floor should be dry. We climb the staircase out of the water. My heart sinks when I open a drawer in the first bedroom. There are no clothes in the drawers, though it's clearly a kid's room. Maybe no one is currently living here despite the stocked kitchen.

"Nothing?" TJ is looking in the closet.

"No, let's check the other rooms."

In the largest bedroom, we hit the jackpot. Judging by the clothes, I'm guessing it belongs to grandparents. Maybe the grandchildren come and go, so no clothes for them. Of course, that means the clothes for us are grandparent-in-Florida style.

"We should clean up a bit before we try them on."

"Do you think there will be water?" TJ asks.

"No, but even rubbing down with towels will help, I think. Plus, I'd like to find a first aid kit."

TJ follows me into the bathroom. "Did you get hurt?"

"A little." The scratches on my stomach feel like fire, and I think I've done something to my shoulder.

We luck out with flushable wipes and a large first aid kit in addition to towels. I hiss a little as I pull off my shirt. My shoulder doesn't like that motion, but I'm pretty sure there's nothing wrong that a little rest won't fix. When my head emerges from the bottom of the shirt, TJ is wincing while examining my stomach. There are three bloody scratches and a couple red lines. I have no idea what the anatomy of an alligator is, but it looks it got me good with three middle claws and mildly with two outside claws.

"I don't think I need stitches this time, so that's a plus."

She looks at me with a small smile. "I guess, but the hydrogen peroxide is going to hurt. Sit down."

I follow instructions. She's not wrong. But after that, she touches me gently while dabbing on antibiotic ointment, and my stomach muscles tighten.

"Am I hurting you?"

"No." It comes out soft and filled with desire. TJ looks up at me, and her hands move to my sides. I cup her face and pull her in for a kiss. I slide a hand around to the back of her head as our mouths meet, open to one another, wanting. I want to let this progress, but I listen to the part of my brain that's telling me we've spent too long here, been too loud. I pull back and touch my forehead to hers. "We should get moving."

It takes some time to clean me up, which includes a new bandage for my arm. By the time she's done, I'm anxious about time. I take a towel and some of the wipes and leave the bathroom to her. We can't get more distracted.

TJ emerges after a few minutes, wrapped in a towel. I've already pulled on an oversized grandpa T-shirt and some elastic-waisted grandma shorts. The grandma clothes are too small for me, but the elastic helps. They should fit TJ well.

She laughs a little. "Looking good."

I give a little bow.

Luckily, the grandma clothes fit TJ perfectly. She puts on a new outfit, and we both take an extra in one of the shopping bags. I find a bucket hat that will hide my hair which, coupled with the clothes I found, should help me appear androgynous.

Grandma's shoes fit me, being just a half size big. TJ apparently has big feet because they're small on her. I have sneakers, but she ends up in sandals, and her toes spill over the front.

It would be very helpful to have some cash for New Orleans, so I look around for a stash. A lot of people keep cash in their houses in anticipation of the possibility of civil war. Banks are likely to crash. The question of if cash will still work is a legitimate one, but plenty of people consider that one way to hedge their bets. Unfortunately, these people either aren't among them or have a very good hiding place. Or it's underwater downstairs, which makes it nearly inaccessible.

We leave, armed with branches again in case of alligator attack. We're both a little jumpy, flinching each time something bumps our legs, but it's always fish or debris or nothing that tries to bite.

We're nearly to where we need to turn into the trees to get to the boat, and I'm starting to feel like we're going to make it without incident when I see a shadow move in a way it shouldn't. I crouch to prepare for whatever may be coming while hoping it's an animal rather than a person.

TJ freezes. "What is it?"

"Be ready to run," is all I have time to say before attackers erupt out of the night around us. "Run!"

TJ splashes through the water in the direction of the boat, a good plan when we were at the house, and the people most likely to come for us were homeowners. I should have given alternate instructions for this situation. I fucked up. I only have a brief second to regret it before all my attention is taken by fighting off the attackers.

They aren't shooting. Probably because they don't want to risk killing TJ. I don't know what happened between when we were first on the boat and now. Maybe Mr. Rice is back in power. Maybe those guys in Florida were acting without orders. But if they wanted us dead now, they'd have picked us off from the shadows. Instead, I get to fight multiple men hand to hand.

One grabs at me, but I block and aim a strike at his solar plexus; they're wearing flak jackets. Great. He comes again, unfazed by me nearly breaking my fingers on his armor. A second is behind me. I duck both. It'll be harder to take them out, but they're also bulkier and much less nimble. If I can get them underwater, all their gear will make it challenging to get up. I dance around, making contact with a third attacker's nose. He bends over, howling, but there is no time to enjoy the victory because the other two are positioned for a new attack. I manage to sweep one's legs, and he goes under, tangling in the legs of the other.

A fourth person punches me in the ribs, forcing all my air out of my lungs. I can't let that stop me, even though it bends me over. I find myself underwater, but I use the new position to drive into his knees, dropping him heavily on top of me. It's been too long since I've gotten a good breath. I roll us over and push off him to get my head above water. I still have to force air in from the blow to my ribs. I have a brief moment to notice another cluster of action nearby but can't do anything to help. The two attackers who took a tumble are up and coming at me again.

I get lucky with a side strike to one's throat. He's down and probably won't be bothering me again. Maybe he'll drown. The second one gets lucky and glances a blow off the side of my head. At least it wasn't straight on, but I still feel a little dizzy. I manage to block the next and land a stomp on his knee. He's down. He pops back up, but he's clutching his knee and howling.

Broken Nose is back up. I dodge and weave, avoiding his blows until I get an opportunity to use his momentum against him and slam his head into a tree. It's a sickening thunk, and he slides under the water.

I draw in ragged breaths as I stagger into the trees to where I last saw movement, but no one is there now. TJ is gone.

CHAPTER TWENTY-FIVE

TJ

When Bailey yells, "Run," I take off down the beach toward the boat, but I know I've made a mistake. It's hard running in the water with ill-fitting sandals. Maybe if I get deep enough, I can outswim them. Unless they have a boat. They must have. How else would they be here?

My panicky thoughts are cut off when I'm tackled from behind. I go under hard, a heavy weight on my back. I flail uselessly for a moment before the weight disappears, and I'm hauled above water. "You're okay, Miss Rice," a male voice says. "Deep breaths. You're safe now. We're going to take you home."

Safe? I'm as far from safe as I've ever felt and on the opposite side of the spectrum from how I felt just earlier today with Bailey's arm around me, on my way to freedom. Tears fall down my face, but I don't have the breath to really cry. I struggle against the hold on me.

"Now, now."

It's useless. I subside. Maybe a moment will come for me to try again.

A second man, maybe the one who tackled me, comes beside us, dripping wet, and reaches for one of my arms. I'm momentarily only held by one, and I try again to pull away. The man who hauled me up has me in a vise grip. "Miss Rice, you really need to stop."

I finally look at him. He's been behind me this whole time. He's wearing a dark baseball cap. I don't know him, but I know from the cap he's Patriot Army.

The other man gets hold of my other arm. "That's enough out of you, missy. Led us a merry chase, didn't you? It's over now, though. You're going to get what you deserve."

"Now, now," the one with the hat says again. "We are bringing young Miss Rice home to the fold. Love the sinner, Lake. Let's see how our fellow soldiers are faring." He looks over his shoulder. "Ah. Let's get Miss Rice out of here."

They hustle me through some trees to a speedboat. How did we not hear this? It has been so quiet on the island, aside from when Bailey was wrestling with the alligator. Maybe they came then. Or maybe when we were in the house, far enough away and insulated. I struggle for a few moments, but there is no point. They way overpower me. I look over my shoulder, trying to figure out what's happening behind us. Is Bailey okay? All I can make out is a blur of movement between the dark trees.

Lake climbs the ladder first and hauls me in while the other man lifts me from behind. It's the only boat I see. I guess we're just leaving the others. And Bailey. I hope she's okay. How can she be after multiple men attacking her? My heart feels like it's breaking, but it has to vie with panic over my capture.

Lake pushes a button, and we start moving, answering my question. The boat is electric. Figures they'd make an exception to the "gas is best" policy red has when it suits them.

"Where are we going?" I twist to look back, but there is no sign of Bailey. The man has my arm again, so there's no jumping overboard. My stomach hurts. I think part of it is from being tackled, but a large part is being separated from Bailey and impending conversion camp. Or worse. Is there worse?

"Camp Redeemer, where you'll get the help you need." The man's voice is still calm. He seems to be trying to inject comfort, but there is none to be had from him or his words.

I'm going to conversion camp.

The ride only lasts for about ten minutes. We circle the island and pull up by the road on the mainland. A Hummer waits. The man with the vise grip passes me out to Lake, who holds on with both hands while Vise Grip disembarks. Lake ties the boat off. Vise Grip puts me into the back of the Hummer. As soon as he lets go, I go for the opposite door, but it's locked.

"You might as well settle in," he tells me calmly. Vise Grip gets behind the steering wheel while Lake takes the passenger's seat, and we start driving.

My wet clothes, panic, and adrenaline keep me awake for hours. I learn that Vise Grip's name is Dillinger. We cross through the Florida wall, and they have papers for me. My father must have approved this. Or maybe it was Preston. Or for all I know, they're both dead, and I'm the property of the church or something now.

I don't want to cry, but the tears slide down my cheeks anyway. I at least manage to keep quiet while I fall apart. Is my father dead, deposed, or did he finally get tired of covering for me and turn me in? I don't know which is worse, to be honest. If he died without turning me in, died for me, then he really loved me, something I've doubted most of my life, especially since my mom died.

If he's been deposed because of his refusal to turn me in, maybe there's a possibility that he will love me for who I am. That doesn't really matter now. I'm going to conversion camp.

If he gave me up...well, did I ever really have a father anyway? The tears fall faster for a while.

Lake talks on the radio to the men they left behind. Bailey got away.

The relief that washes over me is likely responsible for the fact that I fall asleep while he's still on the call. The last thing I remember hearing is that one man died, and the others are on the way to the hospital.

I wake up when the vehicle stops. I look around blearily. We're at a truck stop. Lake is pumping gas, and Dillinger is nowhere to be seen. I tentatively try the door on the opposite side of where Lake is pumping. It's still locked, as expected. Something about my movement must catch Lake's attention because he cups his face with his hands and peers in. He leers and wags a finger at me, even though I'm just sitting here now. He's such a stereotype that I'd be amused if he wasn't in control over me.

Dillinger comes back, exchanges a few words with Lake, then opens the back door while being sure to block the opening with his body. "Miss Rice, do you need to use the facilities?"

I do. Sort of. It's not desperate, but maybe it'll give me an opportunity to escape. "Yes, please." I look down, trying to look meek.

"I'll take her. I need to go anyway," Lake says. My insides shrivel up at the leering tone. While my father may have approved my capture, he'd never approve this. If he was still in power, there's no way Lake would be leering at me. Either way, he's absolutely the worst of the supposedly "devout" men, the sort whom Redeemer regularly turns a blind eye to. He's probably convinced himself that he's doing me a favor, letting me know I'm attractive to men. I shudder.

"You go take care of yourself, Lake. I'll take the young lady."

Dillinger is better. At least I don't feel like I'm in danger of being accosted with him.

Lake grumbles under his breath. Dillinger ignores him, keeping his focus on me. "Let's go, Miss Rice."

I scoot awkwardly out of the back seat. I'm clumsy with exhaustion, groggy from sleep, and fearing what's to come. As soon as I emerge, Dillinger has his vise-like grip on my arm. He guides me to the store and in. We garner a few second glances, but people look away. I'm a woman being led by a man in a red state. He can pretty much do what he wants. My stomach churns at being back in the middle of this instead of free with Bailey.

He takes me to the handicap bathroom and comes in with me.

"Am I supposed to pee with you watching? I don't think I want to drop trou with you in here."

He looks around, sees there are no windows and no weapons. "I'll wait just outside."

He leaves, and I lock the door, reveling in a tiny bit of privacy. He never searched me. If I had a portie, I could use it. I bitterly wish I did, but who would I contact? Bailey doesn't have a portie, but even if she did, I don't know her handle.

I do relieve myself, then wash up as best I can at the sink. There's not much I can do about the salt crustiness of my clothes, but washing my face, neck, hands, and arms helps some. At least I wasn't captured in my swim wear.

It was about twenty-four hours ago that Bailey and I were in the pool shed, hiding out from the hurricane. It was just yesterday morning—unless we've already passed midnight—that we slipped off the dock and swam to the boat to escape the men who'd shown up at the house. So, yeah, two days of being salt-encrusted.

There's a knock at the door. "Miss Rice, how are you doing in there? We need to get on the road. Come on out, and you can get some food to eat in the car."

Great. Road trip snacks with Dillinger and Lake. This is like a dream come true.

Lake is waiting by the Hummer when we come out. He eyes the food I'm carrying. "Did you get something for me?"

"You had an opportunity to get your own, Lake."

He looks pissed as he climbs into the passenger seat.

Food has been in short supply the last couple of days, so I eat the questionable hot dog and bag of chips in short order. I drain a bottle of lemonade to wash it down.

I feel wide awake again and figure that's it for sleep. My mind is roiling with images of everything that happened in the last forty hours. It's full of Bailey. Her getting us to safety again and again. Her kissing me. Her touching me. And now we've been ripped apart. I'm on my way to a conversion camp where who knows what will happen to me. I pull my mind away from thinking about the possible horrors again and again.

But if it's not one horror, it's another. What happened that they came for me? What is going on with my father? As much as he disapproves of me choosing—as if—to be gay, he has always covered for me. I again circle through the possibilities.

At some point, I must fall asleep because what feels like a blink makes the light shift from dark to early morning. We've stopped for gas again. In my blearily and newly awakened state, I mumble, "Where are we?"

I don't really expect an answer, but Lake gleefully says, "Fort Smith. Almost to Oklahoma, where you'll get yours."

I realize belatedly that he and I are alone, and my general feelings of anxiety and grief crystalize into immediate fear. Lake radiates a desire to punish. He's not unique among men in red circles, but I've been protected from them because of who my father is. Or maybe was. If he gave me up, it would be with a strict order that I not be hurt. This man wouldn't dare look at me the way he's looking. Or is he still in power but gave up on me altogether? Was me running off the final straw, and now I'm at the mercy of the wolves? I don't know.

He must have given me up. After all, there was the radio call before the hurricane offering a lesser punishment in exchange for surrendering myself. That would indicate he was still in power, at least then. And why would he have been removed from his position after he gave me up? He should still be in power now.

Or maybe the hurricane offer was a lie. I have no idea. Whatever happened, Lake feels comfortable leering at me. I need to adjust to my new reality.

I straighten and cross my ankles demurely, trying to present as a respectable woman to discourage him. All that does is draw his attention to my legs. He licks his lips. I want to vomit. He reaches back, but before he can touch me, the back door opens, and the gap is filled with Dillinger. He throws Lake a searing look but doesn't say anything. Still, I'm pathetically grateful. And I feel sick for my gratitude.

"Come on, Miss Rice. Our last pit stop. Not much longer now."

That fills me with dread for other reasons.

CHAPTER TWENTY-SIX

BAILEY

TJ is gone.

I get in the sailboat and get away before my attackers can recover. Where did they take her? There's no sign of a boat. I don't hear an engine. I circle the island and see a boat tied up, but it's empty. There's nothing around it. If that's how they got off the island, they had a vehicle waiting.

Someone took TJ and left the others to fend for themselves. I have no way of knowing where they are right now. What I do have is a strong idea of their ultimate destination.

I need a car. I sail west along the coast until I find a town, worrying the whole time. I'm highly unlikely to be able to intercept them along the way, even with an educated guess about where they're going. They have too much of a lead. I have to hurry, I don't want TJ stuck in conversion camp for any length of time. I don't want her stuck there at all. Even orientation can be extremely damaging. My stomach clenches, and I wish I could step on the gas, but I'm at the mercy of the winds and my sailing ability.

TJ was right, sailing, at least this craft, isn't hard. But it's harder than when she was with me. I make some mistakes that only serve to make my stomach clench tighter. I finally pass a city and aim for shore. I overshoot where I was aiming. Yesterday, I was ready to take up sailing as a hobby. Today, I'd be happy if I never again set foot on a sailboat again. I take down the mast and let the boat drift free. People will likely think it came loose in the storm.

The cover of night is a boon for stealing a car. I swap the plates with another car a few miles away and set out, feeling too far behind. I have more stops to make. Outside of Florida, a car is by far the better transportation, not to mention that TJ is being taken inland. Probably. Most likely. I have to believe I know where they're taking her and can rescue her, so, yes. She's been taken inland.

On my way to Tulsa for an important stop at my dad's house, I steal credit cards at every fueling station. While I would give anything to not be traveling alone, it does make it much easier. People may still be looking for me, but TJ was their primary target. I am thankful for my baggy clothes and a hat I find in the stolen car. I lost the bucket hat in the fight. With my hair tucked up, I'm passing for a young man again when I need to stop to charge up the electric car and for food. I use the credit cards I steal once each, then throw them out.

I drive through the night. My eyes burn, but I'm wired with adrenaline and caffeine when I reach my dad's house. After this stop, I'll have at least another hour to drive. I need to hurry. Who knows how fast TJ's captors are going? They won't have had to stop to steal cars or gear up. I don't bother with the front door, going directly to the fortified shed in the fenced backyard. I key in the codes from memory and feel a flash of relief that Dad hasn't changed them.

I close the door behind me, flip on the light, and start gearing up with grim determination. I put on a flak jacket, fill several pockets with magazines, and am putting grenades into the others when I hear the door open. I spin around, ready, although I'm fairly certain it's Dad.

He comes in and closes the door once more. "Bailey. Glad to see you're in one piece."

Face set, I say, "I'm going after TJ."

"I won't stop you. She's at Camp Redeemer. You should know that one of the men in the team that retrieved her is dead. Patriot Army is looking for you, even without her."

That news rocks me back on my heels. I've never killed anyone before.

"It was self-defense," Dad says. It's not a question. I can read him. He's reassuring me that my conscience is clean.

I give a quick nod. I don't like that I've killed, but I agree. It was self-defense, but it doesn't matter. No. It matters. I hate that I was responsible for killing someone. I hate that I will be doing it again, but what I tell Dad is what I believe. "Yes. And I'd do it again. I will kill again if I need to in order to get TJ to safety." They brought this on themselves by taking her.

He nods back at me. "I never saw you this morning. Let me know when you're safe." He taps an assault rifle on his way out. "She's been misfiring. Take a different one." He slips back out the door.

I appreciate the when-not-if statement. I'm going to get her out, then we're going to get out of here together. The fact that Dad and I are on opposite sides of this war is something for me to deal with later. For now, he's playing his loyalties down the middle. Not turning me in but also not helping.

I go back to arming myself. Luckily, Dad has plenty of options when it comes to assault rifles, even if the one he pointed out was one of my favorites when I was younger. I take a different one and a couple of handguns. I open a drawer and pull out a belt with two thigh holsters. I have to take my flak jacket off to put the holster on. I'm out of practice gearing up. Sloppy. I need to slow down and do this right, even though every nerve is screaming at me to go faster. TJ's liberty, if not her life, is on the line. The thought threatens to send me into a spiral. I take a deep breath, center myself, and this time, putting everything back on goes smoothly.

I stand and look around, considering what else I may need. I decide to be over- rather than underprepared. I pull out a duffle bag and fill it with anything that may possibly come in handy. Rope, trip wires, claymore mines, a flashlight, a comprehensive first aid kit and more. There is a battle ahead of me. I need to be ready.

It's only about an hour's drive to Camp Redeemer. I consider a nap before I get there, but I'm running too hot to sleep. And who knows what's happening to TJ while I make my way there? She's likely going through whatever processing looks like.

I step a little harder on the gas before reminding myself that if I get pulled over and caught, she'll be there a lot longer. I force myself not to be the fastest car on the interstate. Or on the freeway. Or on the country road that goes to Camp Redeemer. And the whole time I drive, I work on centering myself. It will do neither of us any good if I go in with chaotic energy. I need to be focused and smart. I need to be prepared to do what it takes. I breathe, I drive, and I plan.

I turn down a dirt road just before the main entrance. Approaching head-on isn't my best bet. I'm one against however many staff this forsaken place. I'll be sneaking in the side, armed for bear.

I take a few branches off the road, finding each one increasingly rougher. I turn the car around for a quick getaway before leaving it among some scraggly trees. The trees here can barely be called trees compared to those in Oregon, where I wouldn't have seen the car from twenty feet off due to the foliage. I set up some surprises for anyone who might approach. I need the car to be here and undisturbed to get TJ and myself out.

It's broad daylight. Waiting until night makes me uneasy since I don't know what's happening to TJ. However, the cover of darkness will be an advantage. Or it will make things more difficult because not as many people will be on the move. Not to mention that the hours between now and then will be difficult ones to get through.

I move through the sparse trees toward the camp to at least scout and plan. I spend a couple of hours watching from different directions. Aside from the front gate, there aren't any guards looking out. There are some moving among the campers and patrolling the fence, always with an eye inward.

At times, the camp looks full, people moving between activities. Mostly groups moving together, but I see pairs or singles at times. The thing that pisses me off the most is seeing a group of kids who range in age from preteen to nearly adult. While it's a crime that anyone is here, I'm most offended by the preteens. What are they doing here? How could anyone send their kid to this place?

Aside from the guards, the male-presenting people are wearing khakis and polo shirts, while all the female-presenting people are wearing dresses. I scan those, looking for TJ, but I know it's a long shot that I'll see her among all these people. Not only do many look alike because of the style of clothing, but she's likely not part of a group yet.

What I'm really looking for is what's keeping people here. There's the fence, of course, and the guards. But some of the men and women are in clothing of a different caliber. There aren't a lot of women who fit the bill, but their dresses look more flattering, more individual. They accompany but stand to the side of the other women. The men who stand out are wearing khakis and button-down shirts rather than polos. They, too, direct. Both groups are of interest, but the ones who will really get in my way are the guards. They're all men. They outnumber me for sure, but there aren't as many as one would expect at, say, a prison. They must count on the high, barbed wire fences; counselors; the tendency of people toward rule-following; and a lack of options for the inmates to help keep people here.

I can do this. This should be easier than some of the exercises we did at kids' camp, particularly in the teen years. If I knew where TJ was, I'd consider going at night and just getting her. As is, I'm going with plan B.

I retreat to the car to get the bolt cutters and weapons I hadn't wanted to carry while scouting. I double-check all my gear and shoulder the bolt cutters. I'm a little over halfway back when I see a person in the distance. I duck behind a slim tree, heart pounding. Encountering a guard right now was not part of my plan. I hadn't seen a one outside the fence. That's what I get for trying to do this quickly. The tree is no real cover. I peek out. He's armed and attempting to move quietly. He's clearly looking for something. Me?

Whether he's looking for me or not, I can't let him find me. Or at least, not live to tell the tale. I gently lower the bolt cutters, draw the handgun with the silencer, aim using the trunk of the tree to steady my arm, and wait for a clear, close shot. My heart speeds at the thought of taking another life, but I take a deep breath and focus. This is war, and they started it by taking TJ. He sees something and starts jogging with purpose. I hear him whisper-shouting, "Get back here, you bitch."

I shoot.

CHAPTER TWENTY-SEVEN

TJ

When we reach the gates of Camp Redeemer, I've had several hours of wakefulness to worry about what's coming next. It will be unpleasant, to say the least, but without anyone being afraid of what my father may do to them if they hurt me, I expect it to be much worse than unpleasant. My guts churn from anxiety and the gas station breakfast. What is going to happen to me? Is Bailey okay? Will I be marrying Allen Baker, or will it be even worse? Will he think I'm contaminated, meaning I'll be married off to someone who needs a wife and can't find one?

If I could roll the windows down, I would. I need the fresh air.

But once we're through the gates, and the door opens, bringing a gust of the very fresh air I was just wishing for, I want to take it back. At least here in this back seat, I only have to worry about Lake. Out there, worse is waiting.

"Come on out, Miss Rice," Dillinger says. "You're here. It's time to get settled in."

Gingerly, I emerge. I'm stiff from so many hours in the Hummer. I stretch involuntarily, then stop when I realize a woman in watching me with serious disapproval in her eyes. Lake is also watching with interest. I lower my arms.

"Welcome to Camp Redeemer," the woman says, not sounding at all welcoming. "You will address me as Mrs. Grant. I'll be seeing to your processing." In a much friendlier voice, she addresses Dillinger and Lake. "Thank you for bringing this wayward sheep back to the flock, gentlemen. There is breakfast for you in the dining hall and a cabin where you can sleep before you go on. Lacy will see to your needs."

I notice for the first time a woman who looks to be in about her thirties standing off to the side in a prairie-style dress. Her hair is long and sleek in a way that looks like it takes a lot of time to achieve. Even though she's looking down, I can see she has a face full of makeup. Her hands are clasped in front of her, and her nails are adorned with pink polish. The resulting look is one of ultra feminism.

"All our needs, is it?" Lake asks, eying Lacy up and down.

Alarm bells go off in my head, but Mrs. Grant just looks at him with an affectionate gaze. To Lacy, she says sharply, "Go on now, Lacy. Show these nice men around. And remember your next step."

Lacy nods demurely in a way that gives me the creeps and leads the men toward what I presume to be the dining hall. Mrs. Grant watches them go for a moment before addressing me once more. "As for you, girl, we'll start by getting you out of those boyish clothes and into something more suitable. Come with me."

The irony is that I'm wearing the clothes of a conservative grandma: khaki Bermuda shorts and a loose-fitting, blue, flowery, sleeveless, button-up, linen top.

She takes me to a pink room lined with dresses and mirrors. Instead of one of the display dresses, she opens a closet and pulls out what looks more like gray sack than a dress. She shoves it at me. "Here."

I take it but am not sure what to do with it. Does she want me to put it on?

She opens a drawer and hands me generic underthings. "You'll have to earn the nicer dresses. I imagine it will be a while. You'll shower before I take you to the cleansing room."

The idea that a shower and a cleansing room aren't the same thing nearly has me laughing, but I don't suppose it would be taken well. Not to mention that my abject fear about the cleansing quickly dampens any amusement I feel.

I follow Mrs. Grant through a room filled with vanities, the stereotypical idea of what any femme wants, and into a bathroom with stalls. I imagine that group showering with a bunch of lesbians would likely not be encouraged.

She hands me a shower kit. "Be quick about it."

Tears mingle with the shower water as I hastily wash, dry off, and pull the sack over my damp skin. I put my underthings on under the dress. There's plenty of room.

I'm just coming out of the shower when Lacy enters. She looks demurely at the floor as she says, "Mrs. Grant, your presence is requested in the office."

Mrs. Grant glares at me, as if I somehow orchestrated that. "Lacy will take you to the cleansing room. Don't get any ideas. She will report you." She turns to Lacy. "Directly to room three, Lacy. How did it go with the gentlemen?"

"They're eating breakfast, ma'am."

"That's not what I asked. Did you treat them right? Was either interested?"

My eyebrows nearly climb into my hairline. What exactly is Mrs. Grant saying? I've heard horror stories about how people are treated at camp, but I didn't realize offering women up for sex was so…sanctioned. Things may be much worse than I'd even imagined.

In a near whisper, Lacy says, "Mr. Lake seemed…interested."

My blood runs cold.

Mrs. Grant pats her on her shoulder. "Very good, Lacy. You'll be married and out of here in no time."

"Yes, Mrs. Grant."

As soon as Mrs. Grant bustles out, Lacy starts whispering to me without changing her outward demeanor at all. "We don't have much time. You'll get through the cleansing quickest if you admit to a few things. Not everything. But admit an attraction. If you can give them a name they already know, that helps. Don't give anyone else up. Play along. You can only leave if you're engaged to a man. Pick one of the men here. It'll be the best you can hope for. Got it?"

I nod dumbly. We start walking. "What did she mean by one of them being interested?"

Lacy rolls her eyes. "She thinks some man who is visiting might ask one of us to marry him. As if. I'm marrying Cameron. It'll be both our final steps, and we're out of here. Find you a Cameron. You'll protect each other."

"Why is Grant pushing for some stranger, then?"

"They like to maintain the fiction that we'll find someone on the outside. The only way that happens is if your family sets it up. And believe me, you don't want to be with someone who wants to reform you." She gives a little shudder. "Plus, she doesn't know about my plan to marry Cameron yet. He has to get to the next tier of rehabilitation before he's allowed to get engaged officially."

My stomach flips unpleasantly. There is so much to be scared of, from what's going to happen in room three to what happens after. And Bailey. Is she okay? Did she escape back to blue?

"We're nearly there." She slows even more. "Just get it over with. Afterward, as long as you pretend, it'll go fast."

I'm not sure she's completely sincere, but I appreciate her attempts to bolster me. My feet drag, but what use is it to put off the inevitable? We're about to enter a building, *the* building, when a harsh male voice calls out, "Hold up."

Lacy shifts subtly to more docile. She's been maintaining the veneer of a subordinate, but when talking to me, her head got just a little straighter, her shoulders a little squarer. Now, they fall back into the positions I saw them in when I first met her. She's good at this. I don't know if I will be. I'm too used to leeway.

We turn toward the voice. It's Lake. "I need a minute with Tatum," he says.

I can feel Lacy not wanting to let me go with him. She says, "I'm supposed to deliver her for her cleansing, sir."

"Loosen up, Lacy. This will be good for her." He grabs my arm and starts pulling me away.

I glance back at Lacy to find her staring helplessly after me. I'm on my own. "Where is Dillinger?" I ask.

"Sitting in the dining hall talking with some of the guards. Don't you worry, he's not going to show up to spoil our fun."

Terror blooms in my chest. I've thought since the first time I laid eyes on him that he will rape me if given the chance, but he's now practically come out and said it. I try to come up with a plan, but I'm having trouble thinking through the fog of fear enveloping me.

I'm surprised to realize that we're going toward the gates we drove in through. Hope shoots little darts through my fear. Surely, the gate guards won't let Lake take me out of camp. When they wave us through with smirks on their faces, I'm once again enveloped by sheer terror.

"Be back soon, boys," Lake calls to them.

One of them replies, "Not too soon, though."

Oh hell. Rape may not be officially sanctioned, but it's clear that at least some of the guards will not only look the other way but encourage it. I'm numb with terror as Lake pulls me past a line of cars to a Hummer, outside the fence.

I'm outside the gate. I should be looking for a chance to escape. Not just from Lake and what's about to happen but from Camp Redeemer.

He opens the door to the back seat while maintaining a circulation-compromising grip on my upper arm. He throws me in and climbs in behind me. "I thought about this the whole drive here. We're going to make my fantasies come true and make a real woman out of you at the same time. Believe me, honey, you're going to like this." He starts unbuckling his belt.

I'm trapped in this small space and about to be raped. I expected the possibility of sexual assault while at Camp Redeemer. We've all heard stories about what they do to women here. At the very least, there is simulating sexual activity with a man, which is horrible enough. Expecting something like this doesn't make it any better. My throat feels tight, and I feel tears gathering. But there's nothing I can do. Nothing. If I fight, I'll get beaten. It'll probably be better for him. I can't run. I'm trapped. I want to scream.

He pushes his pants to his ankles and runs a hand up my leg. "What are you wearing under here, honey? Not much, I see."

It occurs to me that I didn't hear him lock the doors. It's a long shot, but I feel around behind my back, searching for the door handle. He seems too distracted to notice. I pull the lever, heart in my throat, and fall out of the car.

I'm up and running before Lake has a chance to pull his pants up.

CHAPTER TWENTY-EIGHT

BAILEY

The shot flies with a muffled thump. The man screams as he falls, though, which is more noise than I feel comfortable with this close to the camp. I run over and put my hand over his mouth while I assess his injury. I aimed for center mass because he wasn't wearing a flak jacket and because it's the best way to insure I hit something. The bullet hit his hip. He's bleeding a lot, but it's likely not life-threatening. I'm sure it hurts like a son of a bitch, though, and he's not walking anywhere soon.

"Swanson? Fuck."

I finally really look at his face. Jeremy Lake. We were at kids' camp together, and he was always an asshole. I avoided being paired with him because he was one of the boys who thought that girls shouldn't be there while leering at me by the time we were eleven. "What are you doing out here, Lake?"

"Chasing a runaway. Come on, Swanson, you know the best thing for Tatum is getting straightened out."

I bop him on the temple with the butt of my gun. His eyes roll back before the lids close. I may have given him a concussion, but I care not at all. I stand. I'm tempted to end him, but I'm more worried about finding TJ. "TJ?" I call softly. "Are you out here?" I hear rustling, and that's all the warning I get before TJ launches herself at me. I wrap my arms around her. "Are you okay?"

"I am now. You're alive. And you came for me. Also, this is really hard." She taps on my flak jacket.

"Yeah, sorry." I'm crying with the relief of having her in my arms.

She laughs, but as she pulls back, I see there are tears running down her face, too. "Don't apologize. You came. You saved me."

We wipe each other's tears. "It seems that you were doing a pretty good job of saving yourself. Are you really okay? Did he…" I will shoot him if he did.

She shudders. "No. I got away."

It's a mixed answer if ever I heard one, but there will be time to unpack what's happened later. Right now, I need to get us to safety. "Let's get out of here." I feel a brief twinge of regret about all the other people I saw in the camp, but my priority is TJ.

I consider Lake. Should I tie him up or shoot him? He tried to rape TJ, and a large part of me wants to shoot him while another part of me doesn't want to kill if I don't have to. "Let me just tie this asshole up to slow him down."

I drag Lake to a tree and pull his arms around it. I secure them with zip ties. I'm looking around for something to use as a gag when my gaze falls on the oversized dress TJ is wearing. "That's quite the getup they put you in."

She looks down, frowning. "Yeah. It's kind of horrible."

"Do you mind if I cut some off the bottom to use as a gag?"

"Please cut off enough that I can run without having to lift my skirt."

I use a knife to raggedly cut the hem at about knee height. She should be much more mobile. I cut a strip to gag Lake with. None of this will help his health, but I don't really care if he dies.

When I look back up at TJ, she's biting her lip. I gather her into my arms. "What're you worrying about?"

"What about the others? The people being kept in Camp Redeemer."

I glance over her shoulder in the general direction of the camp. I'm not sure what to say. I'm one person, or actually, we're two people, of course, but TJ has no training and was just traumatized. "What are you thinking?"

"Can we save them?"

I consider the question for a few long moments. "I don't know. Let's go back to the car, regroup, and talk about it."

We make it back to the car with no sign of being followed. We get in, and I hand TJ a water bottle. "How long do you think it'll be before they start looking for you?"

She shrugs. "I'm not sure. I think they might start being concerned after an hour. When they go the Hummer and see we're not there…" She shrugs again. "Maybe they'll think he took me off somewhere else. I really don't know."

I'm angry all over again, but TJ doesn't need my anger. I hover my hand above her knee. "Is it okay if I touch you?"

"Please. It makes me feel grounded. Please don't treat me like glass. I'll let you know if something makes me uncomfortable, but Bailey?"

I drop my hand onto her knee. "Yes?"

"You still make me feel safe. I'm so glad you're here." She starts to cry.

"I'm sorry you were taken. I'm sorry I wasn't able to prevent this." I gesture around.

She huffs a laugh. "You're not Superwoman. You survived and came for me. It's all I could ask."

We fall into another hug, both crying now. When we pull back, I'm anxious about my lack of situational awareness. People could show up at any time. We need to focus.

"Let's talk rescue," I say.

Time isn't on our side. I get as many details I can from TJ about what she saw on the inside. We come up with a plan. Everything is rushed. It has to be quick because we want people moving around camp, which means going before dark falls. We need to get campers onboard. Part of the plan involves them creating chaos through various methods but predominantly by handing them the tools to start fires. Without that distraction, the two of us won't be able to do this.

I hate that this plan puts TJ in danger again, but she makes it clear that she can't just turn her back on the people there, particularly after I mentioned seeing the kids. I get it. I don't want to abandon them, either. I think the plan has a solid chance of success, or I wouldn't agree to it.

"I wish you'd thought to pack clothes for me," TJ says as I help her strap on the extra flak jacket I brought for her in case we were being shot at as we escaped. She's still wearing the loose gray dress with the ragged cut around her knees. We're working with what we've got.

"Yeah, sorry about that. But remember, this thing doesn't make you bulletproof." I tap the front of the jacket. "So don't take any huge risks, yeah?"

"Okay."

"I'm serious, TJ. Don't get shot."

"I don't want to be shot, no worries." Her voice is too playful for my taste.

"I just…want you here after, okay?"

Her eyes turn serious. "You too, Bailey. Let's both make it to the other side."

I grab the armholes of her newly donned jacket and pull her in for a kiss. "It's a pact."

She's a little flushed when we pull back, be it from the kiss or the danger, I don't know. I put a couple of grenades in her pockets. "Remember. Pull the pin and throw. It's not dangerous until you throw because the handle falling off is what triggers the explosion. The pin's job is to keep the handle on, but your hand will do that until you throw it. All that to say, take your time and aim."

"Sure." She sounds nervous.

"I'm sorry."

She looks at me sharply. "For what? Rescuing me? Going along with my scheme to liberate the camp?"

"For putting a weapon in your hands." I hold my hand over hers on the grenade.

She straightens her shoulders. "I'm the one who wants to save them. I can do this."

I also want to save the people in the camp, but I'd have gotten TJ out of here and then worked with NoFa to do it. TJ's conviction and bravery steels my nerves.

"You'll do great." I hand her a shotgun. "This one is a wide scatter, so you need to be close for it to do any real damage, but the benefit is that you don't have to have good aim." She's never shot a gun before, so it was a debate about arming her at all. "Here's how you load it." I show her and put some shells in her pockets. "Got it?"

She nods, eyes wide but determined.

"But your main tool is this." I hold up the bolt cutter. "So strap the shotgun to your back and only use it if you have to."

I help her adjust the shotgun so it's out of her way. She looks a lot more comfortable with the bolt cutter.

"Ready?"

I expect her to be nervous like she seemed when I was arming her, but she looks resolved. Her tone is determined when she says, "Yes."

My heart surges in my chest, and I'm torn between charging into battle with her and driving away with her to protect her. "Let's do it, then," I say, choosing battle.

CHAPTER TWENTY-NINE

TJ

I follow Bailey through the sparse trees to the fence line. She's such a vibe all strapped up. I didn't know I could think that was sexy, but Bailey is pure sex appeal. The way her butt moves in her jeans. The gliding way she moves that radiates competence.

This isn't the time. We've got a job to do. A job I want us to do. The grenades in my pockets and shotgun across my back feel like the heaviest things I've ever carried. I want to rescue the campers, but I don't know if I'll be able to use these weapons. I grasp the handle of the bolt cutters to anchor myself. This I can do.

At the fence, I start cutting while Bailey keeps lookout. It's harder than I thought it was going to be, but I keep going. I'll be doing more of these holes, and I need to figure out how to be proficient with it. Bailey has another job. When I've cut a several-foot-high line, Bailey grabs one side and pulls. I pull the other with a little more effort.

She looks around, then turns to me. "Cut the holes and go back to the car, right?"

"Right."

"Remember to avoid the trip wires."

"Bailey, I will absolutely remember not to get myself blown up." I do have a sense of self-preservation, even if it's not so strong that I want to abandon people to this camp.

"Okay. I'll meet you there as soon as I can."

"Go. I'll be fine."

She looks around one more time, kisses me, then ducks through the hole. I watch her hide behind a building before I move along the fence to cut more holes. It's scary without her. I have to keep an eye out for danger. If a guard shows up, I'm supposed to run. The weapons are tools of last resort. It's just that there isn't much to hide behind around here. I'm not sure I can outrun a guard. If one shows up, I may have to defend myself. I don't want to have to hurt anyone, but the thought of the guards just allowing Lake to take me to the Hummer makes me even more determined to do what I need to do to keep myself safe and help the people trapped here.

Even so, I try not to think about having to use the weapons.

At the first cut of the second hole, the sound jangles my nerves further. It seems louder without Bailey. I look around. Nothing. I keep going. I pry the sides up and move down the fence.

I'm about halfway through my third cut when movement catches my eye. I throw myself to the ground. I'm cursing my choice and waiting for bullets to start flying, or at least for the yelling to start, when a voice says furtively, "What are you doing?"

I look up. A man in khakis and a polo shirt is standing there. He's lean and trim, somehow managing to make the uniform look good. He's probably not a guard. He's not obviously armed. He could be a counselor, but why would he have asked the way he did if so? I stand, feeling stupid, and retrieve the bolt cutters. "Staging an escape. Want to get out of here?"

"Oh hell, yes. Is it just you?" He looks around as if there may be an army behind me. Well, Bailey is a one-woman army, so he's not entirely wrong, but she's not here at the moment.

"Not entirely. But there are only two of us. We need help. We need everyone who wants to get out of here to leave and if possible, set things on fire before they go. Interested?"

"Didn't I already say hell yes?"

"Okay, then. The most helpful thing you can do is take this." I pull a bottle of lighter fluid from one of my pockets. "Go tell people to make for the holes in the fence. I'll be cutting more. Burn things down behind them."

He takes the bottle. "Got a match?"

"Oh, yeah. That'd be helpful, right?" I nearly laugh at myself and how bad I am at this stuff. I feel around for the matchbook. It's rattling around with the shotgun shells. That gives me an idea. "Do you know how to shoot a shotgun?"

"No, but I know someone who does."

"Want to give them this?" I heft the shotgun.

"You don't need it?"

I marvel at the trust I'm putting in this man. But we share a bond. The bond of being who we are in a red state. The bond of being captured and imprisoned for it. I can trust him. He hasn't raised an alarm, has he? The look on his face, fierce hope and desperation, is one I recognize. "I've never shot a gun of any sort before," I admit. "If you know someone who can use it to aid the escape, that's where it should go."

"All right."

I finish cutting the fence, and together, we pry the sides up. I hand the shotgun over with relief. He puts the shells in his pockets. "What happens after we get out?"

"That's up to you. Run for blue, I say."

He nods. "Okay. Let's create some chaos."

"That's the idea. Hey, if you see a blond woman in a flak jacket with lots of guns, don't shoot her. She's on our side."

He laughs softly. "Fair enough. Good luck to you."

"Same to you."

He looks around and makes for a building. I move on to my next patch of fence. It's amazing that this place isn't a hornets' nest of activity already.

In the next moment, I realize I should have knocked on wood because all hell breaks loose.

First. I hear shouting, then an explosion from somewhere in the camp. I'm not well-versed enough in explosions to know if it's from a grenade or if someone shot up a car. I am pretty sure it wasn't just from setting fire to a building, even with lighter fluid. People are pouring out of buildings now, and the word about heading to the fence seems to be spreading. Many of them are running for the perimeter or yelling at others to do so. The fence is tall, with razor wire at the top. They need the holes I'm cutting to get through, and the more of them there are, the fewer bottlenecks there will be. I hurriedly start cutting again. I wish I there were more bolt cutters so I could give them away, but there's just the one.

A big buff man comes directly to where I'm working. "Hey, hand those over. I can cut faster."

I'm not sure if he's a camper or a counselor. I realize I'm stereotyping, but he doesn't look gay to me.

He grins and winks. "Come on. It's a lot of cutting. I can help."

When a second man joins him, grabbing his arm as if for protection, I make up my mind. I shove the cutter through the hole. He pulls it through and starts cutting, making quick work of a huge hole. It was the right choice.

Only now, I'm standing here useless. I'm supposed to meet Bailey at the car. Going back would be the prudent choice, I know. However, I haven't seen any kids yet. They may already be out the first exit, or they may be holed up in some building, scared to come out. I can't leave without knowing for sure.

Before people start pouring out of the hole that the man just cut, I go in.

"Hey, where are you going? We're supposed to be getting out," someone calls after me.

I'm glad to hear that the word is spreading, but I don't stop. I pass a group of campers disarming a guard. Off to the side, a couple of people are on the ground bleeding. I pause, but there are already people there helping.

I dither. I hate that people are getting hurt, but of course they are. To think we could pull this off without injuries was some seriously naive thinking. Besides, it's far too late to stop it.

Someone else pauses next to me, evaluating the situation as well. When I look fully at her, I realize it's Lacy. "Hey, do you know where the kids are?"

She regards me, taking in the flak jacket over my hacked-up newcomer's sack. "I won't waste time asking how you got away from Lake. I know where the boys are, at least. Follow me."

We start jogging farther into camp. People are running everywhere. It's hard to tell who is a camper and who is staff. Buildings are on varying degrees of fire. Everyone jumped on the setting fires bandwagon, it seems. I just hope they've also jumped on the "get out of here" bandwagon. There's no way that backup isn't on the way.

"Why just the boys?" I ask, panting a little.

"They keep us away from the girls because we're a bad influence. This place is all kinds of fucked-up."

I hear a car approaching and grab Lacy's arm, pulling her behind a building. I don't have to pull too hard. She must have also heard the engine. We watch a Jeep go by with armed guards. I wish I could warn the people in their path. Again, I question if we should have started this.

"Let's go." She pulls me farther between the cabins. She looks around before stepping out the other side.

We come to two cabins, both flame-free. An intact stretch of fence stands behind them. The man with the bolt cutters must not have made it this far. Is it slow going? Was he caught? Maybe he cut a few big holes and decided it was enough. Maybe he's heading away from here right now.

Lacy slows. She indicated the cabin with a Jeep in front of it. "That one is the boys' day room. The other might be for the girls, but I'm not sure."

"There may be guards keeping them there, so we should approach carefully," I say.

Lacy doesn't say anything to that obvious statement. We approach from the opposite side of the neighboring cabin in a low crouch, although I'm not sure what good it does. I suppose if no one is directly looking out the window, we're less likely to catch anyone's attention. And yet, my nerves are screaming the whole time, waiting for a sign that we've been seen. We make it to the wall under a window with no calls of alarm.

I attempt to use hand gestures to tell Lacy that I'm going to look. She rolls her eyes, and I suspect she knows what I was trying to say more because it's the obvious thing to do than because my signals were readable. I ease upward until I'm looking over the sill. I hurriedly drop back down.

"Were you seen?" Lacy whispers.

I put my finger to my lips and shake my head. I'm pretty sure I wasn't, but there was a person with his back to the window inside. An armed man. My heart is thudding in my chest. How are we going to get the kids out when there's an armed guard?

I ease up and take another look. The man is walking away from the window. There are maybe ten kids, ranging from preteen on up, who are watching his every move. I don't see any other adults. I crouch and tell Lacy what I've seen in a whisper so soft, I'm a little surprised she hears me.

We check the other cabin and find a similar situation with the girls. Here, though, there are two adults. One armed man and one adult woman who must be their counselor.

"We need a distraction."

I touch the pocket of my flak jacket. "I have an idea."

CHAPTER THIRTY

BAILEY

I need to focus on my job, not who I just left at the fence. TJ is smart and capable. I do not need to baby her. And this forsaken camp needs to be shut down. I force myself to be aware of my surroundings and move carefully.

The first cabin I come to is empty of people and full of beds. I squeeze a little bit of lighter fluid inside and throw in a match. It's a small fire now, but it will build.

The next two cabins are the same, except that the third is under repair. There aren't people working on it right now, but there is some detritus on one side. I repeat the actions, feeling a little antsy because while the fires will be a distraction, they will also alert the staff to a situation. They'll be on guard. I'd like to liberate some people and get them in on the plan while I've still got the element of surprise on my side.

The fourth building is larger and looks less like a cabin. It contains multiple rooms and has a large AC unit on the outside. It is a camper space or office space for staff? I peek in a window. Office.

I run back to the last cabin I passed and grab two two-by-fours. I block the front and back doors of the office building by sliding the lumber into the door handles. It won't hold for long, and they can always go out the windows, but it'll slow down a response.

The next cabin is a jackpot. There are a group of people inside. Men on one side, women on the other, listening to a speaker at the front. There are no guards to be seen.

I time my entrance for when the speaker has his back to the group. He's spouting some nonsense about men's and women's roles in society. He doesn't notice my entrance, but several of the people in the back do. I pat the air with my free hand, hoping they understand I want them to stay quiet.

I'm nearly to the front when the man turns and sees me. He opens his mouth to say something or yell or whatever, but before he can make a sound, I leap forward and strike his head with the butt of my rifle. He crumples.

The people behind me, who heeded my request to stay quiet, are silent no more. They're murmuring to each other, gasping, and scraping chairs as some stand. I turn and address them: "This is a liberation, but I need your help."

Briefly, the sound increases until a few people shush the others.

"The plan is to get everyone out and burn down the camp behind us so it can't be used anymore. I need you to spread the word, burn down any empty buildings, and make for the fences. There are holes for escape. Hopefully all around, but for sure to the south of the guardhouse. Get out and scatter."

"Sounds like a half-baked plan," a woman calls out.

"Is it better than staying here?" another woman responds.

About half the people stand and start for the door. The rest hesitate, but as more people get up, the stragglers follow. That was fast. I drag the counselor as I go so I can set the cabin on fire without burning him inside. After throwing the match, I notice the first cabin I lit a fire in is burning merrily now. I hear shouts. I head for the guardhouse near the gate. My job now is to keep as many guards away from the escapees as possible.

There's one Jeep and a line of three golf carts outside the guardhouse. Earlier, there were two Jeeps. I don't like not knowing where the other is. Doing rounds inside the camp? Out getting supplies? I don't know, but I can take out this one. I have to hurry because even as I watch, a couple of guards emerge from the guardhouse. One is shouting into a walkie-talkie. I take aim and shoot.

The Jeep doesn't explode, but I didn't expect it to. I have gotten the attention of the guards, who look around and unsling their weapons as they move to take shelter. More guards run over, crouching low. I count five. They haven't figured out where the shot came from, so I flip to burst mode and wait patiently for more fuel to pour out of the bullet hole in the Jeep. Perhaps feeling brave because there have been no more shots, the guards begin to fan out, looking for me. When some men are closing in on my location, I shoot rapid-fire. It's using a lot of my limited supply, but I need one bullet to make a spark, and finally, one does.

The Jeep explodes spectacularly.

There are a variety of responses from the guards; some hit the deck, some jump and stare at the Jeep, some duck for cover. I flip back to single-shot mode and take aim at one of the guards who is staring at the Jeep. I hit one and sight for another shot, but the next time I pull the trigger, there's just a click. I have to reload. Or switch weapons. Either will take time I don't have. The shot alerted the guards to my location, and some are advancing. I need to move.

I scoot back, stand, and run for the other side of the building. I take stock while reloading. They'll be coming around both sides if they have any tactical skills at all, and I have to assume they do. There are no other buildings I can get to before that happens. Well, shit.

I look up, considering going through the window, but someone is hanging out of it. "What's going on?"

"Liberation! Get out while you can."

She ducks, and I hope that the distraction of killing me gives her and whoever else is in there time to get away, even though they're right next to the guardhouse. I edge to one side, thinking I can at least take out anyone coming from that side. There's no one to guard my back, so it's only a matter of time. I peek around the building and take aim at the guard creeping my way. Before I can take a shot, he grunts and drops his weapon to cover his head. It takes me a half a second to realize that someone just dropped something from the window above.

The guard yells threats, and I shoot him. It's getting to be easier, shooting at people. While it's good for this situation, that thought makes me uneasy. The woman in the window gives me a thumbs-up, and I nod at her before advancing to take out more guards. When I get to the front of the cabin, I see people emerging armed with mops and brooms. It's not a lot to fight men with guns. A guard shoots at the group, and someone drops. The others scatter. I return fire.

It's a chaotic op, but the fact that people are out here participating shows it was the right move. They're being given a chance, and they're taking it. Still, I hate to see people on the ground bleeding. I move to check the person in front of the cabin, but two people carrying makeshift weapons beat me to it, and I decide my job is covering them.

There are two guards still shooting and lots of what I take to be people freeing themselves. And me. I'm sheltering at the edge of the cabin. One of the guards is in a similar position with the guardhouse. The other is behind a toppled golf cart. It was rocked off its wheels by the Jeep explosion. The other golf cart is gone. I have no idea when that left.

I could run. Maybe they'd follow, maybe not. But me staying and keeping them busy is giving people a chance to get out. How many holes was TJ able to cut? Are there bottlenecks at the fence? Maybe I can open the gates to give people more access to freedom. In theory, if I take out these two guards, I can figure out the gate. There has to be a remote control for it somewhere. Maybe even in the golf cart.

With renewed focus, I take aim. However, behind my target is a woman with a two-by-four. I take my finger off the trigger as she hits the guard over the head with the piece of wood.

I move my sights to the other guard, only to find he's getting similar treatment. Maybe I'm unneeded. I should open the gates, then go meet up with TJ.

Just as I'm thinking that, the gates slide open. Okay, then. Things are covered here. Off to get TJ. I move, directing a few people here and there to get out. The place has mostly emptied, as far as I can tell. Fires burn all around. People are few and far between.

I come to a pair of people wandering around, and I direct them toward the fence. The man shouts back, "You? Is this all because of you?" He stands between me and the woman. "I won't let you hurt her."

I have no interest in hurting unarmed people, even though these two must be counselors who have inflicted plenty of damage on the people being kept here. I keep my eye on them just in case I've missed a weapon, but I skirt them while enduring nothing more than the man yelling at me and continue on.

There seems to be nothing left for me to do. I turn to head toward the first hole in the fence and back to the car when I hear an explosion behind me. I run toward it instead.

CHAPTER THIRTY-ONE

TJ

When the grenade goes off, it's followed by shouts and cries from both cabins. I threw it at the fence, hoping to blow a hole in it for the kids to escape. I wasn't sure if the explosion would do anything to the fence, but I figured it was as good a target as any. I don't wait for the smoke to clear to see if it worked. I charge into the cabin containing the girls while I assume Lacy does the same next door. That is the plan, at least.

I go straight for the armed man looking out the window to see what blew up. I tackle him. He's taken by surprise, but he starts fighting back immediately. Additionally, someone jumps on my back, and I can only assume it's the counselor.

I've overplayed my hand, been too confident, and I'm about to pay for it by being recaptured. At least we've won the liberty of most of the people here. Or made the opportunity for them to take it for themselves. Maybe Bailey will come for me again.

All of a sudden, the weight on my back is gone. I have a fighting chance. Not much of one against this trained man who is bucking me off but a chance. Quicker than I can process, I'm underneath him. I go for his eyes with my fingers, try to knee him in the groin, suggestions Bailey made.

He grunts and easily restrains me, holding both my hands in one of his and sitting on my legs. There is nothing I can do. I feel so helpless.

Then, his whole weight is pinning me down. It doesn't make sense. He already had me contained and had a free hand. Why would he...

"Miss, miss, are you okay under there?"

The man is pulled off me, and I assess. "I'm fine. Thank you."

The kids have come to my rescue. The guard seems unconscious. One teen holds what looks like a souvenir paperweight. The counselor is being tied up and gagged by a couple of kids. Several of the teens are missing strips of their dresses, making it clear where the materials came from.

"Thank you," I say again as I stand. "We're getting out of here."

They cheer.

"First, let's check next door and see if Lacy needs help."

One of the older girls frowns. "Miss Lacy is over there?"

"Yes, liberating the boys. Let's go help."

Another cheer and they start streaming for the door. In the next second, gunshots ring out, and they're running back inside screaming.

"Get down, get down! Take cover," I yell, but it's too late. The girls are already knocking over desks and pulling them into corners to create barricades. Like me, they've grown up with active shooter drills. They may have screamed, but their training is kicking in.

I crawl to the window that looks into the boy's cabin window and hope Lacy is looking back. I need to know if they're safe over there. But when I crawl past the guard, I realize we're not unarmed.

"Does anyone know how to shoot?"

One teen pokes her head out from behind a desk. "I do."

I take the rifle from the unconscious man and hand it to her. There's also a pistol. "Anyone else?"

Another girl's hand tentatively pokes up over a desk. I hand her the gun. The girls switch weapons for reasons that seem clear to them and take up positions by the door. I start for the window again, but before I'm there, gunshots ring out again. It all sounds much closer. The guards are advancing, and the girls are shooting back.

This time, when I look out the window at the other cabin, Lacy is looking back. At least she's okay. We communicate what we can with hand signals. I get the idea that a couple of the boys have armed themselves and are defending the building. I try to tell her the same. There's not much else I can do aside from making sure the guard we knocked down stays down. I enlist the help of some girls to tie him up.

A change in the pattern of gunshots accompanied by exclamations from the girls at the door catch my attention. I make my way to the side of the girl with the pistol. "What's happening?"

"Someone else is shooting at the guards."

My heart leaps. It has to be Bailey. I risk peeking out to see it's not such a risk anymore. The guards aren't shooting. They're down. Dead or just injured, I don't know. Rifle out and ready, Bailey is walking cautiously toward the cabins. I should wait. Just in case the guards are still a threat. Or someone else is out there waiting.

I throw myself out the door, down the steps, and into Bailey's arms. Her rifle is jammed between us. Perhaps I didn't think this through.

"TJ. You're okay." She sounds as relieved as I feel. She shifts the rifle and hugs me back.

"Yeah. We've gotta get these kids out of here."

"They're already working on that." She jerks her chin at the cabins.

The kids are coming out with varying degrees of caution. There are a couple already checking out the fence. It seems the grenade did a lot of damage but kind of sporadically. The kids are kicking at the fence, and large chunks are falling to the ground. Lacy emerges and waves, the last out of her cabin.

"Right. Okay. Let's all get out of here," I say.

Bailey squeezes me. "I'm entirely on board with that. I can't imagine that backup is far off. We need to move."

By the time we get to the fence, several of the kids are running into the woods as singles or in small groups, including all the armed kids. I silently wish them good luck. Lacy and six of the younger kids are lingering just outside the fence, apparently waiting for us. One kid is clinging to Lacy.

I watch Bailey take stock. "Okay. We've got a car. I don't think we'll all fit even if we squeeze. Hang on."

She goes back through the fence. I consider going after her. I don't really want to be separated again, but she's constantly doing things that would be a struggle for me to do, so...

She pauses just on the other side. "Come be a lookout?"

I sprint after her.

We sneak through the two buildings, keeping them as cover as long as possible while she explains the plan, which is to steal the Jeep.

"Stay here, keep watch, and call out if you see anything. If you hear something...well, use your best judgment."

"Got it." I wait at the corner of the building while she runs over to the Jeep. They must have left the keys because it starts right away. Just as she gets to me, I see something over the horizon. "Bailey! A helicopter's coming."

"Shit." She steps on the gas. "Hold on." She slams through what remains of the fence and skids to a halt in front of the waiting group. "Everyone, climb in."

They do. There are nine of us in a Jeep with seating for five. Two kids are in the cargo area in the back, three are in the back seat with Lacy, and one is on my lap.

"Hold tight, everyone." Bailey starts dodging between the sparse trees.

"Are we going to the car?" I ask with one arm wrapped around the kid on my lap whose name I don't even know, and the other hanging on to the handle for dear life.

"No. No time. We're getting out of here before we're spotted." She swerves around a cluster of trees. "I hope. Tell me if the helicopter is following us."

I look behind us. The helicopter appears to be following us, and I'm about to say so when it starts lowering, and I realize it's landing. "I don't think it spotted us."

Bailey slows a little, which I'm glad about. This is an open-sided Jeep, and I have visions of kids tumbling out. Plus, while there is still light, the sun went down sometime during the battle for the cabins, and it's getting dark. That can't possibly help with the safe driving situation. But it probably helps disguise us out here, particularly since Bailey has the lights off.

"Everything okay back there, Lacy?" I twist to look.

She has a kid on her lap and a kid on either side. The two in the back are looking wide-eyed but are holding on and seem intact. "Okay as they can be while we're fleeing for our lives in the back of an open-top Jeep, I think."

I laugh a little. "Lacy, this is Bailey. And those are all the names I know. What's your name?" The last is addressed to the kid on my lap who is wearing a dress.

"Taylor. But I prefer Ty, if that's okay."

"Ty, I'm happy to call you whatever you like."

Shyly, so I can barely hear, Ty says, "My pronouns are he-him, then, please."

Bailey doesn't interrupt, but she lays a hand on my knee in an apparent show of support.

"Okay, Ty. I'm she. So is Bailey. Lacy?"

"She-her for me. Hi, Ty. Nice to meet you. And how about you?" she asks the kid on her lap.

Everyone in the Jeep shares their name and pronouns. There's an air of jubilance in the SUV, despite the circumstances. The two girls in the back seat holding hands are Regan and Tatum. That's exactly why I prefer TJ. Tatum is a super common name for girls in red. At first, I chose it to differentiate myself from the others. Later, I was happy to distance myself from anything red in any way I could.

Bailey finds a dirt road, and the going becomes a little smoother. "We will be very obvious in this. We need to find another vehicle. Two would be better. Where does everyone want to go?"

At that question, a few of the kids start crying.

Bailey slows. "Does anyone want to go back? This isn't a kidnapping."

"No."

"Never!"

"No, but I don't know where to go," followed by a sob.

The answers overlap, but I get the idea. No one wants to go back to camp, but it seems no one wants to go home, either.

"Lacy?"

"I'm getting out of red. I should have done it years ago, but... well, it doesn't matter. I'm here now, and I'm getting out." She sounds stubborn, but when she speaks next, it comes out worried. "I wish I knew that Cameron and the others made it out. I don't suppose we can try to find him?" She answers her own question before Bailey or I can. "No. We have to go while we can. Where are you two going?"

"We're running for blue," I say. "Listen, there's an organization I know about that helps people relocate from red to blue. People like us. Maybe they can help if we can get there."

"What about us?" Ty asks. "Will they help us?"

Honestly, I'm not sure. These kids range from eleven to fourteen, at a guess. I never talked to the rescue org about kids. Will they help them? Place them with foster families? Or is the risk of prosecution for kidnapping too high?

Maybe no one will look for these kids. Maybe they'll be written off as dead in the liberation of Camp Redeemer. Their parents gave them up because of who they are or who their parents think they are. Kids younger than high school age just aren't taken without voluntary parental surrender. It's likely they were hoping to get them back all adjusted to being the gender they were born into and attracted to the opposite gender. If instead, they were tragically killed, maybe their parents would prefer that. I've heard people say often enough that they'd rather their kid was dead than gay. If they could send their eleven-year-old to that place, that's probably what they think. At least one of the parents. And that parent will likely just surrender them again. Still...

"Are you all willing to leave your families behind?" If any of them say no, we won't take them with us. I don't know what we'll do instead, but I'm not down for kidnapping.

Ty is hard faced when he says, "Yes."

Not everyone looks so sure. There are more tears but also more yeses, and everyone is nodding. The two kids next to Lacy in the back seat are still holding hands. I look to Bailey to see what she's thinking about all this. She must feel my gaze because she looks back at me. "We'll figure it out."

We drive on into the twilight.

CHAPTER THIRTY-TWO

BAILEY

There is no way that an open Jeep bursting with people, particularly dressed like we are, will escape notice if we're on main streets. I stick to dirt roads and back streets as much as possible while driving north and west and also keeping an eye out for someplace with cars I can steal. It's a delicate balance. I'm grateful it's dark, even though it's slowing us down considerably.

There was a lot of chat at first with introductions, very rough plans, and questions about the journey ahead, most of which I can't answer. We're going to have play this by ear. What I think we'll need to do is steal two cars. I'd consider three to split up even more, but I can't stand the idea of parting from TJ again. So, two cars. Lacy will take one and some of the kids. We'll take the other and the rest of the kids. It would be safest to travel separately in terms of not garnering notice, but I'm concerned Lacy won't have the skills to procure food and fuel on her own.

It's quiet in the Jeep now. Several of the kids have nodded off, including Ty on TJ's lap. She's awkwardly holding him. It can't be easy. He's not a little kid. I'm also a little jealous. I'd love to be sleeping in TJ's arms. I haven't slept since the night before last, and that was in the middle of a hurricane. I'm exhausted.

I really need to get us in a different mode of transportation, something where everyone can have their own seat and where TJ and I can take turns driving while the other sleeps.

"Did you get any sleep last night?" I ask her softly, only now wondering if she's as exhausted as I am.

"Yes, surprisingly. I did have the entire back seat of a Hummer to myself. I won't say it was an excellent night's sleep, but I got several hours, I think."

"I'm glad of that, at least. Are you really okay?" I've been thinking about having left Lake alive and regretting it. That man tried to hurt TJ. Even if he wasn't successful, leaving him alive only serves to put other women in danger. But if he actually did hurt her…well, I may never forgive myself for not killing him.

"I'm really okay." Her voice is calm and comforting. She shouldn't have to comfort me. I'm still berating myself for that a few minutes later when TJ says, "Look, a cabin."

I slow as we pass it. No lights. No cars. It looks like someone's hunting cabin. I stop and back up. Eyes open in the back seat at the change in direction. "We're stopping to see about some supplies," I explain.

I park on the side of the cabin away from the road, just in case someone happens to be passing but also to make sure there isn't a car over there. There isn't. That's both good and bad. On the good side, it means there's likely no one here. On the bad side, it means no car to steal.

I sit for a few moments, tapping on the wheel. I'm both waiting to see if any lights come on or there is any other indication of habitation but also thinking about the best way to handle checking out the cabin.

"I think it's best if you all stay here so we can have a quick getaway if we need to. TJ? Can you come sit in the driver's seat and be ready to go?"

One of the kids in the way back says, "I need to go to the bathroom."

I nearly laugh. Of course everyone has needs. I'm traveling with six kids. We haven't seen another car nor heard chopper blades since we got on our first dirt road. I'm likely being paranoid. I'd rather be paranoid than caught, but we can take a real pit stop.

"There's an outhouse," Ty says, pointing.

"Okay, change of plans," I say. "Everyone out. Stretch your legs, use the bathroom, but stay close and alert. Keep your eye on at least two people at all times." I consider the literalness of children. "Unless you're in the outhouse. Keep quiet. Inside voices. Be ready to get back in the Jeep at a moment's notice."

In answer, everyone starts piling out. I make for the cabin. The windows have curtains drawn over them on the inside, so I can't see in. All signs point to it being unoccupied. No one has made themselves known, and between the engine and now the sounds of people moving around, someone would have noticed us if they were here.

The kids are trying to be quiet, I think, but they can't seem to help making some noise by simply being awake and existing. It's clear none of them have been to kids' camp. Well, maybe one of the boys has. When I sweep my eyes over the group, he's standing off to the side on alert. I suspect most of the kids who had training of any sort were the ones who ran off on their own as soon as they were able. But he stayed. His name is Curt, if I remember correctly. I'd put him in his early teens.

I turn back to the cabin. Still nothing. I try the door. It's locked, unsurprising. There's a dead bolt. I can pick it, but it'll take a while. It'd be much faster to break a window, but I don't like the idea of leaving the cabin open to the elements. Sure, I'm about to raid it for whatever we need, but it could be months before the owner is back. The place would likely be home to many a critter if it were open.

I move around the cabin, trying all the windows. When I get to the back, I see there's another door. This one doesn't have a dead bolt. I chuckle at that. What's the point of the one on the front if they're going to have the back practically wide open? Whatever. It's good for my purposes. I jimmy the door open.

I pause to see if this is the moment an occupant shows themselves, but nothing. There's no light switch. I suspect there's no electricity. The only light is coming through the door I just opened, and it's not much. The moon is about half-full. It's enough to see outside but not enough to penetrate into the cabin. I start feeling around, hoping for a flashlight or lantern. I get lucky with a flashlight on a counter just to the right of the door. Or maybe not lucky. If it was my cabin, I'd leave a flashlight near the door.

Before clicking it on, I set myself. Someone could still be lurking in here, waiting for this moment so they have a clear shot. I push the button and shine the light around the small space. I'm the only person here.

There's a bed with a bare mattress in one corner, a small built-in table with a chair in another, and a small rustic kitchen that spans the other wall. It looks pretty bare. There may not be anything of use in here. I'd been hoping for food, at least.

Well, if nothing else, the flashlight is nice. I start looking through the cupboards. In the end, I find a box of granola bars, some homemade jerky, a couple of gallons of water, four flannel shirts, one pair of jeans, and a few other odds and ends that may come in handy. It's not nothing.

I exit the way I came, closing the door carefully behind me. TJ is waiting.

"Should we maybe stay here and get some sleep?"

"I'm anxious to put miles between us and anyone who may be looking for us. I think we push on."

"How are we doing on gas?"

"So-so. The tanks were nearly full when we started."

"There's more than one tank?"

"Yeah. Some backcountry vehicles have a second, smaller tank. Luckily, this one does, although I don't know what they were playing at thinking they needed it."

"Handy, though."

"Honestly, I'm hoping for replacement cars before we need to fill up."

"It seems like we might need to go someplace more populated?"

It's something I've been thinking about for sure. I've been hoping to find a place far from anywhere with a handy car in the driveway, but it seems that's wishful thinking. It's just that we're so very noticeable with all of us. And I wouldn't be surprised if there's been push notifications to watch out for escapees and particularly this Jeep, which means towns are dangerous.

"I've been thinking about that, and I think I have an idea," I say.

CHAPTER THIRTY-THREE

TJ

We're stopped again. If I had to guess, I'd say it was about three in the morning. Daylight isn't far off. Bailey wants to steal cars under the cover of darkness, which makes sense to me. We're just outside a small town. I lean down to cuff the stolen jeans one more time. When I straighten, I have to pull them back into place. They're way too long but only a little too wide. I tuck the flannel in, which helps.

When I look up, Curt is adjusting his flannel, too, the only thing that betrays any nerves.

"Everyone knows the plan, right?" Bailey asks.

Lacy says, "Most of us just need to sit here and not draw attention to ourselves, so, yeah, I think we've got it."

I see a flash of Bailey's teeth in the moonlight when she smiles at that. "True enough. We'll be back soon."

Lacy gives a curt nod and puts her arm around Nancy, the kid who has been sitting on her lap. I don't love that we're separating, but I get why. Three of us in the Jeep wearing much more normal-looking clothes will be much less noticeable.

Curt claps Derick on the back. They've been sitting in the far back together, and I suspect that Derick is why Curt didn't go off on his own. He climbs into the Jeep. I get in the passenger seat, and Bailey drives toward the lights of the town. She points out a stand of trees. "That's where we'll leave the Jeep. Think you can pick it out?"

I turn and look at it from the other direction, the direction I'll be coming from when we return from town at which point we'll each be driving separate vehicles if all goes to plan. It's the only clump of trees I can see, and there is a limb that sticks out at an odd angle. "Yes, I've got it."

When we're at the outskirts of town, nerves are getting the best of me. To distract myself, I ask, "How old are you, Curt?"

"Fourteen," he says in a matter-of-fact tone.

"And you drive?"

"I do."

"He was a kids' camp attendee," Bailey explains.

I want to ask how he ended up at Camp Redeemer, but that feels intrusive. However, it seems to me that a boy who goes along with the program enough to go to kids' camp probably masks well.

Curt must sense my curiosity because he says, "I spent some time on some *unsavory* websites and didn't cover my tracks well enough. My parents found out and sent me away. I think they suspected for a long time and were just looking for an excuse."

The idea of parents who care so little about a kid as to send him to Camp Redeemer wrenches my heart. My father and I have our problems, but he never wanted me to have to go through cleansing. Of course, he hoped I'd come around on my own. Now I have no idea where he stands. He may well have offered me up for conversion to save himself. Or maybe the fact that he sent me away to protect me meant his downfall. I itch to get my hands on a terminal, not only to find out what's going on in the world but also to check on my accounts.

There's no radio in the Jeep to listen to whatever propaganda the local radio stations are putting out. I try thinking of other things to distract myself. "Do you think they'll know it was us who led the liberation of the camp?" I ask. Maybe in the confusion, no one will figure it out.

Bailey shoots me a look, then looks back at the road. She puts her hand on my knee. "I'm sure they'll put it together. Is that a problem?"

I sigh. "I just wonder if the fallout will be a problem for my father."

"Is that a problem for you?"

I glance back to see that Curt is listening with interest. "Not so much of a problem that I regret doing it. But I…things with my father are complicated. I wouldn't want to be responsible for his downfall, I guess."

"My parents can die in a fire as far as I'm concerned," Curt offers up.

"That bad, huh?" Bailey says. "Sorry. That really sucks."

"It does," he says. "Hey, what about there?" He points at a house that has several cars in the yard.

"Nah. Most of those cars probably don't work," Bailey says.

"I meant for license plates," he says.

"Good point." Bailey pulls over several houses down. She hands Curt a screwdriver. He pockets it, which I wouldn't have thought to do. I'd have just carried the thing down the street, looking like I was up to trouble. He has plausible deniability about just being out for a walk *without* a screwdriver in his hand. He's back in a few short minutes with the license plates from two different cars.

Bailey drives on to a different residential area. This neighborhood has a lot of cars parked on the street instead of in garages, which makes sense from a convenience-for-theft perspective. I chuckle to myself. Or maybe not so much to myself because Bailey says, "What?"

"Nothing. I just never thought I'd be thinking about the best neighborhoods to steal cars from."

She shoots me a wry grin. "Life offers up new adventures every day."

"It does these days, that's for sure." So much so that it feels like I've lived a year since the moment that my father walked into my dorm room, but it was something like a week ago, I think.

"Okay, you remember the rendezvous?" Bailey asks.

"Yes."

"We'll meet you there."

I don't love this part of the plan. I hate leaving them, but Bailey says they'll be more clandestine without me lurking around. Still, it's hard to drive away.

It's even harder to sit and wait by the stand of trees. It feels like forever before I see lights coming down the road. My first feeling is relief, followed by worry that it's not one of them. I hide behind the trees away from the Jeep. The car pulls off the road, and my heart thumps. It should be one of them. Unless it's someone come to check on why this Jeep is here. The door opens, and I relax. It's Curt.

I step out from behind the trees, and he gives me a nod. "Good thinking."

"It went well, I take it?"

He shrugs. "Fine. Easy enough."

Now we're waiting for Bailey. At first, it's easier because Curt is there, and the fact that he made it makes me think Bailey will, too. After a while, though, I start running out of reasons for why it's taking her so much longer. I start pacing nervously. It bothers me that Curt is calmly leaning on the hood of the car he stole.

"Maybe I should go look for her," I say, as if asking for permission from the fourteen-year-old.

"I'm sure she's fine. Just picking the right car." I catch a note of nerves in his tone, though.

"Or she got caught."

"If she did, what will getting yourself caught do to help her?"

I pace some more, thinking. She came for me when I was taken. I should go for her. But Curt has a point. If I'm also arrested, what good will that do anyone? How can I help her? I find I don't care. I have to go after her. I'm walking to the Jeep when I see headlights.

Curt and I hide behind the trees. The car approaches, pulls off the road, and I nearly collapse with relief. It's Bailey.

She looks around, pausing at the trees as if she knows where to find us. I suppose it is the most obvious hiding spot. When we emerge, she beckons us to hurry, greeting me with a hug.

"I took a little extra time to pick up some resources." She hands Curt a small stack of credit cards. "Only use each once. Get food with fuel. You know the drill."

He accepts them with an equanimity that indicates he does know the drill, and I marvel again at the childhood these kids' campers had. While I spent my summer days learning about how God doesn't want us to talk back to our parents, they spent theirs learning to hot-wire cars, blow things up, and go on the run. What exactly does the Patriot Army think is going to happen? But I can answer that question. We've all been preparing for multiple things: the government to turn on us, civil war, invading the heathen blue states, and the rapture, to name a few. They've just been on the military action side of things while us girls were supposed to let the boys get on with it and not sully ourselves. Mostly. There were exceptions, like Bailey.

She eyes the Jeep and moves it more fully under cover. When she gets back out, she says, "The hiding job won't last long in daylight, but that should at least keep it from sight for a few hours. Longer if this road doesn't get much traffic."

We get in the cars—Curt driving the one he stole, me with Bailey—and drive to pick up the others.

"How'd you get the credit cards?" I ask. It's the middle of the night. It's not like she could have gone to a shopping center and pickpocketed a bunch of people.

"That's what took some time, sorry to keep you waiting. I went to an apartment complex and picked a few doors. It was a last-minute decision." She sounds almost defensive about it.

"I'm not arguing with having the supplies we need. I'm just glad you didn't get caught." We're on a serious criminal spree. Stealing credit cards is the least of it. At least the owners should be able to get the charges reversed when they report them stolen.

"There was a close call with a barking dog." She gives a quick grin.

When we get back to the others, there's a short conference during which we agree that Curt, Derick, and Nancy will go with Lacy in the car that Bailey stole. It's a gas vehicle, which means that it'll be faster to fuel. It's also an SUV, so the kids can hide in the back when they need to. The other three are with me with Bailey. We're driving an electric sedan that will make fueling more complicated. It's generally agreed that Bailey should be in charge of the riskier car.

"Here." She hands Lacy a piece of paper.

Lacy unfolds it and reads. "Isn't this dangerous to have out there?"

Bailey shrugs. "They can find where I live pretty easily. And there's nothing they can do with the handles. If you get a phone before you arrive, give Greer a call. They can help smooth the entry."

"Greer before you?"

"Yes. I don't know if…" They look around at the kids, who are watching the interaction. "I don't know if we'll beat you there. Plus, Greer has contacts who can make sure you have a safe landing, so to speak."

Lacy makes a move as if to put the paper in her pocket before remembering she doesn't have one in her Camp Redeemer dress. She hands the paper to Curt, who pockets it, then pats his pocket as if to indicate he'll keep it safe. Then it's time for good-byes. While the kids are busy with that, I whisper to Bailey, "Greer?"

"They're my friend with NoFa."

It's scary to think that we may get to Oregon and still have to worry about Patriot Army. But if we can get over the border, so can they. And Bailey says the Oregon border is easy to slip through. It's also hard to say good-bye knowing we won't know the fate of the others until we all, hopefully, get to Oregon.

We don't share our plans for the trip. It's safer for the other car if we stay independent and unaware.

I insist on driving. Bailey hasn't slept in forever. She's asleep before I separate from Lacy's car, which I do at the first opportunity to go north while they go west. From here, going north and west is the bulk of the plan. We will have to decide if we are going to try to get into Colorado or skirt it at some point, but Bailey can get some rest first.

Pretty soon, I'm driving under a lightening sky with a carful of sleeping people I'd give my life to protect. I can't protect them the way Bailey can, but I can get us closer to safety while they sleep.

CHAPTER THIRTY-FOUR

BAILEY

I wake up to the sound of rapidly changing music and voices. When I sit up, TJ says, "Sorry. I've been wondering about what's being said about the camp for hours now and couldn't hold off anymore. Also, we need to charge soon. I need your input on where to stop. And where to go next."

"'S okay," I say, words slurred with sleep. "Where are we?"

"Still in Kansas. We're not far from Colorado, but we can't make it across the border before we need to fuel up. If that's what we want to do."

We'd crossed into Kansas sometime while navigating the back roads in the Jeep. The red states bleed into each other with only token border checks, same as the blue. It's only between red and blue that things get dicey. Or in and out of Colorado, the Switzerland of the US. They've remained staunchly neutral as the other states have become more and more polarized. Like Oregon, they've shrunk. Much of the flatlands on either side of the mountain range voted to separate and join the bordering states. Colorado is now basically the defensible mountain range, with limited ways in and out. We're still deciding if we cross into Colorado and then fly to Portland or drive all the way. Both options have pluses and minuses.

The problem with flying out of Colorado is IDs. We'd have to figure out those for at least TJ and me. Procuring them will be risky. Also, there's crossing into Colorado. I'm guessing this border is heavily patrolled on the red side, thanks to the downfall of Camp Redeemer.

The border into Oregon will be less guarded because it's so much farther away from Camp Redeemer and because there are simply more ways in, but we'd be in red territory the entire way there, which puts us in a vulnerable position.

Instead of figuring it out, I fell asleep, leaving TJ to worry about it for hours. "I'm glad you woke me up. We're getting to the decision point if we're close to Colorado."

The kids are stirring in the back, too, rubbing their eyes and looking around. Everyone is going to need a bathroom and food, too.

"Okay, what we want is a truck stop with a lot of people coming and going so we can blend. We can also take care of all our needs at the same stop. Have you seen any truck stop signs?"

"Yes. There's one that must be pretty big in about twenty miles. I've been seeing signs for over an hour now. 'You're almost to Trucker's Heaven! Family friendly! We have showers and snacks to die for at Trucker's Heaven!' Stuff like that."

"Perfect."

I take over tuning the radio and stop when I hear news. "Stay tuned for more weather at the bottom of the hour. And now to Mark for an update on the situation at Camp Redeemer. Any new information, Mark?"

Even the kids, who had been talking among themselves, quiet down.

"Crusade of the Redeemer would like everyone to be on the lookout for both NoFa forces and members of our flock who may have strayed during the chaos at the camp yesterday, Gary. They ask that if any of your loved ones from Camp Redeemer show up that you alert the church immediately. The safety of our people is their top concern. The new head of security, Preston Rice, who recently took over for his father, Thomas Rice, has this to say."

TJ stiffens, and the voice coming over the radio changes again. "It is a great tragedy that our men and women who so desperately need help have been so profoundly hurt. It is clear that NoFa is getting more brazen with attacks on the operations of the Church of the Redeemer. Make no mistake, we will not stand for this. Reprisals will be swift and more than reciprocal. We will not rest until we gather all members of our flock and avenge those who have fallen."

Mark comes back on the line. "All of us will be sending hopes and prayers to the families who are suffering, I am sure. Back to you, Gary."

"And now, for our eight a.m. prayer. If you will all bow your heads if it is safe to do so. Our God, who art in—"

I turn the radio off.

"Well. I wonder if Preston figured out where I was and used that information to push our father out of his position or if our father was pushed out first, and then Preston took over and figured out where I was. It doesn't likely matter, but it's clear who turned me in."

"I'm sorry, TJ. Your own brother. That sucks."

"If I'd known he knew where I was, I would have guessed it was him. He's been a real asshole ever since our mom died."

It's the first time I've ever heard her swear. I glance in the back seat to see wide-eyed kids looking back. I don't know if they're surprised about the swearing or the situation.

"Wait," Ty says. "You're Tatum Rice?"

It must be the situation.

"That's me," she says. "I prefer TJ."

Tatum the younger says, "Yeah, I'm always called Tatum P or some stupid thing."

"But if you're Tatum Rice, won't they be looking for you?" Ty persists.

"They're looking for us all, Ty," Regan says like he's said the stupidest thing.

But it's true. Being in a car with TJ likely does make these kids vulnerable. But with the other option being that they're out in red territory on their own, I don't regret our choices.

"And Bailey will keep us safe, right?" Tatum the younger says.

"That is my plan." I need to keep them all safe. TJ, Tatum, Regan, and Ty. I need to get all four of them to a place where they can live full lives free from fear. At least once they all deal with the traumas they've endured. That could take a while. The first step is to get them to a place where they can start doing that. But I can't promise nothing will go wrong. "And with everyone from the camp going in all different directions, it's my hope that Patriot Army will be too busy to be focused on us."

"Right, but they'll still be at the border to Colorado. More than usual," TJ says.

"I agree. I think it's probably better to road trip." But my gut churns at the idea of shepherding everyone across another thousand plus miles of red territory. It's going to be a long day.

First things first. Fueling up both car and bodies. We have another ten minutes or so before we'll get to the truck stop.

"TJ, you start fueling and stay with the kids." I turn to the back seat. "You guys stay in the car." They start protesting. I hold up a hand. "Just at first. I know. You probably all need to go to the bathroom, and I'm sure you're tired of sitting in this car. But your clothes are way too obvious." They look down and at each other, seemingly realizing they're in their Camp Redeemer dresses still. "I'll go in and get some supplies. At a place like this, they're sure to have T-shirts. Hopefully, I'll also find shorts or something. I'll get food and clothes and bring it all back out. Then, while the car finishes fueling, we'll go in to use the bathrooms. Ty, you'll go with TJ. You two are with me," I say to Regan and Tatum. "Pretend you don't know each other. That won't fool anyone who sees us all get out of the car together, but it'll be less obvious we're two women traveling with kids."

That might be okay if TJ and I looked enough alike to be sisters, but we don't. Two moms with kids in red is suspicious. We might be trying to flee our husbands or something. I am still in baggy clothes, making me look androgynous, but even if I pass for male, I look more like a teenage boy than an adult man. That'll be fine when I'm in there on my own, but me with kids? People are more likely to assume I'm a woman.

"Everyone understand?"

There are nods all around.

I'm nervous as we pull in, and TJ drives to the charging stations. I honestly hope everyone in the car is nervous, too, at least a little. It'll keep them from doing anything stupid. Unless they're overly nervous, in which case, that can cause stupidity. A look in the back seat tells me they're on the side of too nervous. I smile at them. "Be wary, but also pretend you're on a normal family trip as much as possible. Jerky movements can draw attention. You're all going to do great. We're going to be fine."

TJ and I get out and start the charging process. Here there are only a few charging stations, and they're off to the side. In Portland, fueling stations are mostly charging stations with a solitary pump off to the side. It really only matters in this moment because I have to walk past the crowded pumps to get to the store, which will provide more opportunities for notice. It's also good for us because no one else is charging at the moment, which means we have a little privacy. If we were at the gas pumps, people would for sure be looking in our windows. The "see something, say something" campaign red has been pushing for years means everyone is on the hunt for deviant behavior. There are rewards.

Alone, I draw no attention as I browse the store. I find T-shirts and an aisle that sells underwear, socks, and flip-flops. I stock up but only for the kids. I've concocted a cover story for the clothes in case the clerk asks. I grab food, drinks, and a pack of wet wipes. I fully expect the clerk to look at me funny, but he doesn't bat an eye. I'm probably not the first person to buy this assortment of things. I'm relieved and a little disappointed not to need to tell my tale of an exploding Coke dousing my siblings.

On the way out, I casually throw away the credit card. Now that we've used it, the owner is likely getting an alert about it, and it would be a red flag if we tried to use it again.

At the car, I pass the bag of clothes to Regan and leave the bag of food and drinks on the passenger seat, out of the way. We'll get to it after we get away from here.

"All good?" TJ asks.

I casually lean against the window to block the flurry of movement caused by the kids changing in the small space, facing TJ across the top of the car. "Yep. So far, so good."

"Good. Because I have to pee like a racehorse."

I smile at her. "That's quite an image."

"I know. I practically ooze sex appeal."

I laugh, relieved she's calm enough to joke. "How much longer?" I jut my chin at the readout on her side.

"Fifteen minutes."

That should be about perfect. The door moves against me, and I realize Regan is trying to get out. I step back. She and Tatum come out my side. They're dressed in oversized T-shirts. I can just see the bottom of the boxer briefs peeking out. It's exactly what I'd hoped for. It looks like shorts. Flip-flops are on their feet.

I toss my hat into the car. I'd rather be clearly a woman because we'll be using the women's bathroom. "I'll take these two, then you take Ty in a minute. We meet back here. Okay?"

"Got it." She looks nervous but in control.

"Let's do this," I say to the girls, giving them a smile to remind them to be easy.

They give me weak smiles in return, which will have to be good enough. There's a line in the bathroom, which I don't love. TJ and Ty join the line behind us with a teenage girl in between. The kids do a good job of not acknowledging each other. By the time we've washed our hands, I'm feeling like things are going well. We just have to get back to the car.

We come out of the bathroom, me in the lead, and I see a face look around the corner. It's just one person looking, then pulling back. It could be anything. A husband wondering what's taking his wife so long, for example, but I know that wasn't it. I know we've been made. What I don't know is how many more are out there waiting.

I push the girls back inside. TJ and Ty are washing their hands. "We've got a problem. Everyone with me."

There are a few people still in the bathroom with us, but no one is in line anymore. They must have stopped people coming in after us. One of the women washing her hands says, "You can't keep these kids away from their father. Just go back."

I ignore her and pull a gun out of my pocket. I hold it low by my leg, but the people in the bathroom back up anyway. I guide my group out the door and point them down the hall the other way. I'm hoping for a back door. It doesn't matter if there's an alarm as long as we get out of the trap of a building.

TJ is leading them down the hall while I block for them when someone shouts, "Hey. Stop!" Then, in a different tone, "They're headed your way."

Shit. They must have people on the back door, too. Of course they do. At least they aren't shooting at us. Yet. As soon as we get around the corner, I see a door. It's our best bet. Maybe there's a window we can work with. Options are becoming very limited.

"In here." I push the door open into what appears to be an employee break room. There are no windows, but there's a door on the other side. I lock the door behind us, which won't hold long but may buy a minute or two, and direct everyone through the other door. It's an office. There are no windows. I deflate. Three faces are looking at me in varying stages of panic and fear.

TJ isn't. She's looking at the terminal sitting on the desk. "I think I can make this stop," she says.

CHAPTER THIRTY-FIVE

TJ

W hat? How?"
I sit at the desk and check to see if the terminal is locked. It isn't. Sloppy, but it's just the manager's terminal, so it's probably doesn't really need to be secure. I pull up a browser and start typing. Distractedly, I say, "It's ultimately Preston in charge. I can get to him. I just need a few minutes."

Bailey doesn't bother me with more questions. I hear her directing the kids, furniture scraping, and banging, but I ignore it all to focus on my task.

It's a matter of minutes to get to my blackmail file on my brother. I've kept one ever since he started ratting me out to our father about stupid kid stuff. He was eleven, and I was eight when our mom died. He seemed to decide the best way to deal with his grief was to ingratiate himself with our father, not only leaving me to fend for myself but actively throwing me under the bus. I was labeled the problem.

When I started figuring out computers, I started spying on his online activities. There was enough typical teenage boy stuff there that I was able to amass enough blackmail that he stopped getting me in trouble all the time. He changed the passwords to his terminal, but I hacked them again. So when he told our father that he caught me drinking when I was fourteen, I sent our father an email from

Preston's account with the porno clip he'd been watching that day. We both got in trouble. Preston changed his passwords again. I hacked them again.

He stopped tattling on me, but I never stopped tracking his online activities. I kept an active file on him at all times. When he started embezzling funds from the church, it was like I'd struck gold. I siphoned off some for myself and kept meticulous files on how he did it.

I quickly set up an email to be sent on wide release to the church, our father, and red media if I don't stop it. Then, I spam Preston with emails, texts, and a variety of direct messages on accounts he doesn't want the church to know about, just to hammer home the point.

Dearest brother,

Call off your dogs, or I send out proof of your embezzlement.

There is no way he's not monitoring this attack on us. He'll be online and can't miss my message. I add the files to the email as proof of the goods. There is a splintering noise, bringing me back to the present. My head snaps up, wondering if they're in the room with us already.

"They just broke through the break room door," Bailey says. "It won't be long before they make it through this one, too. Whatever you're doing, I hope it's fast."

There's pounding on the door to the office. The filing cabinet that Bailey and the kids apparently wrangled to block the door is shaking with each bang. They must be using a battering ram. The three kids are huddled next to me behind the desk. Bailey is standing in front of it, gun at the ready. I believe she will defend us to the death, but it would be a waste. If this doesn't work, we're trapped here. Her death will do us no good.

"Bailey—"

There's a ping on the terminal.

Fine. You win. For now.

I message him back: *Safe passage to Oregon for me and my traveling companions.*

There's a long pause during which I notice the banging has stopped. Baily is staring at me in amazement.

Fine. Go. Get the fuck out of my business. But I can't let you take the kids.

No deal. The kids don't want to stay. I'm pushing my luck, but I can't abandon these children. *All of us or nothing.* I don't say anything about Lacy and the other kids. Maybe he doesn't know about that carful.

There's a long pause during which I listen hard for resumed sounds of forced entry. But finally, Preston messages again. *If any of this leaks, even drips, I'll know it's you and come after you and those kids with everything I can muster.*

Deal. I'm not sure I mean it. If it would be useful again, I'm pretty sure I'd use it again, but that's what needs to be said right now.

Just go.

"We should be able to walk out of here now," I say.

"How?" Bailey asks. "What did you do?"

"I made a deal with the devil. Also known as my brother."

"What kind of deal?" She sounds suspicious.

"Don't you trust me?"

The kids are looking between us like it's a tennis match.

"With my life. I'm just not sure I trust you with yours in this situation. You didn't offer yourself up or anything, did you?"

"No. Not that kind of deal. I'll tell you when we're out of here."

"We can seriously just…go?"

I nod. I hope so. I'm betting my brother's desire to stay in power and out of jail is stronger than his desire to see me suffer or to score some sort of win by getting me back. I'm just a little nervous that the Patriot Army men who are outside that door won't follow his orders. There's nothing to do but try. "Let's go."

Bailey shoves the gun into her pocket and starts pushing on the filing cabinet. I help. The door is off its hinges, and when the filing cabinet is out of the way, it falls. No one rushes us. No one shouts. Bailey holds a hand out, indicting we should hold back while she steps cautiously out. Still nothing.

"Stay close," she says.

I shoo the kids in front of me so they're between us. We step out. There's no one there. That stays true as we go into the hall. The back door is hanging open. Bailey leads us through it. Still no one. It's not until we get to the front of the building that we see anyone. There are people pumping gas as if nothing happened. And maybe for them, it didn't. It's surreal.

We pile into the car, and Bailey pulls out. It's not until we're pulling onto the street that we see the Patriot Army. There are a couple of trucks and a cop car sitting in the empty lot across the street. Bailey's hands tighten on the wheel, but she keeps us moving. No one chases.

We're ten minutes down the road with no apparent tail before Bailey takes a deep breath and lets it out in a long, slow exhale.

"I don't know how you made this happen, TJ, but you are a wonder."

"Are we safe now?" Ty asks.

"I think we are," I say, "but let's get to Oregon as fast as possible to be sure."

"I second that," Bailey says.

CHAPTER THIRTY-SIX

BAILEY

A few miles after my fingers unclench, my shoulders loosen a little. We're not home free by any means. We're still in Kansas, at least the part of Kansas that used to be Colorado, and we still have a long way to go to Oregon, but the victory at Trucker's Paradise is hard to ignore. The mood in the car is jubilant. TJ is clearly and rightfully proud of herself. I'm beyond impressed with her. I had no way to get us out of that situation, but she did. I was already aware that she is competent, but now, I fully know I can lean on her. It's all very heady. The high carries us a long way. All the way to Casper and afternoon traffic.

Which is when I notice a person in the car next to us peering in.

Shit. Just because Preston called off the Patriot Army doesn't mean that we can sail free to Oregon. There's still a lot of "see something, say something" country to get through. We're still two women traveling with three kids. This woman sitting in the car next to us, staring at us disapprovingly, is probably about to report us. Who knows if Preston really put the word out that we should be granted safe passage or just called of the Patriot Army at Trucker's Paradise. In fact, it's in his best interest to have the Patriot Army capture us and keep TJ away from a terminal.

"What's wrong?" TJ asks, voice pitched low. The kids are chattering in the back seat and probably don't hear her.

I smile, putting on a show of normality. "Don't look, but there's a woman in the car next to us checking us out. I think she's…yeah. There she goes. She's on her phone. She's reporting us."

"Oh." I hear her understanding that we're not free yet in the single syllable.

I should have stuck to less busy roads. Being on the freeway in the middle of a city during the day is inviting trouble with traffic congestion, meaning looking into cars is easy. On the other hand, it means I can exit the freeway and have a network of roads for evasion. I take the next exit. It'll make us look even more suspicious, but the harm is already done, and staying on the freeway will make it that much easier for the local cops to find us.

At first, I drive with an eye to blending with traffic while making turns that don't follow a pattern. But then I notice a black SUV of the sort Patriot Army uses for official purposes down a side street. Then another. We're being hunted.

"I should have known Preston wouldn't keep his word," TJ says.

The kids have gone quiet in the back. I want to promise I'm going to get them out of this, but honestly, it'll be hard. I can maybe evade these pursuers and get us out of Casper, but there's still a good nine hours of driving to the Oregon border, which doesn't guarantee safety unless there's someone there to enforce it. If Preston is motivated enough to send out a large number of forces, I'm going to have my work cut out for me, to say the least.

I take a turn to see what will happen. I'm followed by two pickup trucks and a black SUV. The pickup trucks are certainly Patriot Army, also, just privately owned vehicles. A cop car pulls onto the street in front of me.

"Everyone make sure your seat belts are fastened," I say. TJ turns to check on the kids. I give her a second, then say, "Everyone, face forward. No twisting. Heads against headrests."

Someone starts crying softly in the back seat. I have to ignore it for now. I have a job to do, and that job is to get us out of Casper, preferably without being followed, for what good it'll do. I'm pretty sure all roads leading west will be monitored. One step at a time.

I turn abruptly across a lane of traffic and into a parking lot. The sound of crunching cars followed by sirens trails behind us. A glance in the rearview shows that a pickup truck crashed into a car in an attempt to follow us. Another is following. The cop car made its own hasty turn and is moving toward the exit from the parking lot around the corner from where I turned in. All more or less expected. I could have wished for more crashes, at least into each other—as I don't want bystanders hurt—or some overshooting, but losing one is something.

I turn as if heading to the exit the police car is blocking. At the last minute, I turn again, skidding into it, and head for the corner of the lot that abuts the intersection. This car is much smaller than the SUV or pickup truck, so I aim for the space between the streetlight pole and a parking sign. It'll be a tight squeeze.

"Hold on. Face forward."

There's a small scream from the back seat as we speed toward the corner. I thread the needle, and we fly off the curb, landing roughly in the mostly unoccupied intersection. Traffic is stopped from the left where the pickup truck crashed into a car moments ago, the direction the light is green for. There are a few cars coming from the right. I steer behind them and proceed down the street perpendicular to the one we were on before the parking lot.

There's another crash behind us. I look back to see the SUV on its side. SUVs are notoriously top-heavy, and this one seems to have hit a parking curb while trying to avoid the poles I drove us through. The pickup truck is on the sidewalk, having slowed down but is still in pursuit. The cop car is turning out of the driveway it was blocking in pursuit.

"Look out," TJ calls, drawing my attention back ahead. Two black SUVs are pulling into position to block us at the next intersection. I don't slow. When I reach the intersection, I make a hard right, only to find a pickup truck and a cop car ahead. I swerve left into oncoming traffic. Traffic helps me, providing cover and things for our pursuers to crash into, but I can't help but wish someone had thought to block traffic. As I weave my way between oncoming traffic, the cars peel off, trying to get out of my way and frequently crashing into one another.

The cars that were blocking all maneuver into pursuit.

I go back to the right side of the street, leaving mayhem in my wake. I furiously cast about for my next move. I wish I knew Casper better. As is, I'm trying to evade multiple pursuers who know the city much better than I. And I'm not the only one who went to kids' camp, presumably. I have to assume their local training was equal to mine.

My advantage is a smaller car. Period.

I need a narrow alley, although the chances that they won't have the end blocked are slim. Unless I can get more of them to crash into each other to reduce their numbers. I speed up. I notice an airplane taking off ahead and slightly to the left. It looks like a small commercial plane and probably has nothing to do with us. The intersection ahead has a red light, and there are stopped cars. I slow a little, then see my chance and gun it, narrowly avoiding cars as I slip through cross traffic.

The sound of screeching metal behind me is music to my ears. That's a couple more out and more slowing. I also see the pale faces of the kids in the back seat. I am confident in my evasive driving skills, but I need to remember that I'm not doing those kids any favors if I get them killed in an effort to avoid recapture. I need to finish this.

"I need a terminal," TJ says.

I glance at her, not sure how to make that happen, before taking a sharp turn at the next intersection.

"It's the only way to stop this. I should have thought of it before, but I've got an idea. Can you get us to a, I don't know, an office or something?"

I take another sharp turn and consider. Just running is a fool's game, as I already surmised. If TJ can really make it stop, which she did once, maybe she can come up with another miracle and get it to stop altogether; that's the goal. But first, I need to lose the pursuers, then I can worry about where to find a terminal TJ can use in peace.

Currently, I see three vehicles behind me, gaining. Like I said, the advantage of this car is that it's small. It's not fast. The longer this goes on, the more people they'll muster and the more danger I put the kids in. I weave through another intersection, gain a little distance, then turn abruptly, hoping something in the next block will provide an opportunity. It doesn't, but after another such maneuver, I've gained a little distance and shaken off one pursuer. Also, a gamble I've made pays off. I've been moving in the general direction of where I saw the airplane originate, and we're near the airport. It's even smaller than I hoped. I'd been looking for a parking garage, but we've come to the other side of the terminal, and it has a parking lot rather than a garage. However, there's a mall, and it does have one. Before that, there's a Walmart with a huge parking lot. I pull in, weave through narrow openings to temporarily lose our tails, then whip to the back.

"Everyone down. No heads showing. Make it look like I dropped you off here."

They all comply.

I zoom out the other end of the back alley to find an SUV waiting. I don't know if it's new or one of the followers, but it's bad news. I hoped I'd lost them. Worse, it's blocking the exit. I throw the car into reverse—there's no room to turn around—and go back the way we came. That entrance is also blocked. I messed up. We're trapped.

"Why did we stop?" TJ asks without straightening.

I tap my fingers on the wheel, trying to think. "We're cornered at the moment." I don't know why I added, at the moment. We're cornered period. I'd planned on using the gap in the sight line I'd been hoping to earn with this trip behind Walmart to get into the garage. I figured we could find a terminal in the mall. Time would have been limited, as they'd certainly search the building, but maybe TJ could have made it happen.

"Are we going to have to go back?" Tatum the younger asks. That's her designation in my mind not only because she has TJ's first name but also because she's the youngest kid at twelve. "We are, aren't we?"

She sounds so sad, so resigned her to her fate that it decides me. There's one option. It's risky, but I think I can do it. "Everyone assume crash positions," I say.

I floor it. At the end of the alley, there's a garbage can. Someone left a crate leaning against it, making a ramp. I aim just to the side of it. The left wheels go up it, tipping the car nearly on its side. It makes it narrow enough to squeeze through the gap between the SUV and the wall. The wheels hit the wall, making controlling our progress difficult. I wrestle with the wheel and manage to just scrape the SUV as we squeak through. Once past, I jog the wheel, and we fall back on all four wheels with a jolt. There are grunts and gasps. I hope everyone is okay, but I don't stop to check. The SUV has some maneuvering to do before it can chase us. The others are stuck at the other end of the alley. Now's my chance. I join traffic as casually as I can, and when we get to the garage, I pull in.

I'm torn between letting them all out and hiding the car in an attempt to buy us more time or staying together. One look at TJ decides me. I park between two large family cars. "Everyone out. Act casual. You three act like TJ's kids. I'll trail you." They're frozen for a moment, and I can't blame them. It's been a wild ride, but I need them to move quickly. "Now. Let's go."

Everyone scrambles out.

CHAPTER THIRTY-SEVEN

TJ

We enter the mall, and I don't know where to go. Bailey's idea to follow may seem like a good one, but I have no idea how to procure a terminal. Then it hits me. I don't have to steal one or break into an office. All I need is an electronics store with terminals on display. I check the mall map near the entrance, trying for casual when I feel like I'm wide-eyed and disheveled like the kids. There's a Tree store on the second floor. Perfect. I take Tatum's and Ty's hands and give them a reassuring squeeze. Regan is looking the most confident. While looks can be deceiving, confidence is what we need right now. After consulting the map, I lead the way up the nearby escalator. I can't help looking behind to make sure Bailey is coming. She's lingering near the map. No one else seems to be paying us any mind.

"I'm so excited about my new portie, Mom," Regan says, startling me.

She's being smart, though. Buying my kid a portie is a good reason to go into the store. On the other hand, Regan, the oldest of our group of kids, is fourteen. How could anyone think I'm really old enough to be her mom? I'd have been about eight when I had her. I play along and muster up a smile. "Which one do you think you want? Remember the budget I gave you."

Regan rolls her eyes and says with all the distain one would expect. "I remember."

Ty, who went stiff when Regan first spoke, seems to have caught on. "I want a new portie, too."

"When it's your birthday, we can talk."

That gets us to the top of the escalator, where I have an excuse to look behind me. I need to make sure all my kids are with me, right? And I see that Bailey is now on the escalator. Good. She looks relaxed, bored even.

I take a deep breath to steady my nerves. "Let's go find you a portie."

The kids do an admirable job of chatter. As we turn into Tree, I glance behind and get a shock. There's a person in a red hat just behind us. Red hats are emblematic of Patriot Army. My hand clenches on Tatum's. She clenches back. Then, I realize it's Bailey. She's somehow procured a hat. Her shirt is different, too. Did she steal them out of a store she passed? I have no idea, but it's a good disguise. It had me for a moment there. I squeeze Tatum's hand again in reassurance this time.

I saunter to a terminal with a keyboard. The kids huddle around me at first, which feels like it will draw attention. "Look around, see what looks good to you," I say to Regan.

She gets the hint. She loops her arm through Tatum's and pulls her to look at the porties on display. Ty goes off in another direction, the picture of a bored sibling. He pokes at a screen between glances at me. I give him a small smile and get to work.

I quickly override the block on accessing LiFi that store models have installed. What I have in mind will take a little coding. I navigate to my virtual computer, log in, and get to work. I have no idea how much time I have, and my attention is torn between coding and watching the wide entrance to the store. As I get close to done, I focus more and more on the screen in front of me. When on the third try, I compile the code, and it goes through error free, I turn my attention to contacting Preston again.

"How much longer do you need?" It's Regan.

I look up and around, feeling panicked. Did I miss something? "I'm not sure. I'm done with the hard part, but I'm waiting for… something out of my hands." I don't want to say my brother's name, as if he's Voldemort or something. "Can you keep looking around?"

"It's Bailey who asked. She said there's Patriot Army activity in the mall now."

I must have really been involved in my task. I didn't even notice Bailey coming in or Regan going out. Also, I need more time. I glance around the store and see a salesperson approaching. I've been here too long. I close the window I was working in, even though I haven't heard back from Preston.

"Can I help you with something?" he asks. "Are you interested in this terminal?"

"No," I say. "Just poking around while my kid looks for a portie." I put my arm around Regan and try to look old enough to be her mom. I also want to focus attention on her. We're all a little bedraggled, but she has somehow managed to stay more or less put together. It helps that her curly brown hair looks like it's meant to be a little messy.

Regan smiles. "Yeah. I'm getting a new portie for my birthday."

He looks between us, skepticism written all over his face, but he finally says, "Okay, what do you have in mind?"

When I look to the entrance, Bailey is gone. She was leaning against a railing that overlooks the lower level most times I looked. She'll be back.

The salesperson is talking to me as much as Regan about various models, and I feel like I have to play along, even though I'm itching to check for a response from Preston.

The store phone rings, and another salesperson answers. After a moment, he looks up at me, then at the kids, a frown on his face. He speaks quickly into the phone, looking excited.

"Regan, we have to go. We're out of time. You can think about it, and we'll come back to pick it up." The salesman who was on the phone is coming toward us now. "Kids, let's go."

We start for the entrance.

"Stop them. They're fugitives," the phone salesman calls to the other.

He comes after us, and we start running. The security gate begins to lower. We're sprint for it and duck under. I pull Tatum out and don't let go as we run. The man following us is stuck on the other side, but mall patrons are looking at us, and I don't see Bailey. The man behind the gate yells to the shoppers, repeating the call to stop us. The mall isn't hugely busy. It's mostly women and children, and none of them seem inclined to grab us, but there's a man just a few stores down who moves our way. I lead the kids the other direction.

One woman holds up a hand. "You should stop."

I ignore her and jog on, hoping Bailey can find us. We're causing enough racket that it shouldn't be a problem. Shouts from below indicate that the Tree employees have updated the searchers. Going down and out of the mall isn't going to work. They likely have people on all the exits, so getting into the garage is likewise out. I stop. I don't know what I'm doing or where to go.

"Come on," Regan says. "We have to keep trying."

She's right, but I don't know what to try. If I can get my hands on a terminal again, I can enter negotiations with Preston. If he's even gotten my new threats, he should be calling these people off without further negotiation. The fact that they're still in pursuit means either he hasn't gotten the messages or he's not in power anymore. If he's also been deposed, I have no cards left to play. But also, why would anyone care that much about me unless it's to make an example of the whole family?

"Let's go," Ty pulls on my free hand, and I let myself be pulled back into a jog, squeezing Tatum's hand in an attempt to reassure her.

It's as useless as I thought. The man behind us catches up and grabs my arm just as Patriot Army men come charging from the top of the escalator.

We've been recaptured.

"Thank you, sir, we've got it from here," the red-hatted man in the lead says to my captor. He has a silver bar across his cap, indicating he's in charge. "Come along, now, miss, kids."

Men in red hats surround us while my erstwhile captor speaks excitedly to a Patriot Army member who stays behind. I feel numb. Tatum is crying softly. Ty looks utterly defeated. Regan is scowling.

They take us downstairs to the same entrance we came in maybe twenty minutes ago. We stop just before exiting. The man in charge pats my shoulder in an apparent attempt at comfort. I don't know how to take this. No one has laid a hand on us since the man upstairs. He called me miss. They seem almost protective instead of aggressive.

And where is Bailey?

"You're safe now, miss," he says. "You and the kids. It'll all be all right."

What is he talking about? Of course it isn't going to be all right. Even if Camp Redeemer is destroyed, there are other conversion camps. We're for sure headed for one. I don't say anything.

Someone next to us is talking on a portie. "Yes, we have them." He nods at the leader, who fishes in a pocket and hands me the portie he pulls out of it. I almost drop it, I'm so surprised. He wraps my fingers around it. "Your brother asked that you be given this so he can contact you. It's really okay, miss. You did it, getting away from your captor like that. Your brother will get you home safely now."

I look at the portie. It starts ringing. I hit accept and put it to my ear. "Hello?"

"Hello, Tatum. Is it only you listening?" It's Preston using his public voice.

"Yes."

"You win, for real this time." His voice is now his private for me, pissed off voice. It's somehow comforting, like at least this part of the world makes sense again. "These men are going to provide you with a car. They've been instructed to let you go on your own. The story is that you're jumpy because your 'captor' pretended to be Patriot Army. They think you'll be driving home, but go where you want. No one will stop you in a Patriot Army SUV. Go, live your depraved life in blue but keep your mouth shut. Do we have a deal?"

I let out a deep breath. He got my message. The code I wrote was simple. If I don't stop it each day before noon, all of my blackmail on him will be released. I don't expect it to last forever. I imagine Preston is already making plans that will result in that data being destroyed. There are hackers out there who are better than me, for sure, and given enough time, someone will succeed. I hope to one day be good enough I'll be unassailable, but that means school. For now, it's enough that it at least gets us to Oregon.

"Yes."

I want to ask where Bailey is, but I don't want to give him or anyone standing around me any information. It's killing me not to know if they have her, but if they don't, I need to keep them from looking. I'm still debating when he hangs up. I remove the phone from my ear and wait to see what will happen next. I don't completely trust that they're really going to just provide us with a car and send us on our way.

The leader gestures toward the door. "Shall we? I hate sending a young woman and some kids off on their own, but Mr. Rice thinks it will be less traumatic for you than traveling with a strange man." He holds the door open for me. I step into the garage to see an SUV parked right by the curb. The kids follow on my heels. "I get where he's coming from, but still. Are you sure you don't want at least a car to follow you?"

I shudder. "No, thank you so much for your kindness. I…my brother is right. I will feel better without any strange men watching me. Sorry." I grimace at him to show it's not personal.

He hands me a fob. "All right, then, miss. Safe travels."

I hold the back door open for the kids, who climb in looking shell-shocked. I get how they feel. I'm shaking as I adjust my seat and push the start button. Everything works, nothing explodes. So far, so good.

Except that we're missing Bailey. Where is she? How can we possibly reunite? I hesitate before driving away, concerned that we're abandoning her, but she'd never pop out and jump in the car in front of these Patriot Army members, would she? I drive out of the garage.

"Are we really leaving Bailey?" Tatum asks.

"I hope not." I'm scanning, looking for any sign of her. Nothing.

I turn, cruising slowly in front of the mall, hoping against hope that she'll be there, waiting for us. Nothing.

What can I do but drive away?

CHAPTER THIRTY-EIGHT

BAILEY

I watch TJ drive away in disbelief. She pulled it off. Somehow, instead of taking her captive, these Patriot Army men have given her a car.

I left my post outside the Tree store to attempt to head off the searchers before they got to her and the kids and so as not to draw attention to that particular store by standing there. I delayed them a little by planting false information, but suddenly, they were all charging up the escalator. I felt my best action at that point was not to get caught myself. Maybe I'd have an opportunity to free them. I trailed, watching.

Then, they drove away.

Fuck yeah.

Now all I have to do is catch back up with them. I don't want to run and draw attention to myself as much as I want to run and jump into the car as she drives slowly in front of the mall. Worst case, I'll steal a car and follow. I know their ultimate goal, but maybe can catch up enroute.

I walk down the street after them as quickly as I can without looking like I'm rushing. TJ stops at a red light, and I see my chance.

I run.

The back passenger side door opens as I approach. I jump in, crowding the kids, and TJ takes off.

"Bailey!"

"You made it."

"They gave us a car."

"TJ saved us."

"Ouch, you're squishing me."

The kids' voices overlap, filling me with joy. I scramble to right myself and move to the front, where TJ beams at me quickly before focusing back on the road. "Bailey." There's a world of emotion in my name.

"You are amazing," I tell her. "It worked. Whatever you did."

She grins. "It did. I think we're really going to make it this time."

I look around at the tinted window SUV we're in. "I imagine you're right. Who will dare report on a Patriot Army car?"

❖

"There. Behind that car." I point to a nondescript black car parked at the curb. We're pulling up to my apartment building. The sky is just lightening in the west. The kids are asleep in the back, but both TJ and I are awake and alert. TJ woke me up when we were getting close to the Oregon border in case there was trouble, but we sailed on through using a backcountry road. It was only another two hours to get here after that, and we've been keeping one another awake.

We drove twelve hours in shifts, with only fuel stops to get here. Neither of us wanted to test Preston's promise of safe passage more than necessary.

As we come to a stop, Greer steps out of the black car. They're sporting a huge grin. Normally, Greer would be yelling their excitement, but we're trying to sneak in here. Instead, they greet me with a hug as I emerge from the passenger seat, and they keep their voice low when they say, "You are a rock star, breaking up a conversion camp. We'll make a NoFa out of you yet."

"Hi, Greer." My smile is just as big. I'm so happy to be home. When I extricate myself from the backslapping, TJ is standing nearby. I take her hand and pull her over. "This is TJ."

"Nice to meet you, TJ." Greer eyes our clasped hands. "I see you have more to tell me than how to take down conversion camps."

"Thank you, Greer, for doing this," TJ says.

"It is quite literally what I am all about." Greer is solemn and utterly sincere. It's one of the few times they are, when they're talking about anything related to their childhood in Idaho. They came to Portland as a teenager, joined NoFa, and never looked back.

The driver joins the group, and I see it's Vali. Another wave of introductions and greetings ensue. "We've been patrolling the neighborhood and specifically checked out your apartment, Bailey," Vali says. "Everything looks clear. There's even some food in there for you."

"It would seem that I gave my spare key to exactly the right person."

Greer rolls their eyes. "Yeah, your mom is the best."

She is, and I can't wait to see her. She's going to love TJ. "Is there any word from Lacy or Curt?" When I called Greer after buying a phone at our last fueling stop, they hadn't called.

"No. I'm sorry."

I squeeze TJ's hand. We've both been very worried about them, and it seems rightly so.

"We'll keep our ears out for them. Meanwhile, we've got work to do." Greer claps my shoulder. It's too close to my injured arm for comfort, and I wince. "Are you injured?"

"It's minor. I'm fine."

"She got shot," TJ offers.

"It was a graze."

"And wrestled an alligator."

I shrug. "Bruises mostly."

Greer raises an eyebrow. "Maybe get that checked out."

"It's fine. TJ sewed up the bullet wound for me."

Greer looks impressed. "Nice. Now, wake up those kids and get going so we can make this car go bye-bye. Eat, get some sleep, and put on some of your own clothes. You look…bad."

"Gee, Greer, thanks. That's exactly what I needed to hear."

They clap my shoulder higher this time. "Listen. You know you'll always get truth from me. When you feel more human, we'll start figuring out what to do with all these little ducklings you brought us. Are you sure you don't want to send them off now? We've got people volunteering beds."

I'd originally told Greer they could stay with me because I'm finding it hard to say good-bye. But staying with me isn't a permanent solution. I'm simply not ready to be a mom of a teenager, let alone three, and they'd all have to sleep on the floor at my place. "Let's ask them."

TJ and I wake the kids with little shakes to their shoulders. They come awake quickly, looking around, wide-eyed. "Are we here?" Regan asks.

"We are. And I have a question for all three of you. Do you want real beds, or do you want to crash in my living room? At least for today," I clarify.

They look at each other.

"Can we go together?" Regan asks.

"Will they be our new families, or is it temporary?" Tatum says.

I look at Greer for the answers, although I suspect I know the answer to the second question.

"And what about the others?" Ty asks.

"We don't have word on them yet," I say. They look worried. "I know. We'll all keep our fingers crossed."

Greer says, "Definitely. As for accommodations, I can't offer anything permanent yet. That will take a little doing. But there's room for two one place and one another." They straighten and address TJ. "I also found a place for you, but I'm guessing you'll want to stay with Bailey?"

I look at her. I'm hoping we're on the same page. She looks back at me as if asking what I want. "I want you to stay. If that's what you want. Still, no pressure." She doesn't owe me anything, but I think we've gotten past thinking either of us thinks this is temporary.

"I'm with Bailey," she says decisively, still looking at me. My heart soars.

The kids, meanwhile, have been whispering together. Ty speaks for them all, "We've decided to go to real beds and leave these two alone."

I opt to own it. I put my arm around TJ and say, "These two appreciate your consideration."

The kids all groan. Then there's a flurry of them tumbling out of the car and hugs and good-byes, and my heart breaks a little to see them go. They pile into the other car with Vali and drive off. I swallow a lump in my throat.

"Go get some sleep," Greer tells me again. "Everything will be better after food and sleep. And seeing to any other needs." They bump me with their shoulder. "TJ, it was lovely to meet you, and I look forward to meeting again when you're not exhausted. Bailey, let me know when you're ready to talk about your future."

They hop in the car that I'm sure smells a treat from having been lived in for twenty-four hours and drive away.

"What do they mean about your future?" TJ asks.

"Greer has been trying to get me to join NoFa forever."

"And exactly what is the purpose of NoFa? I know what I've read and what I've heard, but what is the real deal?"

"The real deal is to protect people from the Patriot Army. To build communities that can defend themselves."

"So, for example, they might rescue a carload of people who want to escape red?" There is a decidedly innocent tone to her voice.

I put my hands on my hips. "I mean, if you want to put it that way."

"I mean." She mimics both my words and my pose. "I think you already are. Also, do you think there's room in NoFa for someone who knows her way about computers?"

She's so cute, even rumpled and travel worn. I pull her into a hug. "I'm sure there is. Come on. Let's go in."

CHAPTER THIRTY-NINE

TJ

I wake up feeling cozy and safe. I can't remember the last time I felt truly safe. Maybe before my mom died. I'm in Bailey's bed, and that's Bailey curled around me. This much I know. I crack my eyes open and see sun around the edges of the curtains. It looks bright. I think I've only slept a few hours.

The last thing I remember was lying in bed after my shower. I must have fallen asleep before she was done with her shower. I'd wanted to shower together and wanted time to really get clean, so when she said she was going to call her mom, that settled it. We took separate showers. I've been too tired to eat any of the food left for us.

Now, I'm hungry, but I don't want to move. I want to stay curled up with Bailey forever. Forever? Maybe that's too much too soon. That thought propels me to my feet.

Bailey stirs and mumbles, "Is everything okay?"

"Yes, fine. Go back to sleep." Although now that I'm really awake, I'm worried about Lacy and the kids with her.

She sits up and blinks. "No, I should get up, or my sleep schedule will be all off. Besides, I have more calls to make." She yawns and stretches, eliciting a matching yawn from me. "Are you sure you're okay? You're kind of faraway." She pats the bed beside her.

"I was just thinking."

"Bad things?"

She's so attentive and thoughtful. I'm drawn to her and find myself crawling back onto the bed. "I'm worried about Lacy, Curt, Derick, and Nancy."

She bites her lip. "Me too. If they don't make it…well, I guess that's more reason to join NoFa."

"Yes." I lean toward her, then remember my thought about forever and shift back.

"Is there something else?" She sounds worried.

"Yes, no. I'm not sure."

"Do you want to share?" She rests on one hand and lightly touches my shoulder, as if not sure if she's allowed to, even though we were just curled up together.

"I…" I bite my lip. I need to just ask. This is an unusual situation. It's not like we can date for a while and let things progress naturally. Or I suppose we can. I do have money. I can find a place to live. We can date and see what happens. I don't want to impose. "What do you want? I mean, with us." I move a hand back and forth between us as if there is a different us I might have meant.

She straightens and looks serious. "Like I said in Florida, I don't want you to think you have to be with me."

"I don't know if that means that you don't want me to be here."

"I said last night that I do." She looks almost wounded. "I want you here. But I don't want to put any pressure on you to be here if that's not what you want."

I put all my cards on the table. "Bailey, I feel like I've gotten to know you, the real you, in an intense way. I know we have things to learn about each other still." I bite my lip again, then force the words out. "But I want to be with you. I was just lying there and thinking, I wish I could do this forever. But that feels soon. Like it's too much pressure on you." I stop and hold my breath. I'll be okay if she isn't there. I will be.

She blows out a breath and puts her hands on my shoulders. "TJ, you're right that it's so soon." My heart feels like it may shatter. Maybe I won't be okay. "But I don't care. I've watched you come through a harrowing ordeal and show so much bravery. You care so much about other people. The way you wouldn't let me walk away from Camp Redeemer? You're the real hero of this story, TJ. I am the lucky one if you want to be with me."

That sounds ambiguous enough that I'm still not sure where we stand. Yes, she admires me, but she also said it was so soon. My heart is thudding in my chest. "So does that mean…"

"It means I love you, TJ. And I don't care if it's too soon. I want you to live here with me. I want to build a life together. But I also don't want you to feel like that's what you have to do."

"Stop saying that. You've never forced me to do a single thing. If we're in this, we have to be in this together. Stop saying I don't have to. I know I don't have to."

"I'm sorry. I just…" She puts her fingers under my chin and brushes a featherlight thumb across my lips. "I love you. I hope you'll stay."

The simple declaration undoes me. I push her back and kiss her.

"Does that mean yes?" she asks against my lips. "Because I feel like I said some things and…"

I laugh. "You said some things? I started this, I'll have you know. But, yes. I want that, too. I love you, Bailey. Let's build a life together."

I kiss her again, losing myself in the feel of her. I am the luckiest woman alive to be here, to be free, and to be in love with Bailey. The future is scary, but if I'm facing it with Bailey, I know we've got this. We make the best team.

About the Author

Sage is a board game enthusiast and occasional hiker who enjoys reading and writing books about women. When the weather allows, she's further distracted by her stand up paddle board.

She always makes time to snuggle with her beloved dog and chat excitedly about books with her daughter. Sage lives in Portland, Oregon.

Books Available from Bold Strokes Books

A Wolf in Stone by Jane Fletcher. Though Cassilania is an experienced player in the dirty, dangerous game of imperial Kavillian politics, even she is caught out when a murderer raises the stakes. (978-1-63679-640-6)

New Horizons by Shia Woods. When Quinn Collins meets Alex Anders, Horizon Theater's enigmatic managing director, a passionate connection ignites, but amidst the complex backdrop of theater politics, their budding romance faces a formidable challenge. (978-1-63679-683-3)

One Last Summer by Kristin Keppler. Emerson Fields didn't think anything could keep her from her dream of interning at Bardot Design Studio in Paris, until an unexpected choice at a North Carolina beach has her questioning what it is she really wants. (978-1-63679-638-3)

StreamLine by Lauren Melissa Ellzey. When Lune crosses paths with the legendary girl gamer Nocht, she may have found the key that will boost her to the upper echelon of streamers and unravel all Lune thought she knew about gaming, friendship, and love. (978-1-63679-655-0)

The Devil You Know by Ali Vali. As threats come at the Casey family from both the feds and enemies set to destroy them, Cain Casey does whatever is necessary with Emma at her side to bury every single one. (978-1-63679-471-6)

The Meaning of Liberty by Sage Donnell. When TJ and Bailey get caught in the political crossfire of the ultraconservative Crusade of the Redeemer Church, escape is the only plan. On the run and fighting for their lives is not the time to be falling for each other. (978-1-63679-624-6)

Undercurrent by Patricia Evans. Can Tala and Wilder catch a serial killer in Salem before another body washes up on the shore? (978-1-636790669-7)

And Then There Was One by Michele Castleman. Plagued by strange memories and drowning in the guilt she tried to leave behind, Lyla Smith escapes her small Ohio town to work as a nanny and becomes trapped with an unknown killer. (978-1-63679-688-8)

Digging for Destiny by Jenna Jarvis. The war between nations forces Litz to make a choice. Her country, career, and family, or the chance of making a better world with the woman she can't forget. (978-1-63679-575-1)

Hot Hires by Nan Campbell, Alaina Erdell, Jesse J. Thoma. In these three romance novellas, when business turns to pleasure, romance ignites. (978-1-63679-651-2)

McCall by Patricia Evans. Sam and Sara found love on the water, but can they build a future amid the ghosts of the past that surround them on dry land? (978-1-63679-769-4)

One and Done by Fredrick Smith. One day can lead to a night of passion…and possibly a chance at love. (978-1-63679-564-5)

Promises to Protect by Jo Hemmingwood. Park ranger Maxine Ward's commitment to protect Tree City is put to the test when social worker Skylar Austen takes a special interest in the commune and in Max. (978-1-63679-626-0)

Sacred Ground by Missouri Vaun. Jordan Price, a conflicted demon hunter, falls for Grace Jameson who has no idea she's been bitten by a vampire. (978-1-63679-485-3)

The Land of Death and Devil's Club by Bailey Bridgewater. Special Liaison to the FBI Louisa Linebach may have defied all odds by identifying the bodies of three missing men in the Kenai Peninsula, but she won't be satisfied until the man she's sure is responsible for their murders is behind bars. (978-1-63679-659-8)

When You Smile by Melissa Brayden. Taryn Ross never thought the babysitter she once crushed on would show up as a grad student at the same university she attends. (978-1-63679-671-0)

A Heart Divided by Angie Williams. Emma is the most beautiful woman Jackson has ever seen, but being a veteran of the Confederate army that killed her husband isn't the only thing keeping them apart. (978-1-63679-537-9)

Adrift by Sam Ledel. Two women whose lives are anchored by guilt and obligation find romance amidst the tumultuous Prohibition movement in 1920s California. (978-1-63679-577-5)

Cabin Fever by Tagan Shepard. The longer Morgan and Shelby are stranded together, the more their feelings grow, but is it real, or just cabin fever? (978-1-63679-632-1)

Clean Kill by Anne Laughlin. When someone starts killing people she knows in the recovery world, former detective Nicky Sullivan must race to stop the killer and keep herself from being arrested for the crimes. (978-1-63679-634-5)

Only a Bridesmaid by Haley Donnell. A fake bridesmaid, a socially anxious bride, and an unexpected love—what could go wrong? (978-1-63679-642-0)

Primal Hunt by L.L. Raand. Anya, a young wolf warrior, finds herself paired with Rafe, one of the most powerful Vampires in the Americas, in an erotic union of blood and sex. (978-1-63679-561-4)

Puzzles Can Be Deadly by David S. Pederson. Skip loves a good puzzle. Little does he know that a simple phone call will lead him and his boyfriend Henry to the deadliest puzzle he's ever encountered. (978-1-63679-615-4)

Snake Charming by Genevieve McCluer. Playgirl vampire Freddie is on the run and a chance encounter with lamia Phoebe makes them both realize that they may have found the love they'd given up on. (978-1-63679-628-4)

Spirits and Sirens by Kelly and Tana Fireside. When rumored ghost whisperer Elena Murphy and very skeptical assistant fire chief Allison Jones have to work together to solve a 70-year-old mystery, sparks fly—will it be enough to melt the ice between them and let love ignite? (978-1-63679-607-9)

A Case for Discretion by Ashley Moore. Will Gwen, a prominent Atlanta attorney, choose Etta, the law student she's clandestinely dating, or is her political future too important to sacrifice? (978-1-63679-617-8)

Aubrey McFadden Is Never Getting Married by Georgia Beers. Aubrey McFadden is never getting married, but she does have five weddings to attend, and she'll be avoiding Monica Wallace, the woman who ruined her happily ever after, at every single one. (978-1-63679-613-0)

Flowers for Dead Girls by Abigail Collins. Isla might be just the right kind of girl to bring Astra out of her shell—and maybe more. The only problem? She's dead. (978-1-63679-584-3)

Good Bones by Aurora Rey. Designer and contractor Logan Barrow can give Kathleen Kenney the house of her dreams, but can she convince the cynical romance writer to take a chance on love? (978-1-63679-589-8)

Leather, Lace, and Locs by Anne Shade. Three friends, each on their own path in life, with one obstacle…finding room in their busy lives for a love that will give them their happily ever afters. (978-1-63679-529-4)

Rainbow Overalls by Maggie Fortuna. Arriving in Vermont for her first year of college, an introverted bookworm forms a friendship with an outgoing artist and finds what comes after the classic coming out story: a being out story. (978-1-63679-606-2)

Revisiting Summer Nights by Ashley Bartlett. PJ Addison and Wylie Parsons have been called back to film the most recent Dangerous Summer Nights installment. Only this time they're not in love and it's going to stay that way. (978-1-63679-551-5)

The Broken Lines of Us by Shia Woods. Charlie Dawson returns to the city she left behind and she meets an unexpected stranger on her first night back, discovering that coming home might not be as hard as she thought. (978-1-63679-585-0)

Triad Magic by 'Nathan Burgoine. Face-to-face against forces set in motion hundreds of years ago, Luc, Anders, and Curtis—vampire, demon, and wizard—must draw on the power of blood, soul, and magic to stop a killer. (978-1-63679-505-8)